SOUNDING

**HANK SEARLS'S MAJESTIC NOVEL ABOUT
A WHALE AND A MAN**

"A poignant novel about one of history's most
ill-treated and least understood creatures—the
whale. Whales have all the better qualities of
humans and few of their worst, and Mr. Searls
captures this scientifically proven fact with
obvious fondness and warmth in SOUNDING.
...Although this enthralling little book is
fiction, its power of realism completely enfolds
the reader in arms as soft as pillows."

The Kansas City Star

"THE MOST WIDELY APPEALING WHALE-
CENTERED NOVEL YET...
The whale lore is stirring, the projection
of sonar-based whale intelligence is strong,
and readers with whale empathy will find
this a clear, densely imagined, unsoupy
dramatization of the whales' life-cycle and
their survival crisis."

The Kirkus Reviews

SOUNDING

Also by Hank Searls
Published by Ballantine Books:

JAWS 2

OVERBOARD

SOUNDING
HANK SEARLS

BALLANTINE BOOKS • NEW YORK

To the sperm whale, largest-brained creature the world has known, who swims—like the human sperm—against the odds, with the last faint hope of earth.

Hank Searls,
Newport Beach, California,
1981

Library of Congress Catalog Card Number: 81-48297

ISBN 0-345-32526-5

Grateful acknowledgment is made to the following for permission to quote from previously published material:

Dodd, Mead & Company: Four lines from "Whale" from *Golden Fleece* by William Rose Benét. Copyright 1933, 1935 by Dodd, Mead & Company, Inc. Copyright renewed. Reprinted by permission.

Manufactured in the United States of America

Trade Format
First Edition: May 1982

Mass Market Edition
First Edition: October 1985

Cover painting by Tom Hall
Cover design by James R. Harris

PART ONE

South-Southwest

"I hereby separate the whales from the fish, on account of their warm bilocular heart, their lungs, their movable eyelids..."
—Carolus Linnaeus,
System of Nature, 1776

✺ 1 ✺

All the starless night he cruised joyfully south, butting through rising seas at a steady four knots, his enormous flukes stroking upward in power and sinking in rest.

He had been traveling thus for days, in growing excitement, churning awash for a half-mile to breathe, submerged for the following four.

Tonight he was blatting, from spring-taut internal lips in his headcase, a loud and repeated peal: "*Blang ...blang...blang...*" The sound, like a mallet slamming an empty steel drum, would have deafened a man in the water.

The sperm whale was echo-scanning peaks of the Mid-Atlantic Ridge below him, listening for reverberations from the walls of an undersea canyon that scored the ocean bottom and was the ninth mark he must fix in his mind before turning southwest.

He seemed alone but knew that he was not.

Twenty fathoms beneath him, on an erratic course that he knew would end off the shoals of Newfoundland, swarmed a school of cod. He echoed on them curiously at his low-frequency cruising range, swept them finally with a ratchety *put-put-put-put*—like the sound of an ancient outboard motor—which told him there were hundreds: good-sized, aimless and mind-less as krill.

The massive bull was aging, and sometimes dove on cod if they were large enough, for they were never deep and the fat expended was negligible. But he had taken three giant squid, the last one twenty feet across, over the Iceland Basin less than an hour ago, and he had a rendezvous to make. And so he plowed onward.

He belonged to the largest species of all toothed whales, and that species most easily distinguished by man, who had at first called him the emperor. His head—squared bluntly in profile, steep-browed, cylindrical—extended backward for a third of his length. It held hidden within it the internal lips, which were generating the loudest and farthest-ranging of his sonar peals, and seven tons of acoustically perfect light-yellow oil.

The head-case oil was so slippery that primitive whalers had confused it with semen, called it *spermaceti*, and renamed his species sperm—"sparm" in the dialect of New Bedford Yankees who had deci-mated his ancestors. They had hardly noticed that in back of the oil lay the largest brain the planet had ever known.

The aging sperm's head had been slashed and scarred in battle with giant squid and with other sperm as well. His narrow jaw, hinged to drop straight down and swing sidewise as well, was a beaming device for his sonar as well as a weapon, dredge, and clamp for squid. It was only five feet wide at the hinge, tapering forward, closing smoothly along the bottom of his head-case. Fifteen feet long, it was armed with curved and pointed eight-inch teeth, of which only one had been cracked in fifty-nine years. Two had been lost in combat.

His eyes were set above the hinge of the jaw, near small pectoral fins—all that remained of his genus's terrestrial forelegs. With eyes so placed, twenty feet back from the front of his snout, he was blind dead ahead and aft. His vision in each eye was acute and independent, but he was much more a being of sound than sight.

A remora hung writhing from his lip; he had been alone for days, and there had been none of his own kind to remove it.

A crust of barnacles rode his back, and whale-lice he seldom noticed. Two-thirds of the way to his flukes was a mound that his species believed had once been a dorsal fin.

The sperm was sixty-five feet long and weighed, fresh from arctic feeding grounds, almost seventy tons.

For the moment, he eased the motion of his flukes. He could hear the thump of a vessel's screws twelve miles west and he echoed on it for a moment. It was making twenty-three knots.

Last year he might have veered away cautiously. This year was different, so he maintained his course, taking no action other than to drop his own frequency a dozen octaves to a pulsing, sonorous groan.

Now, with his ears attuned to his own deep notes, he picked up the moans of a finback herd. Listening passively in a sea of sound, he had no way of estimating their course of distance—perhaps fifty miles, perhaps half an ocean away. But he knew that at this time of year they would be heading north.

Cetacean legend told him that in the quiet days before propellers one could hear a finback bellowing from Greenland to Cape Horn. And the fin remained, along with the gloriously singing humpback, the most reliable long-range communicator in the seas.

Playfully, bored in his isolation, the sperm clanged out a mighty chain of bangs, hoping for an answer from the finbacks. This failing, he tried a roar from his nasal chambers, but heard no reply, for his range was no match for that of deep-groaning finbacks or blues or humpbacks, as if the millenniums that had split the sperm from the toothless grazers had penalized toothed whales for their far-reaching, larger brains by limiting their voices. Besides, his own years had worn smooth the septums and tongues of his larynx and phonation cavities—had perhaps enfeebled his lungs—and he knew that his bellow, once good for a dozen miles, was weakening.

He blasted one last time, listened, and gave up.

He began to scan the bottom again. Ahead, he thought he sensed the faintest of echoes from the canyon walls. He sent out a signal, glided for a moment, but heard no return.

The slap of the waves on his steep brow distracted him. A storm was whipping up.

In a few minutes he began to swim again, and soon he passed into a trance, one eye open, the other closed.

He had a brain biologically identical to man's but seven times its weight and volume. His kind had already possessed it for thirty million years when man's microcephalic ancestors tottered from African forests onto the savannas of the veldt.

His brain's nonmotor, thinking cortex had five times the convolutions of man's, and ten times the nerve cells.

Now half of it slept while the other half sounded ridges a mile below.

❧ 2 ❧

The leaking blue-black submarine teetered in darkness on a saddle of basaltic rock a hundred fathoms beneath the North Atlantic swells. Her hull lurched suddenly, swept by a current from above. In her sick bay, Lieutenant Peter Rostov, her tall, brown-eyed officer, barely kept his feet by clutching at a chain suspending one corner of a creaking bunk.

Strapped to the berth, his friend the navigator—who yesterday had broken from tension—strained against leather cuffs. He glared at Rostov in the ruddy glow of a battle lantern.

"She's rolling off!" he spat.

"No, Nicolai," murmured Rostov. He grabbed the older man's wrist, managed to slide the shirt-sleeve up, and silently begged the surgeon to hurry with her shot.

"We're drowning in a sewer pipe," moaned the navigator. His eyes clung to Rostov's. "*You* put us here, Peter Rostov!"

"We'll be fine," Rostov whispered. With an effort he overcame an impulse to ask the surgeon to hurry. What was keeping her? He felt the forearm tensing beneath his grip. Struggle had always appalled him; he had avoided physical combat all his life.

The day before, the navigator, spurred by panic when he realized he was to be restrained, had slammed the surgeon's corpsman across the compartment, which was why Rostov, who thought he might calm him, had come today to help.

"We're supposed to be grateful you got us here?" the navigator grated, his voice rising. "You should have let us sink!" He began to sob in racking convulsions, and his arm went limp. Gently Rostov blotted the sweat from his friend's brow. He sensed the surgeon behind him and, when he looked up, saw that her own eyes were full of tears.

When she had injected his friend, he threaded his way forward among the great trunks of the missiles to his cramped sonar chamber in the bow. He relieved his technician at the sonar console. Soon, sitting at the panel, he drifted into one of the trances that came more easily as the days passed by.

"Sonar compartment! Comrade Rostov?"

He snapped awake, swiveling his chair to answer. He had been dreaming, teaching his tiny daughter to hop-skip-jump in the park by Leningrad's Neva River. She had been piping with excitement. Now he was back to the plink of dripping water and the growl of boulders chewing on the hull.

Reluctantly he pressed the switch on the intercom. "Yes?"

"Meeting. Wardroom. Five minutes."

Rostov winced and turned down the volume. The *zampolit* political officer had a voice like a rusty hinge, and the intercom squeezed it of what life it possessed. Death itself must speak in such tones. "I know," Rostov muttered. "Thank you."

He arose, stretching in the dark. The submarine

rocked beneath his feet so that he had to grab at handrails along the passageways.

He was a sonar officer, not an oceanographer, but he knew the ocean currents well. He suspected that they were being jostled by an undersea tributary to the Gulf Stream flowing above. He was beginning to fear that the flow, disturbed by the submarine's presence, would undercut the silt on the cliff beneath her and hurtle her into the abyss. He had no way of knowing exactly how roughly the terrain, a few feet from his console, was grinding away at her thin titanium hull. But last week, as they were approaching, he had scanned the bottom with sonar, and his display on the console had suggested rubbled stones and silt.

The submarine had floundered, turbines dying and ballast valves jammed, while cruising at 200 feet, making 18 knots on routine patrol 500 miles east of Manhattan Island and 450 miles north of Bermuda, not far from where she rested now. Rostov had somehow guided her, sinking, to her perch, terrified of undershooting the ridge and dooming them all to the submarine's crush depth. Bathed in sweat, hands clapped to his earphones, he had conned the skipper into the saddle that was grinding them now. Here, miraculously, the old man, with his usual skill, had landed her like an airship captain six hundred feet below the surface, on the highest undersea mountain range between the Bermuda Rise and the Newfoundland Rise.

A hundred yards astern spiked the tip of the Great Wallop Seamount. Fifty feet off her bow rose the highest step of the crags that mounted to its peak.

To any eye that could pierce the eternal darkness, she must look like a child's toy, dwarfed by soaring spires both fore and aft. She was only 450 feet long and her beam was less than 40. The ridge between peak and crag on which she teetered was not much wider.

Three days earlier, while hearing the crest, Rostov's sonar screen had shown that to her port the saddle fell steeply down what seemed a jumble of boulders, toward lesser mountains of the range. Fifteen feet to starboard the ridge was a vertical cliff dropping sharply to a plain two miles down.

The submarine was very old and far beyond her depth. She was built to carry 12 underwater-launched missiles with a range of only 1,300 nautical miles. She had been lurching in and out of Severodvinsk since 1967, making six-month patrols through cold war, détente, and cold war again, each time submerged from the moment she had departed until the day she had arrived back.

She was one of the first of the nuclear class. She had been launched in the sixties from Gorki, in the heart of the motherland, then cradled to the ocean in the arms of the Volga River. Submarines born so far from salt water traditionally leaked at sea. She was so wet below that Rostov, who had entered the navy through the reserves and had always lacked reverence, had remembered a sputtering piccolo player piping behind him in his university orchestra and named the ship the *Plutonium Piccolo*.

The nickname had stuck. Their lovely new surgeon, Natasha Poplova, had first heard it at dinner the night before they struck. She had been amused and had flashed her heart-stopping smile. Still, Peter Rostov wished he had never thought of the name, for it seemed suddenly disloyal to the steel plates and ribs that were—so far—resisting the squeeze of death.

He told himself now that the leaks meant nothing:

The ship was strongly designed. And her auxiliary systems—fueled with nuclear energy, like the mains—had so far kept them breathing and furnished them feeble light.

She had balanced here almost four days. He adjusted the dim red console light and glanced at a scratch sheet he had taped to the panel. On it were penciled all variations on the theme of time: 3 days, 14 hours, 50 minutes; or 86⅚ hours; or 5,210 minutes; or 312,600 seconds, as of noon today.

One-third of a million seconds, almost. It seemed a third of a million years.

During all the long days and nights he had been plagued by the submarine's movement. The current teased her continually, jouncing her toward the edge, then rolling her back like an oil drum in high winds. Nineteen officers and a crew of 113 lived in various degrees of terror in her hull, and all knew that if she rolled off the edge, the pressure would crush her like a tin of caviar under the tread of a tank.

Her missiles stood in vertical silos aft of her conning tower, which stood far forward, near Rostov's compartment in her blunt and rounded nose. Two nuclear-tipped torpedoes lay in tubes in front of the tower. Torpedoes in two other tubes were armed with conventional Torpex warheads. The last two of the six tubes remained empty, a normal peacetime procedure for reasons of diving stability that he had never understood.

In almost the very bow of the vessel was his own little world of sound; in a bulge to the rear of the forward torpedo room, and in this chamber his sonar crew bunked between the active echo-ranging and passive listening gear. Here, in the ears of the ship, the clanking on her plates was deafening. To Rostov,

who had been a talented student of the cello and had
once aspired to the Leningrad Symphony, the last
three days had been like a month seated next to a
mad cymbalist.

He knew that the nuclear engineering officer, a
burly Latvian lieutenant who had trained at the Sevas-
topol Higher Naval Engineering School, was working
stubbornly with his crew, all stark naked and bathed
in sweat, in the main propulsion reactor chambers.

After the grounding, the captain, over the objec-
tions of the *zampolit* political officer, had released a
transmitter-buoy with a coded message to the Havana
Submarine Depot and the Riga Communications Center, giving their location. The communications officer,
who had joined in the *zampolit*'s dissent, assessed the
chances of the message being heard by either at one
in ten thousand. The captain, a chubby and benign
old Muscovite whom Rostov deeply loved, was trying
to decide whether to release another buoy.

But they were very close to the New York–
Southampton steamship lanes, with weapons and codes
that the *zampolit*, the executive officer, the missile officer, and the communications officer, as well as every
well-indoctrinated petty officer on the boat, consid-
ered highly sensitive.

Peter Rostov, who believed that the weapons were
actually obsolete and that the codes could be easily
changed, had learned long ago that the captain was
a man who longed to look well in the eyes of everyone.
And the *zampolit*, who seemed capable of bullying him
into trying to win them all the Order of the Red Star—
posthumously—was playing on the old man's weakness.

It was dawning on Rostov that the commissar and
those who believed in him clearly advocated dying

where they were, if the engineer failed, rather than crying for help.

The *zampolit*'s paranoia was impressive, even for one of his kind. Their Pavlovitch-Momsen lungs, the only means of reaching the surface if the engineer failed with the turbines, were widely thought to be a fraud and useless at half their present depth. But the *zampolit* had not trusted that bit of widely held lore. He had sealed the inner door of the escape hatch to the pressure lock, which was their emergency exit. It was dogged and padlocked with a chain—as if anyone would try to grab a Pavlovitch lung and rise through six hundred feet of pitch-black water to die of bends on the surface, rather than suffocate quietly in a bunk here below.

When Peter Rostov had questioned him, with some amusement, on why he had bothered to cut off their escape, the *zampolit* claimed that even the traitor's floating body would be a sufficient clue to bring the CIA or US Navy charging to the scene.

And had hardly spoken to Rostov since.

Idiot. Fanatic. Fool.

In Rostov's eyes the guardian of their morale was eroding it, piece by piece, admittedly with help from the leaks, the seamount's awful, grinding boulders, and the Gulf Stream's jostling from above.

All submarine men and women were screened for mental stability, but the rolling and clanging were upsetting the balance wheels in almost every head.

The night before, two long-time shipmates had fought over a slice of sugar cake in the crew's mess. When people laughed at this, their laughter was too shrill.

The Lithuanian galley steward, who spoke no Russian, had finally given up trying to understand their

predicament and had unsuccessfully—so far—slashed
his own wrists. Surgeon Poplova, their resident angel
of mercy, had confided to Rostov quite seriously that
she did not think she could pull the steward through
shock.

When the navigator, who had shared Rostov's stateroom, broke, she had had to call for Rostov to help
her corpsman strap him, screaming, to the bunk in
sick bay.

The *zampolit*, who on the last cruise had seemed no
more dangerous than any of his kind, seemed to be
taking increasing command. He had yesterday passed
the word for officers to assemble in the wardroom,
where he promised to explain to them whatever tortured arguments lay behind his resistance to a full-
scale cry for international help. The breakdown of
the navigator had perhaps shaken him, and he was
entitled under naval and Party regulations to lecture
on matters of morale to both officers and crew.

Whatever reasons he was going to give would be
as leaky as the submarine around them.

The sonar officer glanced at the lighted clock on
his panel. He changed the tapes on the ship's inter-
communication system, substituting a Bach clavier
concerto for Beethoven's Sonata in D Minor. It was
time for the meeting. He made his way aft in the red
glow of battle lanterns which had been dimmed to
save power.

He had been doing what he could with music, for
the spirits of the crew. And he had taken to sitting at
the sonar console for watch after watch while his leading technician slept in her bunk and his sonar men
lay in theirs. There they minimized use of recycled
oxygen, grumbling at the darkness that kept them
from their pornographic paperbacks.

He himself found isolation from the clanking hull when he donned the earphones to listen for passing ships and discovered an escape from his coffin in the voices of the sea.

For days he had been listening to the songs of humpback whales.

From their mournful sobs and distant trills, he was composing a symphony himself.

In his mind he dedicated it to his wife Anna—a flutist with the symphony he had tried so hard to join—and their tiny blue-eyed daughter, Marina.

He sat always in the dark, for light was like gold, too valuable to spend.

He was trying to cling to hope, but was coming to fear, in the midnight hours, that his opus would remain unplayed, heard only in his head.

〰 3 〰

A solitary, often out of communication with his kind, the sperm had nevertheless been among the first of the Atlantic cachalots to sense that the carnage was easing, that finally it had almost stopped.

Man seemed to have ceased spearing whales from ships at sea.

It was to lay his judgment on this matter before his old herd that the aging sperm had traveled one thousand miles south from the arctic, against the stream of normal sperm migration. He had still two thousand miles to go.

During this last northern summer, that of 1981, many sperm had noticed that man seemed to be refraining, for almost the first killing season in a century and a half, from sending whaling ships to sea.

There was need, of course, for caution. The moratorium on murder might be only temporary. For there had been two other amnesties in recent times. Only a few sperm and blues were alive who remembered the original one, sixty-five summers past, when the first noisy submarines had invaded the deep and harpoons had rested for four seasons.

And the last had been forty summers ago, a five-year reprieve during which hardly a single blue or fin or sperm had been speared.

During these short seasons whalers had seemed distracted from their work by strange and endless tragedies that stalked the vessels of man. As if struck by thunder, surface ships and submarines would plummet to the bottom, and the reasons for it were as foggy to cetaceans as the hills of the Newfoundland coast.

But during those respites the carnage to whales had only changed from swift bloody death to a slower and more agonizing end. Eardrums were ruptured by the shock waves of these strange explosions. Deafened, blinded aurally, the victims—dolphins and orcas, too, who had seldom felt the bite of harpoons—were without the sonar they relied upon to home in on prey and navigate. Dependent on their mates and pod fellows to feed and lead them, they would finally beach themselves to die before they weakened the group.

This time seemed different, though. If the explosions had driven whalers from the seas before, the whales now apparently had stopped their spearing for some other reason, because ships—which during those short periods had erupted like undersea volcanoes gone insane—seemed safe enough for man today.

Perhaps man had ceased to eat cetaceans, had found easier prey to stalk on land, or tired of gnawing any living flesh. It was well known that he was omnivorous and that he swept up the plants on his coasts, and possibly inland, just as blues and grays and the other distant baleen cousins of the sperm gulped krill in the polar summer.

The respite was a happy puzzle to sperms, from the aging males who ranged the arctic to the harem bulls and cows who swam the tropic seas. But it was a mystery that, like all others dealing with man, might be solved in time.

For there was a prophecy, believed by almost all sperm, by the massive, gentle blue whales, too, and certainly by every dolphin in the sea. The prophecy was that someday man, most promising of the mammals Cetacea had left ashore, would evolve enough to understand cetacean beings, who had returned to the primal waters that the ancestors of both whale and man had left so long ago.

Sometime before dawn the sperm, still scanning in his sleep, picked up an echo that matched memories deep in his cortex. The memories had been stored during his adolescence, almost fifty years before, in some long-forgotten discourse with an adult, probably the beloved pod bull who was his sire.

He awakened instantly, opening his closed eye. He had a clear and concrete vision of the canyon he was looking for; he had last probed it with sound on his way north in August two years before.

He was on schedule, but had drifted to the left of his invisible path. He had automatically compensated for the effect of the rising wind on his course, but the current from Labrador that was easing him east was stronger than he had estimated.

There was a full gale blowing now, straight from the southwest. Gusts whistled past the blowhole on top of his head. The whip of spray cresting his great snubbed nose became painful on skin so sensitive that it could feel underwater noise. He sank a yard lower in the water and pounded onward.

When he was directly above the canyon he banked, turning southwest, crashing directly into growing seas. He cast his right eye skyward, searching for the moon; its elevation would give him the time of his turning, which would be valuable as he set out from the Mid-Atlantic Ridge across the barren bottom of the Northwestern Atlantic Basin. It would be sparse in landmarks anyway, and so far below him that at times none of his varied voices would reach its gullies.

But clouds obscured the moon. Besides, he was almost blind with the driving foam. He sensed the scud skimming by in the blackness, low to the water. In his weightless environment he could sometimes sense the hour from the tug of lunar forces, if the water was calm. But not tonight.

So he was starting across a trackless waste without a time of departure, and his path would grow more and more uncertain over the weeks until he picked up shoal water off the Newfoundland Rise.

He could only hope that if he was delayed, the females of his old herd, presumably alerted to his arrival by a southbound pod of orcas he had encountered could prevail on the new herd bull to wait off Bermuda.

He felt a sudden tug of emotion. They would be starting north now for the Bermuda Rise, all nine of the cows he loved, and the new pod bull, who for only two seasons had guided the group. There might be new calves, too, he hoped. They would be the first calves born into the group for many years that he had not sired himself.

There had been a time, it was believed, when the sea was so quiet that he would have been told, even as far north as he had been, whether the calves were male or female, healthy or not, how the mothers had taken the births, and precisely where the family was now. But that was in the day of the white silent ships that leapt with the wind. Now that propellers cluttered the sea with noise, only the swift swimming orcas, if they cared to, could have carried the news he craved.

He heard the finbacks again, much closer now. He queried them, and this time they heard him. In the way of all whales, their answer mimicked first, for his information, their sonar perception of the topography they scanned below, duplicating their own signal and then the echoes they heard. Like all baleens, who needed only the crudest sonar to find their fields of krill, their sonic description was vague, but finally he perceived a three-dimensional picture of the ocean bottom under them. He knew the place: a rocky escarpment off the Azores that he had always found barren of squid.

They went on, their voices echoing along sound channels between layers of cold and colder water. As always, being finbacks, they were busy grazing plankton. They told him, in their deep, slurred notes, of the vessel he had heard earlier, locating it for him nervously as if they did not quite believe that this year whalers had truly left the seas.

He felt a great sorrow for them. Finbacks, he knew, over the last seventy summers had suffered punishment almost as bad as that which his own slow-swimming kind had endured for two hundred years. From an original population of half a million, it was said, less than a hundred thousand finbacks were left. Though much faster than sperm, they lacked his own hunting instinct and were thus less able to understand and elude man, more likely to panic under the chase. It was no wonder that this pod was apparently still skittish when it heard a fast-moving ship.

There were a dozen whales in the pod, and they spoke simultaneously, leaving it for him to sort the input. But they spoke in a code that all whales, and dolphins too, knew well.

First they located themselves, spoke of potential dangers, and only then gave him gossip of the sea.

When finally it came, he listened indulgently. They warbled and grunted of krill swarming in the upwelling current off the Biscay Rise.

The next item in the finbacks' report was a synopsis of water temperature and salinity, still matters of more importance to grazers than hunters. But the sperm listened patiently, and when they were finished with that theme he reciprocated with his own evaluation of temperature, thermolevels, and sea-state to the north.

The finbacks' summary was as rigidly fixed by thirty million years of cetacean communication as the sequential roars of mating sea lions, whose accent might vary island by island, but whose syntax essentially was fixed in the genes. Cetacean forms were different, the product of intelligence, and purposeful:

In the extraneous noise of a world bounded by sound, each increment of information should have its slot, to be left empty and filled later if some outside factor interfered. Even the lovely long-drawn tales of the humpback, echoing through the depths with the history of cetacea, fell into patterns, changing through the years, but in a sequence violated only for good reason. It had been so aeons before man had learned to communicate, and would forever be, so long as whales survived.

The finbacks began to describe for him their own pod, a family he had never sounded or encountered. Their pride in two new calves amused him, and he felt a great love for them, unseen, as he did for all the passive grazers.

They blared faintly and joyfully of a herd of blues they had encountered heading south, eleven cows and, incredibly, four calves. Blue whales were the largest creatures the world had ever known. They had suffered hugely from the killer ships until some sixteen seasons back, when inexplicably man had ceased to harpoon them. What blues remained were prodigious eaters of krill, enormous competitors of the fins in polar seas, and the sperm had wondered for years why, despite this, their baleen cousins wished so evidently for their recovery.

The answer had come to him in the latest song of Atlantic humpbacks, heard last season. The humpbacks sang sadly of a scarcity of blues and a surplus of the minute sea animals that made up the fields of drifting krill. This meant an increase in the faster-breeding polar seals, which ate krill, too. And the seals deposited much of their wastes ashore. Blues, eating the krill, returned it to the sea, in clouds of excrement which nourished new plankton.

So the net result of grazing blues was beneficial to all baleens. Besides, the humpbacks had sung, in the murder of one family was the seed of the death of them all: no small abstraction for so passive a brain as a humpback's.

Perhaps the humpbacks had picked up the concept from a passing pod of sperm.

The sperm, using only two of his voice boxes to communicate with the fins, continued to sound the bottom with mighty *blang*'s through the lips deep in his head-case. Now he picked up the image of a squid, down four hundred feet, less than a half-mile ahead. He blew powerfully, inhaled, jammed his blowhole tightly shut, and dove.

Stranded on a beach, his seventy tons of heart and blubber and muscle would have lain helpless as a hill of sod until gravity eventually collapsed his vessels under the weight of his blood. But in the ocean he was weightless, graceful, mobile as the ebony waves above. And capable, away from surface drag, of almost twenty knots.

Homing in on the squid in a shallow glide, he heard the finback voices change. He was leaving the sound channel that had been created between agitated surface waters and a colder layer a hundred feet below. The finback's grunts and bellows, trapped like his own in this wide sound-corridor, had been distorted by hundreds of miles of ocean, so that a short grunt from one of the finbacks would sound like a long, faint wail. Now, going deeper still, he began to lose touch with them completely. He caught a last warbling message, which dealt with man and therefore tickled his curiosity, though he was not sure that he understood its essence.

But by now his mind and his ears were on the squid, and he had no time to ask for clarification.

It was a giant, a full four hundred pounds of protein moving backward slowly through the water. The longest of its ten arms were two twelve-foot tentacles used for catching prey. At the end of each were clusters of suckers formed into a hand. Its shorter eight arms were the sessile members it used for transferring food to horny jaws in the center of its circle of sucker-studded limbs. The eight were not more than four feet long from their bases in the squid's muscular mantle to their pointed tips. Projecting from the mantle was its beak, horny, indigestible, these days often causing the bull bowel impaction when ingested, always bringing pain.

Probing his target, he instinctively spaced his sound pulses to evaluate the size, speed, and course of his prey. Gliding downward on a curving track that would approach the squid from one side, and which he guessed would startle it least, he quickly stopped clanging and began a high-pitched squeal from his central sound box. This, in his experience, was subsonic to the squid.

He had no desire to alert the animal, though not too many years ago he might have deliberately frightened it for the challenge of chasing it down.

In his youth, when his heart was strong, he would have enjoyed the struggle with a squid this size or larger, down to five thousand feet. But he was beginning to wonder if the fight now would be worth the meal.

He had spent his life balancing effort and result in his mind. He faced a long passage across waters likely to be barren of food, and it would be easy to expend energies, in pursuing and subduing this animal, that would upset the equation of feeding.

In the battle for protein, intake must more than equal energy expended.

He shifted frequencies even higher. Now he perceived from a descending note in the echo that the squid had sensed him and was accelerating, probably already trailing a cloud of ink and using its emergency bladder and jet to squirt itself away. Quickly he raised his voice to truly ultrasonic pitch, of a wavelength so minute that he was able to scan the visceral contents of the squid's stomach.

It was empty. The squid itself would be his only reward. And the squid was plummeting.

He was overcome by a sudden lassitude. The thought of battling, in the midnight depths below, a slashing, panicked animal that might later make him sick discouraged him. Besides, the fight might delay him for hours.

He had gained almost a thousand pounds over the last seven days, in contemplation of the trip south.

His store of blubber should last him across the Northwestern Atlantic and Newfoundland basins, until he reached the Bermuda Rise.

Then, his message delivered and his wisdom heard, he could feed in peace.

He slammed out a last crashing *blang*. The echo returned. The squid was at three thousand feet, plunging faster every moment. Already too deep for his aging lungs.

Slowly he returned to the surface and began the next leg of his passage, estimating, as closely as he could from the set of the rising waves, his course southwest.

He suddenly remembered the finbacks to the south, and the strange final communication he had heard before he sounded on the squid.

In their crude, baleen way the fins had been sending him a sonic image, doubtlessly passed to them through pods of porpoises, orcas, sperm, and right whales.

He blared a question at the finbacks. He heard his voice resounding through the valleys and canyons below. But there was no reply. The sound channel had closed.

Their message had been garbled by distance; he had been distracted, and he had missed most of the picture embodied in its howls and whines. But he realized now that they had sent him, in sound, the indistinct vision of a submarine balanced on an undersea ridge.

And he had the impression that men in the submarine were somehow causing it to sound a song, as full of harmonies and rhythms as those the humpbacks sang.

There were almost a thousand dead and sunken submarines known to Cetacea, lying in ocean basins, wedged in undersea crevasses. They were sonically impenetrable, as most of men's vessels had been for a hundred years. But he knew logically that most were full of human dead, isolated from the food chain by the skins of the great metal sharks in which they had died. A few were empty: Humans, like whales, rescued their kind when they could.

He had sounded the exterior of many of the rusting relics, for they were all part of cetacean navigation, landmarks for far-ranging whales and dolphins, and even for those who seldom strayed.

From the finback's description of the undersea

ridge, he knew that he never sounded this submarine. He had never heard of one that sang, although he had sometimes heard from moving submarines a strange pinging pulse, not unlike the sonar of a baby sperm. This one must have sunk only recently.

The original discoverers had probably been a passing school of dolphins or blues or humpbacks. The submarine, from the lack of detail, was obviously too deep for them to investigate more closely, and they had only scanned it from above. He wondered if it was too deep for even sperm to reach. If not, some young bull would doubtless dive on it out of curiosity, and within a dozen sunrises half the whales and dolphins in the sea would be sounding its picture for the rest.

He had always felt close to men who dove, though they were as unpredictable to his kind as those who sailed the surface, and probably just as dangerous. They were air-breathing mammals who, like whales, had returned to the three-quarters of the globe that had once spawned them all. He wondered why they dove when they seemed to take no squid. Someday, probably after his own brain and body had returned to the chain of feeding, Cetacea would know.

Perhaps, if some part of his mind remained in the Ocean of Thought, that part would know too.

To hear of a singing submarine excited him greatly. He wondered why it sang and where, exactly, it lay.

He slipped down to a hundred feet and dropped back into his trance, letting the croaks and groans of the ocean of life merge with harmonies he knew so well, deep in the Ocean of Thought.

Half-asleep, he drove south-southwest under the rising gale.

⚡ 4 ⚡

Peter Rostov crowded into the tiny, fetid wardroom to find that he was late for the *zampolit*'s introductory remarks, but in time for his pretty guest speaker, the medical officer.

Natasha Poplova was a junior lieutenant, new to the ship, having joined it at Severodvinsk two months go. She had jolted Rostov at first sight. A tawny, humorous young woman of soft Belorussian beauty and a twinkling smile, she had transferred from the North Pacific Fleet, catching this particular subway to eternity just in time.

Rostov had been on deck when she reported aboard, carrying her canvas bag and a ridiculous stuffed bear she had got on leave at the Olympics. She had a lilting voice that attracted him. They knew instant rapport, causing him some guilt, for he was famous on the submarine for fidelity toward his wife.

Within ten minutes, over tea in this same wardroom, he had discovered that she loved music and ballet. And when he had warned her of the daily anesthesia of the *zampolit*'s political lectures, she had chuckled in a low and throaty key that popped her instantly, in his mind, into the bunk in his stateroom.

Whether she had similarly excited the *zampolit*, a

grey-bearded veteran of the Leningrad siege, he could not tell. But today the *zampolit* had ordered her to tell the story of her last assignment to a wardroom full of edgy officers preoccupied with survival, so at least he must think that what she had to say would bolster his position with the captain. She was speaking now, in so flutelike and soft a voice that Rostov, standing in the door of the crowded wardroom with the hull clanking behind him, had to strain to hear her.

She told them that she had been assistant surgeon on the flagship *Guryev*, a communications vessel, when the Americans had used their mighty *Glomar Explorer* to try to salvage the sunken Soviet submarine *Baku* 750 miles northwest of Hawaii.

"We heard instantly in the wardroom that the Americans had headed directly for our poor little dead submarine and found her hulk on the bottom, and therefore that their *Glomar Explorer*—which they claimed was mining the ocean floor for magnesium— was a spy ship, no more 'mining' than we are here. At first we thought that they were only trying to photograph her wreckage on the bottom. So we joined them at sea—their *Explorer* was immense—and I think we photographed *them* every day for a week. From the trawlers and our ship and helicopters and even, I think, from our satellite in the sky."

"CIA vultures," spat the *zampolit*, drumming the wardroom table. Peter Rostov noticed with shock that he was sitting to the right of the captain, where the executive officer should have been: a bad sign, that. The *zampolit*'s eyeglasses were misting in the steamy air. He took them off to wipe them. His eyes blazed. "Northern Forces should have sent a sub to blow them up!"

And started World War III, thought Rostov. God

help them all if *that* one ever got the captain's key to the launch board.

He said nothing. Neither did anyone else.

The girl frowned, shrugged, and continued. She told them that with the admiral and all the captains aboard she had felt like a serving-girl and spent most of her time treating the admiral's sunburned nose and tanning herself in the South Sea sun. "But I must be fair to Fleet Intelligence. Who would have believed that the Americans were actually trying to bring her *up*? So obsolete a submarine? Five thousand tons of junk full of water? From *three miles deep*? In open ocean? Impossible! Or so we thought. . . ."

His heart sank. She apparently hadn't grasped the wardroom politics here, or that she was laying a propaganda groundwork for the *zampolit*, who was nodding professionally. The captain seemed to be hanging on her every deadly word.

"What did we learn of the CIA from their mission?" the *zampolit* asked her.

She said that the Soviet flagship had marveled at the Americans' foolish extravagance. It was believed that to grapple for so outdated a submarine they had given the billionaire Hughes billions to build the *Glomar Explorer*, perhaps more than a nuclear submarine would have cost.

"And their surveillance?" urged the *zampolit*.

"Yes. The fleet intelligence officer told me that their hydrophone listening-network off Hawaii must be widespread and very accurate, better even than our own off Vladivostok, or else how could they have known so quickly that the poor *Baku* had exploded, or pinpointed it so exactly?"

"I find it surprising, Captain," the *zampolit* interrupted, "that they don't know we're *here* already."

Peter Rostov had not found it surprising, a full five hundred miles from shore, but he was beginning to wish it were otherwise.

For discovery—by anyone—might be their only hope.

Though even for US underwater rescue vehicles six hundred feet of water overhead was nothing to laugh at. American undersea experts, if the *Glomar Explorer* was an example, could accomplish anything.

Assuming they would want to....

"They are always searching," the commissar growled. His eyes met Rostov's. "And yet there are persons aboard who want to release another buoy."

Rostov, who certainly did, sneaked a glance at his wardroom messmates, trying to read their faces. The tubby, white-haired captain, at the head of the table, was nodding thoughtfully. With dread, Rostov noticed that in the presence of Natasha, the skipper had developed a brave and noble thrust to the upper of his chins. He had always been a good and sensible commander, but he was a recent widower: Who knew what dreams of heroism so lovely a young girl might incite in him?

Rostov studied the Latvian engineer, a burly ex-enlisted man. He sat shirtless and greasy, eyes far away, lost in a world of turbine blades and shaft seals. Latvians, though solid and dependable, were bull-headed people. He already claimed to have repaired the ballast valve, and probably truly believed that he could repair his engines and get them off their perch. At any rate, he seemed unlikely to argue for another buoy.

Now the engineer was glancing at the clock. Rostov begged him silently to brave the *zampolit*'s anger, leave his stupid briefing, and get back to work. Talk, talk,

talk, as the scrubbers in the oxygen regeneration plant fouled slowly and the air grew heavier every day? Ridiculous!

Rostov glanced at the communications officer, who would ordinarily be responsible for getting word of their predicament to the fleet. He was a tight-lipped blond lieutenant who played chess with the *zampolit*. No help for Rostov's position there.

The exec, a bland and greying Navy administrator, was the only officer Rostov had known who could disappear on a crowded submarine, a truly invisible man who seemed to blend with the paint on the bulkhead. He was terrified of decision and seemed happy to let the *zampolit* take his place.

The missile officer was a scrawny boor who drank too much and peopled his world with NATO plots and CIA spies in every port they had visited to show the Soviet flag.

And the rest of the wardroom officers were too new to the ship, or too weak, to argue.

The hell with it. Rostov took up the banner alone.

"We are safe enough here from discovery," he said.

The *zampolit*'s eyeglasses glittered. "Perhaps if the sonar officer of *Baku* had been alive when he hit bottom, he would have said the same." Her jerked his head at the girl. "Go ahead, Comrade Doctor."

"I think everyone knows the rest," she shrugged. She apparently realized suddenly that she was being used, and would continue only reluctantly to dig their graves for the *zampolit*. But he forced her to admit that the CIA had grappled with partial success, though they had fortunately, and irretrievably, dropped two-thirds of the little submarine as they raised it. She winced and recalled that the Americans had nevertheless brought up, they told the world, the bodies of the Soviet sailors.

"Some crushed to a foot in height," the zampolit interjected. "They also got—what?"

"An intelligence notebook which they claimed was still legible," she murmured. "But this our fleet intelligence officer doubted."

It was this last claim, true or false, that Rostov remembered as having shaken the submarine flotilla to its roots. Enough, sweetheart, he moaned silently. Quiet, angel....

The *zampolit* cleared his throat, as if tuning it, and took up his theme: the *Glomar Explorer* was still afloat, awaiting its next chance. The entire *Baku* operation, he pointed out, had been mounted for a look at an ancient diesel submarine. To what lengths, then, would the CIA go to study *this* one if they knew it was here? With a *nuclear* power plant, the latest codes, and three times the missiles? Lying only one-tenth as deep?

The question was rhetorical, but ridiculous nonetheless. Everyone knew that they, too, were obsolete, almost as outdated as the *Baku*. The Americans, except for their "notebook," had really got nothing for their billion-dollar search in the Pacific. They had probably learned their lesson: to let old subs die in peace.

But no one answered. The *zampolit* glared at Rostov. "We are a clam in shallow water, waiting to be plucked. While you play your tapes for 'morale,' loud enough to drive the crabs away."

There was no use reminding him again that the sound of the tapes to the hydrophones of a surface ship would be as nothing to the clanking of the hull. Rostov had been arguing the matter with the commissar all day, with the captain noncommittal. Now the old man was refusing to meet his eye.

Bitterly, Rostov capitulated. When, and if, Rostov got home, he wanted no Party enemy chipping at his wife's musical career. He could not have cared less for his naval one.

"All right, comrade. No more tapes."

He regretted it instantly. Natasha was watching him. She loved music and might be drawing on the tapes for courage, as he was himself. Where was his backbone?

But she nodded understandingly, and he felt a rush of warmth. Except when he had comforted her in sick bay, they had not so much as touched each other's hand; they had damn well better not.

The *zampolit* accepted his surrender but kept the floor. "I am curious, Captain. Shouldn't we be warned by what she's seen? The Americans are everywhere. If you should release another buoy, you'd be risking—"

"That's a decision *I'll* make."

"Of course. But there's something you should know." The commissar began to gather his notes. "As morale officer I can tell you this: There's not a man on this ship who wouldn't die here in silence. Willingly! For the state!"

Speak for yourself, you old bastard, thought Rostov. And what of the women? As if reading his mind, Natasha smiled faintly.

The rest of the officers in the wardroom were studying teacups and fingernails, embarrassed by the commissar's heroics. But that was not to say they wouldn't participate in them. It was impossible to judge their mood.

"The loyalty of officers and men I've always assumed," the captain murmured. He was stiffening, affronted. Good. The Party should not enter his bubble of command. This was no factory committee room, but the wardroom of a Russian man-of-war. Like any fanatic the *zampolit* was pushing too hard. The captain seemed to grow taller in his chair. "I've commanded this ship for two years! What's your point?"

"That if you release another advertisement, how do we avoid the danger of another *Baku* to the state?"

"A coded, discreet frequency transmitted in secret from a one-meter buoy was scarcely an 'advertisement,'" the captain said coldly. "And I *hope* to avoid the danger to the state by repairing our engines and resuming our patrol."

The wardroom clock struck four bells: ding-ding, ding-ding. Peter Rostov thanked it silently. It was time to relieve the useless watch throughout the ship. The captain arose. "Is there anything else?" he asked the *zampolit*.

"Not now," the commissar answered. He took off his glasses and began to polish them.

Rostov headed back to his tiny world of sound.

No more music.

He wished their *zampolit* to the deepest trench in hell.

Ahead of himself and the rest.

❧ 5 ❧

The sun rose to the left of the aging sperm and set to his right, and rose and set and rose and set again. He plowed through the gale at four knots, and when it abated, churned through the slop it left, making only a tiny correction for the change the storm's passing had made in the set of the current.

In the last few days he had passed close to several ships. He had heard them without fear, for he believed the rumor that the killing had stopped, and he, of all sperm bulls that swam the seas, had reason for a certain trust in man.

The trust had begun in tragedy two summers past, after an odyssey that began north of the Straits of Florida and ended in a cove off Narragansett Bay.

Although he had bred each year with every female in his care at every ovulation, only a single calf had been born that season. His seed had lost its power.

And that one calf, a male, was sickly. Though he and the cows knew instantly, from their first scan through its feeble body, that its heart was defective and that it would die, the mother—the bull's own half-sister and wisest of the cows—had continued to lactate, as if her body would not accept what her mind knew.

So their baby had lingered, protected by all, slowing the pod. Perhaps because of the attention, it had learned quickly. Because it did, and because the bull genuinely feared that his half-sister would refuse to leave it, he had made the decision not to abandon it to sharks and orcas.

It would never have the endurance to dive for deepwater squid, but perhaps, if it could be weaned on cod, it might learn afterward to take smaller squid near the surface.

The bull knew of ancient feeding grounds rich with cod. Though reluctant to leave the safe waters off the Florida Strait during man's yearly killing season, he had nevertheless led the group north, sweeping finally past the Muir and Wallop Seamounts and over Georges Bank into water so shoal that he could hear lobster crunching along the bottom rocks.

He was invading whaling waters that two hundred years ago would have been lethal. His forebears had abandoned them when the first boats from tiny towns growing along Nantucket Sound had braved his ancestral herds: successful pygmies under oars, attacking leviathans larger even than himself or any that swam today.

Here had been giant-cod waters, sheltered from the sea. His own sire had visited them once alone. The ancient bull had been driven by desire for relief from his arthritic spine, for sea motion aggravated it, and some bays and sounds of America's eastern claw were famously calm in southeasterly gales.

The old emperor's heart had failed the next summer, his eighty-third, and he had drowned under ice somewhere east of Greenland, rejoining the chain of feeding and the Ocean of Thought. But his lessons had left the map of America's northeast coast intact in the brain of the younger bull, and that summer of the sickly calf the bull had followed it well.

So one night the herd ghosted silently south of Nantucket Island under a full bright moon, blowing softly, diving carefully, forever conscious of the endurance of the baby. Two cows swam always at its side, for it could not be allowed to dive for more than ten minutes, and it seemed continually to want to stretch its lungs.

They found the bays and inlets precisely as pictured, but the cod much scarcer than the bull had hoped. And since the group could consume forty giant squid a day or ten thousand tiny ones, and since even a full cod-run was only a temporary stopgap, and he himself was twice the weight of the largest cow, he hungered most of all.

But in these sheltered waters the little bull survived week after week. He seemed to make up in quickness and intelligence what he lacked in endurance and strength. His skill as a hunter of fish was prodigious. The pod grew to believe that he would endure the summer. He was active and playful, though the failure of his sire's seed had given him no new half-brothers or half-sisters to sport with in the seas.

But this lack the aging sperm tried to fill by playing with him himself. So did the little bull's mother. The adolescents of the herd loved the infant. He became the living toy of nine cows, five young bulls, and seven young sperm whale females: a tiny uncrowned prince.

The little one was soon diving for a full ten minutes, and though he would slow the pod on its long passage home to southern grounds, he had almost doubled in length and weight when it was time to leave before the winter storms. The hopes of the herd were high.

But the first of those storms came early, with a

heaving swell from the southeast that foretold of hurricane winds.

Such gales were of no concern to healthy cetaceans, except at birthing times. The aging sperm would ordinarily have simply moved the herd offshore. There, existing fifty minutes out of every hour at a hundred feet below the waves, they could forget the tempest above for almost an hour at a time.

With the tiny calf however, it would be different. His lungs could not yet survive giant waves at sea. So the bull kept the herd inside, risking beaching, electing to ride out the gale in a deep, rocky cove with the narrowest of entrances, where the water, he was sure, was always calm. Here the little whale, with his constant need for air, could fill his lungs at will.

And so they had sheltered there, while skies darkened and lightning streaked and winds dashed seabirds against the cliffs. When the bull thought the winds could shriek no louder, the gale backed suddenly to the east, funneling down the neck of the entrance. Monstrous waves began to build.

The tiny cove filled and emptied, again and again, a caldron of angry foam. The bull and his half-sister tried to shelter their calf against the surge. The other cows and the adolescents formed a circle, heads-in, to further buttress them. The lee they formed was impressive, but as the waves continued to rise, the group itself began to swing helplessly back and forth, landward and seaward, in the arms of the racing tideway.

All the while the little inlet sucked and vomited the seas, gulped and spewed them out again. At each surge the aging sperm could feel more and more heavily the grating of sand on his belly. The pod might be beached on the tiny strand or hurled to the boulders around it. He ordered the rest of them into open ocean, but stayed by the little one himself.

The cows and adolescents lumbered through the inlet one by one until only his half-sister was left, refusing to desert their stoic little calf. The bull nudged her and jostled her when he could, and still she fought to stay.

It was not until the largest swell of all tossed the tiny bull ashore that she agreed to leave, with a wail of grief so deep that it lived in him still. She lay outside the entrance half the night, calling for the aging bull to join her.

He could not bring himself to go. Scud raced across the sky, but the moon was full, and when it shone he could see the little bull as a dark mass on the white sand, just beyond reach of the breakers probing at the shore.

He himself was tiring, whirling to meet the entering seas, spinning to hold his position as they receded. He was fighting the Atlantic with nothing but the power of his tail, which was wider than the little calf was long, but weakening fast.

All the while he *blanged* and hooted above the crashing waters so that the calf would know he was still there. In the hiss between the breakers he could hear a tiny guttural voice imitating his sounds.

Once, as the moon shook loose the racing clouds, he saw a finger of water grope for the baby. It was the last chance. No other wave would reach so high, for the wind was abating and the tide running out.

But the Ocean of Thought had waters to reach the highest peaks, and he urged it on with all his strength. It enveloped the calf, who struggled bravely to ride it back to the ocean's edge. Then the sperm bull groaned, for the wave lost heart and left the calf ashore.

So the little one would be doomed, when the sun rose, to die in agony, baking within the coat of baby blubber so earnestly won.

In the grey of dawn, while the wind still shrieked, the bull sensed movement on the shore. He forced his head high from the surface, ignoring the slash of rocks and the grinding sand on his flukes and thorax.

A man was scrambling down the cliff. Ahead of him was one of the four-legged creatures man seemed to love, barking like a seal. It ran across the sand to taunt the stranded calf. The sperm trumpeted a warning. Neither man nor animal seemed to heed.

But the man, whose white hair tangled like eelgrass on his head, drove his animal off, and approached the calf. Something in his bearing gave the aging bull hope, and when the moon next appeared, he could see him clearly reaching up to caress the baby's snout, rub his lips, fondle his pectoral fins. The calf moaned softly, as he did when short of breath and comforted by a member of the pod.

By sunrise the wind had abated and other men had come. Some began to dig a trench to the water, as if somehow they thought they could float the baby to the cove. Another, whom the sperm took to be a female, was trying to suckle him from a bucket through a snakelike tube she had forced between his lips.

All useless. He would die, the sire knew, for his heart was weak. Men were clever creatures, but could not know this. They were far too small to move him, at least without devices he was sure they could never get down the cliffs. Even now, he knew, the weakened heart was pumping against gravity it had never known afloat, and blood that should have been flowing to his brain was pooling in his belly.

To hope that men could save him, for whatever

reasons they had, was useless. He could only wish that the clouds that covered the sun would stay; the baby would enter the Ocean of Thought soon enough, but to see the little body simmer and boil in the blaze of noon would be too agonizing to bear.

Still the bull remained. All high noon the sun peeked through, disappeared, and blazed again. The wind died. The calf began to writhe.

He could not desert him now. He closed his eyes and sank himself into the Ocean of Thought, swam north in his mind to arctic waters with the little one, to play in currents always chill. He sounded a scene of bergs and ice floes to the dying calf.

He heard barking and opened his eyes. The man who had first come stood frozen, watching him from a nearby rock. Beside him yelped his creature. The man reached down and touched the animal, who grew silent.

The sperm continued to echo, as if to the man, his plunge with his calf into arctic seas. He did not know why he did so: Man could not hear such a song in air, or understand it if he did.

But for a long while the human studied him, his two eyes locked to the sperm's left orb. It seemed to the sperm that their minds were locked as well.

The man turned suddenly. He cupped his hands and shouted to those on the beach. They ceased their digging and took the bucket, and found others as well, and soon they were passing them hand to hand full of water. At the end of the the line, through the long hot hours, the white-haired man washed the baby's skin.

As the cliff's shadow fell on the little calf's head, it shivered once and died.

Passing through the entrance, the aging sperm had

looked back. The men had left the beach, but on the cliff, against the reddened sky, one turned and raised his arm.

The sperm whale heard a bark.

He shot an arc of bloodred spume soaring to the sky, and swam to join his herd.

◈ 6 ◈

That was two full summers past. Feeling, in his grief, that his seed could not sustain the herd, he had deliberately lost his cows in ritual battle to a transient young sperm giant. Then he had swum north, to join an arctic band of bachelors, exiles like himself, too weak to win or too old to mate.

But he was not weak, and perhaps not too old to mate. He was still healthy, and had sometimes wondered if he had acted too hastily. Heading southwest now to visit his beloved herd, he knew that if the death of his little calf had not wounded him so deeply, he would have kept the pod until beaten in true combat.

Though he did not intend now to stay, but only to advise, he wondered if he might have to fight the new herd bull again to see the cows he loved. He hoped that the young harem-master was wise enough to take his advice without combat, and to move the pod to European waters rich in squid, now that the harpoons slept.

These things would be answered somewhere off the Nares Deep, still a thousand miles away. Now he had the voices of the sea to distract him from tides gone past and those to come.

Squeaking and squealing somewhere near a pod of his little porpoise cousins, the first he had heard since his arctic self-exile. They were bound for the Grand Bank fishery, on an age-old track that would intercept his own.

As his path converged on theirs, he guessed from the pitch of the leader's signals that she was a female. She had four newborns and nineteen yearlings with her. She was concerned because the gale of the preceding week had somehow disrupted her dead reckoning. At the limited depths she was able to echo, the few bottom landmarks in the silted plains below were beyond her range.

He knew from her fuzzy sound-picture that she was unsure of her location. He had the potential to fix her position for her precisely.

So he dove deeply for the first time in many days, hyperventilating for a dozen breaths first, then rolling mightily, tossing his flukes toward a sky of steel and boring straight for the dark of the sea. He plummeted through water from milky green to deepest grey and finally to midnight black. Every few fathoms he tested the salinity with his tongue, automatically integrating the saltier water with the squeeze on his lungs to determine his depth.

There was almost no life at these levels above the sterile plains, but a half-mile down he glimpsed a phosphorescent gleam with his right eye. He sounded it and found it to be the decomposing body of a squid. It could only have been carried here from upwellings off the continental shelf. He ignored it and pressed

downward. At three thousand feet he was able to scan
the bottom in detail.

He found a hillock that he recognized, transmitted
its position to the porpoise, and continued for ten minutes to swim at depth, enjoying the cold on his skin.

Long before his endurance was tested, he glided
to the surface. The porpoises were out of range, their
tiny voices lost in the chatter of the waves. He wished
they had waited. They were interesting creatures, with
brains hardly larger than man's. Like humans they
were unpredictable, emotional, but adaptable and
clever. He hoped the porpoise leader, when she got
her bearings, was not too far off track from the fishing
grounds she sought.

They were far-ranging animals who loved to pass
on the gossip of Cetacea. He had hoped to ask if they
had heard where the submarine lay singing.

〰 7 〰

The aging sperm churned onward.

Last summer he would have made his passage like
a hunted thing, in a series of long, shallow dives, surfacing every hour to recharge his blood with oxygen.
For a short ten minutes he would have traveled on
the surface, breathing deeply, one explosive exhala-

tion first to clear his blowhole, then once each minute a long gasping breath. In whaling waters he might even clear his blowhole underwater, just before surfacing, to reduce the plume he showed. It was a strategy requiring careful timing, a technique some cachalots could learn and others could not, taught him early in life by his sire. It had saved his life many times.

A whale of no other species could match the sperm's endurance underwater, although blues and bottlenose whales came close. Traveling five miles below for every mile on the surface, he had minimized the odds of detection by whalers. This his ancestors had learned generations ago, and it was a necessary lesson.

He knew that in one thing—the shape of the plume he was forced to blow—evolution had failed him. For in thirty million years the rational laws that had resculptured his kind from land animals back to creatures of the sea had closed one nostril and moved the other to the left side of the top of his head. This permitted sperm babies, with their narrow, awkward mouths, to breathe while they suckled on their sides. But it had left the species spouting through a one-sided hole in a slanted plume unique in all Cetacea.

He had always feared, as all sperm did, the waterspout he left.

For a sperm to confess his species on the horizon was suicidal, because men seemed to value him above all other cetaceans, perhaps for the oil in his head-case: Cetacean lore was full of stories of man bailing oil from the sperm whale's head and abandoning his body to the deep. So the slanted banner of a surfacing cachalot, raised askew within sight of a whaling vessel, was lethal.

The aging bull had learned this early, but the defect

in the blowhole was incurable, structural. His ancestors had evolved in a world free of surface predators, and all of sperm intelligence could not eliminate the flaw.

But now the fear was past. This summer, in the absence of whalers, the aging sperm had abandoned his furtive ways. He had returned in passage to the careless, untiring journeying of the ancients, and now he moved regally on the surface west-southwest.

Relishing his freedom, he pondered his kind's strange bloody link to man, and on how sperms' fortunes rose and fell with the appetites of little creatures who had learned to sail the seas.

He knew that when men had first begun to hunt for whales, they had feared to harm the sperm. For a thousand years before man took his first emperor whale, he had slaughtered other cetaceans. Always his vessels, from the flimsy skin boats of squat northern men who left ice floes to spear with poisoned tips, to the ships from Western Europe with high sterns like sounding flukes, had avoided cachalots and killed only bowheads, right whales, humpbacks, pilots.

To ancient men on tiny boats, sperm must have seemed invulnerable.

Man was obviously a rational hunter, not far below the orca in intelligence. Thus like the orca, his first thought in hunting must have been for his own safety.

For millions of years—since the last of giant megalodon sharks, whose fossilized teeth the aging sperm had often fingered with sound, fathoms beneath the bottom silt—there had been no threat to cachalots. Even orca killer whales, who would tear the tongue from a sick finback or a humpback calf, and who might attack sperm newborn during birthing, would seldom test an adolescent sperm.

But cetacean legend told of the change. One squally day almost three hundred summers ago, a silent sailing ship, apparently kept from the normal hunting of right whales by a storm, had winged from behind Nantucket Island to attack the first startled sperm.

There was no history of the actual struggle: Perhaps the victim had been a lone male out of hearing of the nearest herd. And Cetacea had no memory of the sperm's size, either, but ancestral males had been immense—90 feet and 150 tons, it was thought—bigger, perhaps, than the ships that could take them, almost as big as blue-whale females, bigger than blue males today.

Whatever the size of the first sperm harpooned, whatever lonely struggle he had made or food he had yielded man, his fat and oil must have balanced the human energy. For his murder had ended cachalot immunity. From the western wall of the Atlantic, scores of winged ships followed, spawning rowing boats as herring spewed out roe.

When the first cachalot herds were ambushed by whalers, sperm bulls, though astonished, would decoy pursuit away from the group. Overwhelmed by more and more of the six-oared craft that the ships sent scurrying across the water like creaking crabs, the bulls could die without regret as the wails of their pods grew faint in distant waters.

In the earliest days it had always been the bull that man attacked first, for the whalers seemed insatiably hungry for the head-oil, and the male cachalot's head was twice the size of any cow's. But then man learned to strike first at a calf or a suckling baby and to kill it slowly. So long as it shrieked in pain the mother was unable to leave it, and she and the bull, which must stay to protect them, could easily be speared.

The whalers tortured calves to make them cry and the herds milled helplessly, and a hundred summers passed from that first Nantucket sperm. By that time, of almost a million cachalots who had swum unmolested and unmolesting until the first was taken, less than two out of three remained. Still the white ships swooped silently to kill.

Sperm were dying by the thousands, faster than they could breed. Man was becoming the new megalodon. He must somehow be told to stop.

So some eighty killing seasons before the aging sperm had been born, a conviction had grown among Pacific sperm, in meetings in the hunting grounds, that a message must be sent to man.

If humans had the wit to understand....

It was not certain that they did. Despite the age-old prophecy of someday communicating with humans, cetacean history was already full of failure at human contact.

Two thousand years before, porpoises had sported with human young in Europe's inland sea. They had rescued men who fell from their vessels, and strained to answer the cries of man's children in air, but the human adult seemed deaf to all they did.

The Pacific harem masters decided that where friendliness had failed, perhaps fear—which cachalots themselves were lately learning—would end the slaughter.

They would thrash the tiny six-legged boats to splinters.

They would try not to harm the men in the water. Man was perhaps the most intelligent mammal left ashore. There was no way to know how many of his race existed: To kill even one human, and doom his seed to extinction, would run counter to currents in the Ocean of Thought.

Besides, it was known that, like cetaceans, man rescued his own kind. If humans communicated among themselves—as they surely must, to build their white-winged structures—the survivors' would be carried back to the lands from which they came, and whalers would leave the sea.

If men were inadvertently drowned, perhaps the Ocean of Thought would accept it without storming as the price of herd survival, as when starving orcas had to kill their fellow whales.

And so the battle was begun. Near the islands where volcanoes flamed and harmless bare-skinned humans sailed double canoes, a whaleboat far from its tall mother ship harpooned a forty-ton adolescent sperm, so young that his teeth had not broken through. Knowing of his elders' decision, he sank deliberately beneath the little craft, rose under it, and tossed it skyward in a rain of flashing oars. It broke in half.

He had not been badly speared; a cow tore the harpoon from his back, and though the mother vessel chased him half a day, he survived.

He had been careful to avoid with his flukes the men clinging to their wreckage in the water, so that they would be able to spread the tale when the mother ship saved them.

Porpoises nearby sounded on the rescue of the men. But incredibly the mother ship did not flee: It stayed. Before the next sunset, boats from the same vessel had killed a calf and another bull.

The aging whale's sire had sounded him the pictures of what had happened next, and the bull had passed it on to his own calves through the years; lastly to the sickly little one he'd loved the best of all. All Cetacea knew the story well.

That season long ago, on the Pacific side of the narrow neck between South and North America, swam three groups of sperm with a total of three bulls, nineteen cows, twelve yearlings, and three newborn infants.

The three bulls joined in feeding forays far ahead of their harems, to leave nearby squid untouched for the slower cows and babies. They heard from dolphins of the attack by the island adolescent, puzzled at how futile it had been, and mulled it together, resting awash in the calm southern sea.

There seemed no logical reason why the ship was persisting. Perhaps Cetacea was wrong in hoping for a rational brain in man, and perhaps the prophecy of future contact was a jellyfish dream, beautiful in the distance, slipping away when approached.

Unlikely. They knew men had good brains, for whales had sound-scanned men's bodies in the sea—always distantly, because to panic one in the water was thought to be fatal.

Men's brain size seemed respectable, considering their stature. Penetrated with ultrasonic squeals of curious whales and dolphins, their skulls had echoed clear sound-maps, as any mammal's did. Though the brain itself was of an odd elongate shape, like a tortoise shell, it had the cetacean's two halves and seemed almost identical in density and composition.

If human brain folds were smooth and shallow as those of a newborn calf's, that was to be expected in an animal so recently evolved.

Nevertheless, the brain itself seemed physically capable of reason.

And human brain size was not the only evidence of intelligence. For there were communicative river dolphins with brains even smaller than man's. Though practically blind and not given to abstractions, they had somehow taught men of the rivers to help them fish, and their proximity to riverbank humans made them fine acoustic observers.

The river dolphins had pictured, for larger cetaceans visiting tidal waters, men's own fishing habits, which were clever and seemed to require man-to-man communication.

And man was even capable of cooperating with whales. For all Cetacea knew disquiet with an orca legend.

There had long been a group of orcas—130 of them, in a dozen pods—that patrolled the tip of the great barren island that lay near the Southern Cross. When the group located finbacks or blues, it circled the bigger whales and sent adolescents to a nearby harbor where man kept killer ships. There they had long ago taught men to follow their beckoning dorsals back to the baleens, and to throw them the tongues and lips of the fellow whales that the men speared.

There was no doubt that creatures so quick to learn from whales could reason for themselves. Thus, to the Pacific sperms, stupidity was no explanation for the far-off whaling vessel's refusal to leave their area.

If man could think, he could be taught not to harm mammals, just as a calf, pressed beneath the surface until he moaned for air, would learn never to butt a newborn baby again. Why, then, had whaling not stopped?

The three bull sperm decided that the human's herd master was on the mother ship. The adolescent whale had attacked the wrong men in the wrong ves-

sel, as if a challenging bull had charged a calf instead
of the harem bull.

So the decision had been made among the three
long-departed Pacific bulls to attack again: not the
boats, but the next mother ship they could find.

They led their harems slowly southward over Milne
Edwards Deep, sweeping past the Galapagos and into
the Humboldt Current. They crept over the South-
eastern Pacific Basin to a place where, almost in sight
of shore, the fins on which the Andes rested lay a
mile beneath the waves.

Here, they knew, were rich upwellings from chasms
males could dive, but which during daylight hours
were out of reach of the cows. The frigid Humboldt,
crawling north from the Great Southern Sea, split at
Cape Horn and filled these upper canyons of the
Chilean Trench with krill. After sunset, as the krill
groped helplessly for the dying light, giant squid rose
after it from the bottom ooze. To feed themselves, the
squid had to venture into diving range of the cows,
and to levels where newly weaned calves could be
taught to hunt.

So the bulls dove by day, awaiting a whaler. The
cows hovered, playing with the calves, and when the
sun sank, began their own feeding. By dawn the herd
would be dozing, save for an outriding bull, and it
was one of these outriders who at sunrise one day first
sounded a sailing ship, far beyond the horizon. In
these waters, known to man for their richness, the
vessel would certainly be a whaler, the first of this
killing season.

The bull was the smallest of the three. He awakened the herd and sent it fleeing from the ship directly
into the slap of the southeast trades. Always whales
fled upwind, for they had noticed long ago that man

could sail into the breeze only slowly, in erratic darts and zigzags, like a downed gull with a broken wing.

Then the bull cruised downwind toward the ship. Soon he was far out of sight, and then out of hearing, of the rest.

He homed on the vessel with loud, resonating bangs from his steel-taut internal lips, ligaments placed between two air sacs at the forward end of his head-case. From one sac to the other he expelled short spurts of air, losing none to the water. The explosive crack of the lips, focused by his cylindrical head-case, slammed ahead at five times the speed of sound in air. Each bang was followed by minor reverberations from the back of the bass-drum head-case, which extended a good twenty feet down the length of his body. Reading the echoes of the basic *blang* and its following train as they resounded from the ship, he could distinguish his own sonar from the surrounding clutter of waves, the faint bangs of his departing herd, and the crackle of pistol shrimp.

He could tell from the echoes that the ship was a large one, moving barely faster than his own speed, and that it was approaching him against the wind.

He dove, rose, and spouted, intentionally sending his slanted plume of water high into the breeze, for even then it had been known for a century that man, with what seemed birdlike vision, used sight rather than hearing to find his prey.

He lay spouting and inhaling for a full ten minutes, charging his blood with oxygen. Then he arose to tread water, head up and body vertical, supported by a mighty swishing of his flukes. For ten seconds, his eyes fifteen feet above the surface, he squinted across five miles of shimmering haze. He thought he saw activity among the ship's tiny dwellers, swarming like whale-lice on its back, but could not be sure.

He would wait. He dove for the bottom, almost a mile below, and lay for an hour in the primal ooze.

When his heart, which had slowed for the dive, began to race, he shot for the surface. He breached, leaping free of the sea and shaking his body to clear his eyes of water. Arching twenty feet above the surface, he swept his field of view.

The ship was indeed a whaler, had come to rest almost at the point at which he'd dived, had its six-clawed squeaking boats strung in a line from one end of his horizon to the other.

And the vessel itself was hardly a thousand yards away.

At the peak of his leap he clapped his fifteen-foot jaw, with a crack like a cannon shot that paralyzed for a moment the men on the distant ship. It was the ancient challenge of a furious bull to an intruder threatening his harem, and if those who heard it now did not understand it, they very shortly would.

He slammed back into the water sidewise, in a sheet of spray that would have terrified a smaller male, and centered the mother ship in his sonar. He had independent sidewise vision in either eye, and he could see the nearest boat to his right, claws all out of rhythm and dashing water everywhere. He outdistanced a boat to his left that seemed scurrying to cut him off, five scrawny oars stroking the water and one human in its peak, swaying like a moray poised to strike.

The bull was capable, at full charge, of almost twenty knots. He lunged along the surface in a series of semi-leaps, head up, flukes pounding and sixty-five-foot body planing foam. He was two-thirds the length and one-third the weight of the whaling ship itself. He twisted for a last visual fix on the ship, glimpsed its yardarm above him, saw one tiny human already hurtling through the air, lowered his head-case, and rammed the hull.

For a moment he was stunned, fighting for his senses. To pass out was to smother on the air in his lungs, for evolution had long ago denied whales the automatic breathing of land mammals so that cetaceans would not inhale and drown immediately if they lost consciousness below.

He won the struggle to hold his senses, but found himself on his back. Water was entering his blowhole, trickling past a sphincter valve proved at pressures a mile below. It was entering nasal cavities that had not known salt since he was punished as a calf. He fought his way to the surface, blew gratefully, then forced his head high above the water, streaming blood.

There were humans all around him, clinging to floating bits of the ship, screaming and thrashing. One of the boats was pulling back to help the men in the water. It was true, then, that they rescued their own. He set the scene in his memory: Every such link of man to whale should be observed and reported.

The ship itself was listing like a humpback with a torn pectoral. He could hear water gurgling into its splintered belly. He hoped that the men in the small boats would somehow pull to shore and make the attack known to other men.

Painfully he headed southeast, after his pod.

Only then did he learn the truth. Turning to echo for a last time on the sinking vessel, he discovered that he had damaged his headcase and middle ears. He could no longer sound the pulses he needed to search or hunt, or even hear the distant herd.

He must leave before his pod returned to find him.

He would be a burden, for they would try to feed him.

He swung east. The other two bulls or some new young male could fill his breeding niche.

Two days later he glimpsed a sandy cove under a soaring peak. He beached himself and let the tide run out and joined the Ocean of Thought within three days, on drier land than his ancestors had left, under the Andean sun.

The other two herd bulls rammed three more whaling vessels in the next three years. The smaller of the bulls died in the last attack, and the larger, whose skin was so white that men would mistake him for an albino, opened an eight-foot cut on his skull. Healing, the wound left a scar that would terrify whalers for thirty years from the eastern slope of the Pacific to the peaks of its western wall. But the ship that had marked him went down.

The attack scarred his brain as well. He took his pod to waters notoriously full of whalers, where the Southern Cross rose high. Man soon found them. There were ten days of bloody carnage in which the big bull saw his youngest female calf harpooned and tortured to make her squeal.

In that attack her mother was killed, and he very nearly died as well when he charged a whaling boat. Here he picked up the first of the nineteen harpoons that he would carry to his death. But before he began what most modern sperm regarded as mindless insanity, he organized the other bulls of the migration in a final threat to man, a huge star pattern near one of the whaling ships that had just launched its boats.

Heads in, tails out, they had thrashed the waters,

making mountainous waves that thundered for miles, swamping one of the boats and sending the others scurrying home to the mother ship.

The scar-headed white bull had drawn from cetacean legend the memory of the sperm's ultimate warning—to megalodons and killer whales, too—that the herd would kill to survive. He himself was soon to join cetacean lore, and man's as well.

The next day, while he hunted over the horizon, the whaler ambushed and killed off his harem, from the oldest cow to the youngest baby calf.

Off the island of Mocha, near Chile, the great white whale first killed a man, thrashing him in the water as the splintered boat sank nearby. For thirty summers he terrorized waters from the vale of Typee to the coast of Peru. In his sixtieth winter he crushed a boat off Valparaiso, then charged the craft that came to help it. Two men were mashed beneath his flukes.

A month later, five hundred miles south, he sounded on two boats from a vessel that had sailed all the way from the land that fringed the frozen north. The men were big, black-bearded, and trying to tow a dead sperm cow. He breached between the boats, soaring high over tradewind swells, and crashed in a sheet of spray, which swamped the nearest. The other circled the dead cow, using her as a barrier until the mother vessel returned. He charged the vessel, which he somehow missed. It picked up the survivors and fled.

He wallowed two days by the cow, waiting, but the whalers never returned.

The sun left the equator, flew north, crawled south and north again. He fed in the antarctic, rounded the Horn, and scouted the Falklands off the South Atlantic's western wall. His eyesight was failing now, and an iron that had slammed into his back twenty years before was festering deep in his flesh. But he somehow found a whaler with smoke pouring from its guts as it digested the last of its prey. He spouted loud and long, less than a thousand yards away.

The whaler lowered three boats. He led them to windward, made his rush, and missed: On the surface, with failing eyes and the clutter of waves jamming his sonar, he was very nearly helpless. As he passed he was struck. He sounded deeply, rose, and hauled the boat three miles. Then he sounded again, breached, and crashed down on the boat, demolishing it. He flogged at the men with his flukes, killing two.

A second boat arrived, grappling for the line he trailed. He dove to a level at which his echo location worked, took aim, lunged for the surface, stove the boat's bottom, and sank it. The men escaped in the third and last boat.

He cruised for the rest of the year, searching for victims and missing often. It was said that the festering harpoon was further affecting his mind, but most modern sperm—and the aging bull—believed that he had been insane from the moment he had seen the young calf murdered.

He found his way to the Sea of Japan. He attacked an innocent schooner carrying lumber, a proof to most cetaceans of his madness. He holed it but it did not sink. Three whalers arrived, apparently by chance, and rescued the men of the schooner. He surfaced and lay like a living taunt within their reach.

Each whaler lowered two boats. He led them to windward; he had learned that the men who worked the claws grew weary when they rowed against the wind. He surfaced and took a harpoon. He gasped a last, sighing spout, flinging water fifteen feet into a steely sky. He moved his flukes weakly, feigning death.

The boats were wary. They waited. Finally the one to which he was attached approached.

He exploded into a writhing, roaring mass of muscle and blubber, seventy feet long and weighing almost a hundred tons. He charged a distant boat and splintered it, still dragging the other. He bore down on a second, still tugging his burden, and missed. He whirled, grasped it in his jaws and shook it. In his frenzy he actually gulped down two of its men. They died, thrashing, in the first of his stomachs.

The boat he was dragging cut loose and fled with the other four for their mother ships. He followed, pausing on the way to ram the half-floating hulk of the lumber ship. Then he breached under the bow of one of the whalers, breaking off its beak.

Blind in one eye, he died without a struggle under the bows of a killer ship years later, his scar still blazing white and his back stubbled with the stumps of the nineteen harpoons.

Sperm whale legend held that at the end he had regained his sanity, and like any sick and dying whale, had simply found the quickest way to rejoin the Ocean of Thought.

In orca legend he was said to be heroic, a defender of all the mammals in the sea.

Most sperm whales believed that he had only angered man, and wished that he had never lived.

But in recent years, as the murders continued, certain aggressive young males had ignored the signs of madness in his ancient image and proposed to follow his example against innocent small boats off the busy bays.

Not far from where the three ancient bulls had met

off the Galápagos, two small sailing vessels had recently been attacked by an unknown whale and sunk. The humans and their little ones had drifted for months in the blazing sun. The aging sperm suspected some adolescent, orphaned by whalers, his brain attacked by the legend. Images out of ancient minds could be as dangerous to the young as roundworms in the ear.

Whatever the truth of the scarred one or the other two bulls, their struggles had all been useless, or worse. Man, unlike sharks or other predators, seemed to become more vicious when attacked, not less, as if some cautious ingredient for survival had been left from his evolution.

It was a frightening and lonely thought that the only other mammals that cetaceans could hope to communicate with might be flawed with lethal madness.

Whalers had returned each year with sturdier and faster ships, until finally they evolved craft built of a material so slate-hard and strong that even the three legendary whales of Galápagos could not have sunk them.

And last of all, in pure defiance, the tiny dangerous beings had folded their white wings and begun to make the ocean ring, some eighty years ago, to the maddening churn of ships with whirling flukes, and tipped their harpoons with thunder.

These even sperm had learned to flee, usually in vain.

These last big ships, and the speeding killer boats that clustered with them, were swift as meat-starved orcas.

The lines on spears they spat had threatened for the past eighty years to be the last link in the food chain joining cachalot to man.

Until this recent strange season of mercy...

* * *

Over lonely miles, as the aging Atlantic bull swam toward his rendezvous off Bermuda, he puzzled on what new hunting grounds man had found this season, and why for a time he was leaving the last of the whales in the sea. And he tried to guess the possible locations of the submarine the finbacks had pictured as sunk.

He thought on these things deliberately, to make the miles flow faster. For the Northwestern Atlantic Basin below him seemed to have stretched by half.

He knew the slowing of time as loneliness tinged with apprehension. The cows would welcome him, but the bull might not. He would be bigger now, and stronger, and, after the last three breeding seasons, surely a veteran of dozens of fights.

He hoped that any battle between them would be symbolic and nothing more.

Three hundred years ago, injury or death to either would hardly have mattered. There were plenty of bulls in the sea.

But in the shadow of extinction, every breeding male was a treasure. He would almost sooner damage his own jaw than the younger's.

He glided to a stop, blowing softly, an island of flesh in the waves. He heard the slap of spray on his brow, and the cry of a tern.

Why go on?

Somewhere, hundreds of miles ahead, he heard the faint bangs of a hunting cachalot. The whale was too distant to recognize, even if he had heard it before.

He could not tell if it was a bull or a cow. But he knew that he was too lonely to turn back.

He tossed his flukes into the afternoon sun and

sounded, boring into midnight depths. There he rolled and swam for a while, belly up, grateful for the cold. Then he rocketed to the surface, breached, arcing high in the golden light.

Last whaling season he would not have dared to clear the water for fear of man's harpoons.

Heart booming with strange excitement, he swam on.

〰 8 〰

The blue-black submarine on the Wallop Seamount rolled in the direction of the precipice and clanged against a rock she had jostled a thousand times before. She settled, shivering.

Peter Rostov sat in total blackness at his sonar console. He found himself shivering, too, at the shift in position. He discovered that his fists were clenched tightly. He forced himself to relax and adjusted his earphones.

Some American—Rayne? Cane? *Payne*—had recorded the song of the humpback whales once, off Bermuda, not far from here. A record, scratched and full of clicks, had made its way to Leningrad University, and he had listened with his friends and his Anna, whom he would later marry. She had thought it lovely.

Here on the bottom, the lonely, distant moans of

the living whales themselves had been more beautiful yet. He had found himself wet-eyed in the darkness as one distant basso, in a low and minor key, sang its dirge. The humpback seemed as bereaved as he, crying for contact with a far-off mate.

Or with other sapient beings?

Himself?

Ridiculous. He had been sitting in the dark too long. The gift of music from the whales should be sufficient; to analyze the score was travesty. He was a technician—if not by choice, by necessity—on an instrument of war. To attribute to such peaceful creatures a desire for human contact was to slander them.

At any rate that was yesterday, or the day before. Now they were gone. He decided that they had heard the music through the hull, had stayed only to listen, and had swum off when he had shut the tape deck down.

He wished he had the courage to risk the *zampolit*'s wrath and start the tapes again.

He hummed the prologue to the symphony he himself had been composing. The liquid warbling of his friends and the mystery of their gulps and trills, resonating from the undersea canyons and valleys below, had spoken of eternity, and he had tried and failed to echo their theme in the music he was molding in his mind.

He found himself leading an imaginary orchestra with his finger. He froze suddenly in the darkness. If someone turned a light on and saw him it would be serious. He must remain like an iceberg for the sonar crew, or what might be the last days of their lives would turn to chaos.

To calm himself he groped for his dials, turned up

the sensitivity of his hydrophones, and clasped the earphones to his head.

Nothing outside. The world had died. Even the croaker fish and snapping shrimp had tonight fallen silent.

Tonight? Or today?

He did not know or care. It would be pitch black for the first two hundred feet above, night *or* day. He had stared at the blackness by the hour through the periscope when he had had the purposeless control-room watch.

It was almost as dark within the submarine as outside her. And her lights grew dimmer as her batteries weakened. The skipper had been foolish last night and splurged. He had lighted the wardroom, fully, to celebrate some obscure Allied victory of World War II with a name Rostov could never remember. An American convoy with Soviet escorts had fought off Nazi subs near Murmansk, long before Rostov had been born. The Americans had been friends then; it was worth remembering this, now that the sea itself was the enemy and the *zampolit* was painting pictures, doubtless false, of potential Yankee brutality if he found a helpless foe.

But last night's minicelebration had been unique. Mostly they lived in darkness, except in the engine compartment, where the engineering officer, who was their only salvation short of a cry for American help, was still toiling endlessly.

The navigator, in sick bay, had begun this morning to babble of American destroyers above and divers hammering at their plates.

The Lithuanian mess steward, having survived his slashed wrists for two days, had finally languished and died. The doctor grieved and seemed to blame herself, though everyone knew that her supply of plasma had run out, and the Lithuanian's spirit, too, and that there was nothing she could have done to save him.

Yesterday—or the day before, or the day before that—at the *zampolit*'s command, the steward's body had been stripped of identification, skinned even of a heart tattooed on his arm, because it had a Lithuanian phrase in the roses twined around it. Rostov shuddered. The surgeon had rejected the captain's gallant offer to let the ship's cook do the skinning, and had performed it herself, while the hull creaked and clanked, with a firm jaw and steady little hands, as if in a medical school morgue.

The corpse had been inspected for further clues, weighted with chain, and discharged through the Number Five torpedo tube, with a few words of condolence and regret for the loss to the state by the *zampolit*, who, the sonar officer assumed, in any other navy would have been a chaplain.

Now he heard a bellow of rage from aft, and a cry of fear from the surgeon. He deserted his console and stumbled down the darkened passageway. He burst into the light of the sick bay and found Natasha, her hand to her cheek, clutching a stanchion and crying.

The navigator had both hands free of his wrist-chains and was fumbling with his leather leg cuffs. He swung his eyes to Rostov: They were animal-wild.

"Stay away, you!" he yelled, bending again to his feet.

One foot flew free.

"Stand off!" screamed the navigator.

Rostov stepped across the compartment, drew back his fist, and for the first time in his life hit a fellow human being. He struck him on the side of the jaw.

To his amazement the navigator's eyeballs turned up and he collapsed unconscious on the bunk.

Rostov turned to Natasha. "Where the hell's your corpsman?"

"I let him go to dinner, and Nicolai's cuffs were too tight, he said, and I loosened them and—"

"Give him his shot," he ordered her. "Hurry!" She injected his friend as he rebuckled the leather cuffs, shortening the tether on the chains. He straightened and she was suddenly in his arms, shaking.

He felt his throat tighten. Her body was soft and pliant, but more than desire he felt tenderness, and an ache for the pain she felt. On the eve of this patrol, his little daughter had fallen on the ice and cracked her wrist. She had shaken in his arms exactly like this. He stroked the surgeon's hair, peered at the bruise on her cheek. She swore she would be all right.

"We don't have to report it?" she begged. "He can't help it."

"Of course not."

She bit a fingernail. "If everyone goes mad—"

"They won't."

"Oh, I'm so damn *scared*!"

"We'll be all right," he promised.

He patted her cheek clumsily and groped his way back to his console.

He was as frightened as she. He had sent his final prayer to God the night before his audition for the Leningrad Symphony, when he had gone to his knees to beg for a seat.

No one had heard him then, so he was damned if he'd cry for mercy from the bottom of the sea.

But his mother was religious.

Four days below they'd been....

He hoped she was praying now.

⌘ 9 ⌘

The aging sperm whale heaved his bulk through waters growing milder every hour. The passage, joyfully begun, was turning tedious—a sign of age. And his mind, in boredom, was growing troubled, leaving his body and ranging ahead to the herd he loved.

Far to the south, his cows, with whatever calves the new bull had sired, would be swimming northward now.

He did not doubt that the new calves would be strong. He was sure that the new bull, who was enormous, would have passed on his size to the young.

And that would bring him joy. To be as big as possible was a survival advantage to a sperm, as for any warm-blooded animal in the sea.

The aging sperm had pondered on the bulk of his species, and on the even greater size of blues, and was sure that cetacean growth must have started when the first cetacean ancestors left the land.

Whales' picture of the land mammals from which they had sprung was necessarily cloudy. Camels, pigs, and cattle, found swimming or dead in tidal waters, had been scanned. Their multiple stomachs and identical kidneys were thought to show that they and whales had a common ancestor.

But all of these land mammals were smaller than the largest whales, and lacked blubber.

Sperm understood why their ancestors had found need for mass and fat. Any warm-blooded animal in the sea needed bulk, because water drained heat from skin much more quickly than did air.

In whales, as in other mammals—like man, who seemed to die quickly in cold waters—the internal temperature of large and small individuals was the same and must be kept so. Even in arctic waters a small whale had to keep himself as warm as a large one. To an aquatic animal body heat was life. So the smaller whale, though throwing off almost as much heat to the water around him as the larger, must supply this energy from a smaller store of blubber. In times of stress or famine he died first.

Thus evolution had worked for the greater size of the sperm whales. But man came, and harpoons, and the sperm universe turned upside down, for man killed the largest whales, so that breeding was left to the smaller. Some big bulls, still virile but realizing that they drew attention to their herds, had left breeding to the smaller bulls and had swum alone to polar waters, where they stayed the year around, far from females. With only other males to relieve their sexual pressures, the seeds of super size seemed to have died with them.

Although smaller than his sire had been, the aging Atlantic bull knew himself to be among the largest of cachalots still in the seas. He had, during the last quarter century, met only three sperm bigger than himself. His father was one, and another was a great male his own age with whom he had swum last year in the arctic, and whom he still loved deeply. The young sperm to whom he had given his harem was the third.

The aging emperor had spent his life ensuring the stability and safety of his herd. He had chosen his successor wisely in terms of size and strength: That he had never doubted. But, having abdicated to the arctic, he had learned, too late, from a Pacific sperm that the new herd bull had been an orphan since adolescence, survivor of a famous slaughter off Hawaii well known in the recent history of whales.

A wandering bull, deprived of his elders in youth, was not the successor he would knowingly have chosen, no matter how big and strong. The young herd master, he feared, must have vast gaps in his experience, which nothing now could fill.

And so he had begun to worry. Size and strength were needed, but something else as well.

Young bulls needed long hard discipline under a strong pod leader, or else the massive sperm brain, which demanded use for good or ill, could lead them to strange passages indeed.

In the pod the path to bull-whale maturity was long, frustrating, but essential to survival of their kind. A bull calf, hardly thirteen feet long and weighing less than two tons at birth, would not be weaned until he weighed ten tons and was over a year old. By the age of eight, forty feet long, he would be as heavy as his mother. Although the testicles he carried internally still weighed less than five pounds each, the eel-like penis curled in his ventral slit, when voluntarily erected as he rolled belly-up in show or play, would be a foot in diameter and soar almost as tall as a full-grown man.

He would be quite capable sexually.

But he lacked the teeth and the strength of jaw to

give battle to adult bulls for females. His teeth would not penetrate his gums until he was almost twenty-five years old, and so he would remain on the outskirts of the harem, contributing his hearing as a sentry against man and orca, and his skill and speed to squid hunts.

Always he would long for sex, but if he was intelligent, he would have early learned to defer in all things to the bull who led the harem.

A teething young bull whose intellect was weaker than his mating drive might risk the harem master's anger and penetrate a cow. In ancient years—before man had so diminished the herds that death in combat became an unthinkable waste—he might well have been killed by his elder.

The aging emperor whale had long concluded that it was this harem life of sperms that gave them the intellect to lead Cetacea. The seed of young males unable to accept the brain's dominance over body simply failed to survive: Only adolescent cachalots capable of restraining their sexual drives lived to sire the young.

The proof of his theory was in the blues. Blue whales had brains almost as large as sperms. But blues had no harems. A blue bull found a cow—bigger, in fact, than himself—and mated for life. In none of their ancestral lore dwelt the precept that intellect must dominate passion. They had no reward for discipline to select the strongest mind; no punishment of death or exile to a bull who failed the test.

And so the blues—though gentle giants well loved by sperm—had brains no more orderly than a dolphin's or a man's.

The chain of harem discipline had bound the aging

sperm to the arctic for two years. To return—even for good reason—strained his nature.

And might well strain the nature of the bull he had welcomed—perhaps mistakenly—and fought with, and lost to long ago.

$ 10 $

The aging sperm put their fast-approaching meeting from his mind and drove onward. He had deliberately swung far south until he picked up muffled echoes of the Nares Deep, 21,000 feet below. Now he could ride the Gulf Stream north.

His circuitous route with the currents had swept him onward and preserved the fat he had accumulated in the canyons south of the Greenland Rise. Joining the flow of the Gulf Stream conserved energy, and the warm Antilles Current saved heat. If he did not squander his store of blubber, he could stay with the herd all summer without poaching on limited squid.

Blubber, and the oil it held, was life.

He had good knowledge of the anatomy of his kind. Like all cetaceans, he had since birth been unconsciously scanning, with ultrasonic precision, the internal organs of friend and potential foe, prey and passing fish, harem, calves, and strangers. Instinctively he had searched out sickness, strength, recent diet, and even the churning of stomach gases of high emotional state.

Knowing the organs of others, he presumed that he knew his own. His blubber was a fatty tissue of large cells bounded by fibrous networks, bursting with the oil that warmed, cooled, sank, and buoyed him, depending upon how his blood in turn had transferred its heat to the fat. In his present well-fed condition, his blubber was firm and resilient and made up almost half his weight.

The blubber itself was three quarters oil. The oil, cachalots had known for centuries, was the food for which men hungered more than the flesh of sperm they killed.

His blubber was the only wealth he had, now that he had given up his harem.

He had companions even older than he in the bachelor herds of the north. He had watched them expend fat in play, for sperm whales sported all their lives to remain young and flexible of mind. Some spent their blubber like calves, though they knew that their hearts were aging and their dives growing shorter and the prey, for them, growing scarce.

Perhaps, deprived of females, they no longer even cared.

For months he had refrained from play—even the sexual sport that served males removed from their herds—saving enough fat to bring his message to the herd he loved. When the summer was over he would return to arctic waters, never to see his cows again.

And then he too might frolic, not caring if his blubber was hard with protein or soft from lack of oil.

He pressed his pectoral fins close to his body, testing the consistency of the sheath he wore. When he headed north again, it would be flabby as a beluga's or a starving bowhead's, but now the blubber was firm and solid, and all of the folds and slack, where his skin sagged free, had purpose.

At any velocity above a cruising crawl, the loose flesh filled with the eddies of water that the whale made when he swam, smoothing the flow around the body, saving energy and increasing speed.

Despite blunt brow, bulk, and deeply drafted body, he could rest his flukes and glide for half a mile.

He was grateful for whatever forces had remolded his kind to live again in the sea. For he knew, by the vestigial limbs he saw in Cetacea, that his species had lived long ashore. He wondered sometimes if mankind knew it too, or cared.

Sperm had long asked themselves why the ancestors of man, when once they had evolved intelligence enough, had not escaped like their own forebears from the unforgiving land, back to waters safe from want.

The aging sperm, who loved man while he feared his immaturity, judged that somewhere in the ancestry of these strange and lethal animals must be an errant, stubborn strain.

Cetacea had once pitied them their naked struggles on the shores, imagining the predators and storms they faced. Whales had watched with tolerance, from the safety of unchanging seas, while men tried ineptly to conquer, from the third of the globe that was land, the endless swarming depths.

Whales knew that the chain of feeding was uncaring of what its creatures did, so long as they survived. It was enough that they lived and breathed and died and lived again. To the Ocean of Thought, all living things were tentacles sensing the tides.

None but man tried to change the world or the ocean's surge.

Perhaps man's vision, like an infant whale's, was only of himself. Perhaps his toys were nipples, to feed his newborn mind.

Such blindness had seemed harmless for some twenty thousand years. But now men entered emerald depths, probed and tormented the shore. And stood safely astride their islands of land, while their wastes ran into the sea. Their eyes seemed cloudy: They did not see that when plankton and krill and whales were gone, the human end would come.

It seemed to the big sperm bull that men would be the last to know.

But the last to go.

Perhaps, after all, man's ancestors had chosen more wisely than his own.

He swam through the night and heard no more of the distant hunting sperm. Just after dawn he plucked echoes from a long-remembered wreck on a rise in the Northwestern Atlantic Basin, sunk forty years ago in the last of the explosive epidemics of sinkings that had plagued men's ships. It was a famous bottom mark on the sperm's autumn migrations to southern waters.

When it was first noticed it had been spewing oil like a wounded octopus; afterward, sickening tentacles of it had trailed along the bottom for a decade. Sounding it now from the surface, he noted that its echoes had grown fainter. He would not waste energy diving it—at two thousand feet, it was near his present limit anyway—but he was sure that if he did he would find that oozes and organic sediments were burying its plates. In a few more decades its superstructure would be all that projected from the midnight plain. Like all things of man that sank, it was sinking again, this time under an endless rain of dead sea-life from sunless levels above.

When the vessel finally disappeared, it would be no great loss.

There were plenty of other wrecks in the basin, and there would be more to take its place.

The men who had drowned with it had returned to the food chain forty summers past; he supposed that some infinitely tiny trace of each was in the squid he'd taken here long ago, still in his own body and brain and blood.

His turn to join them in the Ocean of Thought could not be many summers off.

He knew from the wreck that he was only five hundred miles from the Bermuda Rise. His rendez-vous with the herd was above the crest of a ridge some one hundred miles ahead.

He had sent word of his intentions almost six months before, after long and heavy thought, when northern sperm had noticed that the killer ships this year had failed to sail from the Baltic, Petropavlovsk, and the Sea of Japan.

The southbound orca pod to whom he'd entrusted the message would have found his herd months before. Even slowed by its calves, the orcas would have crossed the Atlantic in half the time he had taken. So acute was orca hearing that it would easily have located his herd, from his sound-pictures, in the sparse winter feeding ground in the Equatorial Current.

He swam onward. A swift rise in water temperature

and his own racing pulse told him that he had intercepted the tepid core of the Antilles Stream. In his thick arctic blubber he must either dive deeper for cooler layers or divert his path to the north. His flukes and pectoral fins were cooling surfaces. Increased blood flow radiated heat. But water too warm could raise his internal temperature so fast that his blood would simmer in his veins.

He elected to submerge. Rather than expend energy by diving, he would simply sink. He glided to a stop and began to charge his lungs for the depths.

Though the surrounding water was warm, it was still cooler than the spermaceti oil in his head-case. When sperm oil was cooled, it contracted in volume. Lining the membranes of the great cavity in which the oil was kept were sinewy conduits through which salt water from his mouth and blowhole could be led. He forced water through these channels.

In a few minutes the sperm oil in his head-case became more dense. In arctic waters he could actually have caused it to congeal. But this sufficed: Gradually his head dropped beneath the chop of the Gulf Stream. He began to sink, slowly, then more and more swiftly as the temperature around him fell.

At a thousand feet he flicked his flukes and resumed a horizontal posture. With minute adjustments to the buoyancy of his head-case, and by shifting the air in his lungs and body cavities, he lay suspended in darkness, a thousand feet deep and a thousand feet above the Bermuda Rise, still carried by the current but radiating heat to the chilled levels around him.

He lay so, at neutral buoyancy, for half an hour. He could hear the crackle of pistol shrimp, and somewhere a croaker fish was grating.

All at once he heard what he had longed to hear for two long years: the faint and distant voices of his own herd. Now there was no doubt, for he recognized instantly the sharp-pulsed bangs and reverberations of his half-sister, the cow he loved most of all, calf of his sire, his own favorite mate for twenty years.

She was echoing on a squid somewhere to the northwest, between him and the Bermuda Rise. As he listened, joyfully, he heard the staccato cracks of smaller cows, recognized a daughter and a playful female he adored, and the imperial squeal of a baby bull.

His impulse was to speed toward the group, but he quelled it. He had fat to preserve if he was to stay with them for long; squid were scarce and he must leave those there were for the group.

He ceased the flow of cooling water to the oil in his head, shifted air aft in his lungs, and floated placidly to the surface. There he resumed his ponderous fluking in the easy, powerful rhythm that had brought him three thousand miles in twenty days.

They were a hundred miles off at least. The new herd bull was silent, or foraging elsewhere.

The rendezvous was less than one day away. He began to give thought to the moment of meeting and to what the new herd bull would do.

The aging sperm feared conflict, for the sake of the herd. The younger bull might fear it too. But man was not the only thinking animal that acted irrationally. The older bull knew that his own kind had well-known weaknesses that sometimes defied intelligence.

Its larger bulls seemed always driven to fight to rule the herd.

Much depended on how he approached the harem.

❧ 11 ❧

The sun rose on a sapphire sea. The aging sperm lay twelve feet below the surface, listening silently to the approaching pod, his tiny earholes insulated from the chuckle of the Gulf Stream chop by two fathoms of water still cool from the winds of the night.

He had lolled here in what he estimated to be the path of the herd during all the hours of darkness. Swept gently north by the current, with only a flick of a pectoral fin or a swish of his flukes to maintain position and depth, he had surfaced every hour, lying awash for ten minutes while he sent sixty long sighing breaths into the moonless night, then submerging again to listen.

Listening so, he had already gathered a considerable knowledge of how the pod was faring.

He knew that last night it had hunted poorly.

Poor feeding waters meant sickly calves and a lack of milk, babies born headfirst to drown, and sometimes floundering infants left to die.

Which was why he had returned from the north....

For the last hour he had known that his half-sister was controlling the pod. He could sense this from his offhand bleats to the other cows and occasional signature whistles to the outriding yearlings, which permitted them to gauge her location without alerting squid to their own.

And he knew certainly that the herd master was elsewhere, for he had heard only the echo-bangs of cows, none of them over forty-five feet; this he knew from the short interval between the primary pulse from the sounding lips and the echo from the back of the head-case. The interval varied precisely with the length of the herd. The harem bull's, he knew too well, was as awesome as his own.

The herd's normal playtime was approaching: Barring some unnatural occurrence, the cows would leap and sport with the calves for a while, suckle the young until the sun rose three fluke-widths, then post their sentries for the morning sleep.

He was overcome with an ache to be with them, a longing so powerful that it squeezed his heart and lungs, as if he had dived too deeply and stayed too long.

He forced himself to wait.

If he lay silent and undiscovered until he heard the bull returning, he could intercept him away from the group and visualize for him the evil, to the pod, of real struggle; picture, too, the sensible, not uncommon alternative: a meaningless display of threat, harmless wrestling, and afterward, tolerance.

He himself had once allowed his sire to return without battle. Despite the law of sperm whale nature that seemed to decree social catastrophe to a herd with more than one fully toothed bull, he had all that summer felt only affection for the wallowing giant.

But that had been long ago. And he had detected in this new harem bull, when they had fought, a certain ferocious tenacity that might cause tragedy now.

He sank to quieter water at twenty feet. All at once

he sensed that his half-sister had stopped her sonorous probing ahead of the herd. He heard a questioning whistle, as if she sensed his presence: not impossible, for there had always been a bond between them more mysterious than sound.

She whistled her signature again, inquiringly, with a rising note of tension. When he still did not reply she warbled, in the cetacean way, an exact replica of his sound-echo as perceived from her own angle and distance, so that he saw himself as she saw him: immense in the water, head-case and jaw scarred by a lifetime of battle with squid and interloping bulls, with the ridge of a harpoon-slash behind his left pectoral fin.

The image was blurred and tremulous, shimmering through a half-mile of ocean with the music of their love.

He could wait no longer. He began to rise, powering toward the herd, great flukes moving half a ton of water at every stroke, rocketing for the surface through dancing shards of sapphire from the marching swells above.

He had not forgotten the absent harem master, but he could no more have stopped his reckless charge for sunlight than his pounding heart. He broke surface, scattering a school of wave-dwelling needlefish, soared high and glittering over foaming hillocks of blue, hung for an instant with his head a full thirty feet high, only his caudal trunk and flukes in the water. At the height of his arc he twisted, flinging a sheet of spray at the sun, then slammed on his side into the sea in a booming crash that jarred him from the tip of his flukes to the rounded blunt of his snout.

The ocean seemed shocked into silence for an instant, then came alive with sound. Now all the pod knew he had arrived, the cows and yearlings and even the youngest calf. Their squeaks and squeals and creaks of joy seemed all about him, though the nearest was still a thousand yards away.

Reason returned to him, and a moment of regret.

If the harem master was within earshot and chose to interpret the leap as challenge, all of nature would tell him to accept. When the body spoke to so young a bull, the brain was often silent.

To breach had been a foolish thing to do. But what was done, was done. The fastest marlin in the seas, chasing the setting sun, could not set the day back a single instant.

For now he was surrounded with writhing, joyous females and squirming young, and his great pulse pounded with happiness. He could only wait to see.

◊ 12 ◊

All night she had led the herd in the hunt for squid, scanning waters she had not sounded for years.

Her hunger these days was unending, for the drain on her energy was enormous. Her calf swam always at her side, just behind her pectoral fin, where the pressure wave of her motion drew him with her as if attached to an invisible cord. He weighed nine tons and the laws of fluid dynamics exacted the same toll on her muscles, with the calf dragging at her wave patterns, as if the bond between them were of steel.

He was only ten months old and could not other- wise have kept the pace she set for the herd, so out of her own body she had to provide not only his food but part of his motive power.

He was gaining a hundred pounds a day on the fifty gallons of milk she squirted for him, and he sucked every half hour. It seemed to her sometimes that there were not enough squid in the sea to satisfy her, or enough richness in her teats to satisfy him.

To ease her hunger and that of the other lactating mothers, the harem bull, two years younger than she, had left the pod yesterday to hunt over the bottomless void of the Nares Deep. Food had been scarce all through the long swim north, and it was not his habit to compete with the cows when he might seize bigger squid in deeper water.

For weeks she had verged on panic. She feared that this time hunger would dry her milk.

The tiny herd was used to scarcity; the western soundings of the North Atlantic Basin, from the skinny neck of Panama to the jut of Nantucket Isle, had long been short of food. The school's very presence here was for that reason, for whales congregated where squid were plentiful, and her half-brother, who pre- ferred the risk of famine to the certainty of slaughter in better feeding grounds, had chosen these waters as the safest refuge he knew.

For the group had not always swum here. It had once been part of the great migratory pattern above the Azore, Canary, and Cape Verde Basins off the knob of Spain. Once, the pod had joined the hundreds of thousands of sperm who risked harpoons for the rich upwellings off the coasts of Southern Europe and

North Africa, and fed in teeming waters flowing past Gibraltar from the tepid inland sea.

Then the herd had numbered seventy cows and three young bulls, and an outpost bachelor pod of fifty.

And thirty seasons ago, during these short days of carnage over the Basin of Sierra Leone, it had seen half the cows, all of the bachelors, and two of the young bulls die.

Her half-brother, twenty-five summers older than she and adored above all the cachalots in her sea, had led them here immediately. And was, she hoped, returning to lead them away.

Every night for weeks she had been listening, as she hunted, for the smashing boom of his sonar or the whisper of his voice or the warble of his signature as he lumbered through the seas.

A month earlier, while the new herd bull hunted elsewhere, southbound orcas had painted a sound picture of the aging sperm and of the seamount above which they had left him. She recognized the peak as a well-known mark in cetacean navigation, the highest summit of the Reykjanes Ridge off Greenland, though she had never been so far north herself.

Unless today she was mistaken or the orcas had misunderstood, he was due within a week. She had been frightened of the harem master's reaction to the orcas' news and had not relayed it, but had imperceptibly, through selection of the new day's hunting grounds for the herd, eased the pod to the rendezvous point. She was frightened by what she had done, but she longed for the calm of the older bull's intellect and the great scarred hulk of his body.

When he had led them to these waters she herself was twelve, heavy with the first calf he had given her, and happy, though she realized he was guiding them knowingly from plenty into want.

Since that long migration, against the flow of nature, the herd had not prospered.

But it lived.

Not long after dawn she had sensed him; how, she would never know, for she had not been sounding, the last squid having dived some time before.

The feeling of his nearness had puzzled her for hours. She knew that sharks and other fish had powers beyond intelligence, and that they somehow felt, without hearing, others of their species and predators and prey.

Perhaps whales, who knew the presence of their kind only through sound or sight or sometimes the taste of urine in the water, had once had this mysterious sense as well, but lost it in the sea. And perhaps they had lost other senses even more mysterious as their great brains grew, senses that had less and less value as one whale learned to mimic the sound of his own sonar to make its pictures live in the mind of another.

With such a reliable link as sound available, they needed no primitive channel between mind and mind. But it was strange, and a little discomforting, that between her and her half-brother a vestige of this bond remained.

She had never enjoyed what she did not understand.

The sense of his presence grew stronger by the instant, so strong that she was impelled to raise her head, heaving her upper body half-free of the water while her calf tried to imitate her. She began to turn slowly, scanning the horizon, and was halfway around when the aging bull breached a thousand yards ahead.

Her world became a shattering kaleidoscope of dancing waters, rushing bodies, grunts and groans and shrieks of joy, and a bone-deep chill of fear.

The younger bull had been gone for twenty-four hours. He was sure to return today.

〰 13 〰

For half an hour the school leapt and dove and squirmed in joy. The aging bull, who for years had not felt a female body sliding along his own, or the thump of a calf butting him in play, found himself starved for these things and reluctant to call a halt.

But when he had cavorted and stroked and been stroked by all, sounded his love to each and heard their love for him in the moans of the young and the old, he led them slowly north, stopping every few thousand yards to glide and let the baby rest, until he felt the pulse of the herd stilling and knew that the excitement had ebbed.

They had hunted all night, and soon all but his half-sister and her calf dozed, sleeping with both eyes closed because he was there, secure in his nearness as if he had never left.

Only then did the three—bull, cow, and little calf—

move away, slowly and languidly, upwind to his old post on the outskirts of the school.

He was curious and excited about the tiny bull.

Could she already have been gravid with his bull calf before he left two years before?

She could not know, of course, and so he never would.

Why this made him unhappy he did not know. Whether he or the new bull had sired it, he should now feel only joy at its plump stocky frame and vibrant flesh. In an age when males grew ever smaller, his half-sister had birthed a baby giant.

He caressed the little head with the tip of his pectoral fin and swam away, circling the herd to scan its members individually, quietly, at frequencies so high that no one awakened. He wanted to see what the years had done.

The pod had not fed well. And so his worst fear had come to pass. The waters of the western Atlantic must be nearly drained of squid. Far to the north, where ice growled at the braking seas, he had suspected this from the thin blubber on arriving orcas. He had listened to them hunting, herding seals and Greenland right whales to their deaths, and finally heard their own reports of famine over southern grounds.

If giant squid, which fed on smaller squid, which fed on fish and plankton, were growing even scarcer, then something was harming the local waters more seriously than river waste.

It was not a change in salinity: He could have tasted that. It was not too high a temperature, for he remembered how he used to spend hours in these waters on the bottom to cool his blood, and he felt that same need today.

Neither saltiness nor temperature had changed since he had left.

Oil?

He had heard from orcas who had cruised the Caribbean that man was building more of the platforms that sucked oil from the primal ooze. It was said that a great blazing cancer of it had stretched a mile wide on the surface over the Yucatán Basin.

Oil floated. It coated seabirds so that their feathers could not dry, and they died thrashing on the surface. Baby seals swam in it, crawled out to bask, and died shivering and coughing in the rookeries of the north. Even the young of the least intelligent cetaceans knew enough to avoid it where they could.

But krill was mindless, heeding only light, and could not avoid the spills. Perhaps oil dimmed the twilight that the krill needed to survive, or buoyed and kept away from it the tiny surface organisms it needed in the depths.

He stirred restlessly. Small squid ate krill, larger squid ate smaller squid, and sperm ate the largest squid of all. Man, having ceased to kill whales with spears of iron, was poisoning their seas.

He put the thought out of his mind and probed his half-sister's belly with an ultrasonic moan.

She was thin as the rest, and he saw that she had taken only seven squid, none over five feet long. The gases in her stomach told him that she was full of fear.

He knew why this was, and slid beside her, comforting her with his bulk. She sent him a high-pitched image of the young giant he had honored with the school. From her picture he seemed even bigger than when the aging sperm had left, but he tried to ease her fear with another vision: he and the other bull, far from the herd, playing at a struggle, and then acting together for the good of the pod.

She turned fiercely, countering with her own prediction: a crashing, whirling battle, water boiling red. The baby, though hardly one year old, seemed already able to read simple images, for he squealed in distress.

The aging male slid a fin down the length of the calf's tubby body, and finally the little one slept. His half-sister seemed to become more calm, and murmured pictures of the years that had passed.

As all Cetacea knew, there was no way to speed the tug of the moon on the tides, and he could only wait.

❧ 14 ❧

Peter Rostov stumbled in the dark toward the tiny wardroom, where the captain and the ubiquitous *zampolit* awaited his report of transient surface traffic. He grabbed at a remembered handrail, invisible in the blackness. It seemed to him that the motion was worsening. The creaking of the hull was drowning out the crunching of the rocks beneath it. An immense boulder amidships seemed to be grinding its way aboard.

He felt his way into the wardroom, squinting in the dim light to distinguish the captain from the *zampolit*. With a sudden chill he saw that the *zampolit* was sitting at the head of the table, with the skipper, nursing his tea, to the side.

A thing of no importance, he hoped: This wardroom, and this captain, had never stood on ceremony. Perhaps the captain had been sitting there first, and the *zampolit* simply had taken the most convenient chair.

Or perhaps rank made no difference this close to the grave.

Still, the commissar, who scarcely knew the depth gauge from the master chronometer, seemed to gain more assurance by the hour as the technical competence of the line officers, like their instruments, grew more irrelevant.

"So what have we today?" the *zampolit* asked. His glasses were rosy in the battle-lantern glow.

Rostov knew that it was the *zampolit* who had insisted on the daily sound-surveillance report. At first he had assumed that the commissar had been traumatized by the *Glomar Explorer* incident. Now he knew otherwise, for he had already explained to the *zampolit*, who was typically ignorant of all but the Party line, that their situation here was different.

The poor dead *Baku* had been famous for the smell of hydrogen from her ancient batteries. When she blew, she exploded with a concussion that must have struck the US early-warning hydrophones like an undersea volcano. No wonder they had pinpointed her wreckage on the bottom.

But the *Plutonium Piccolo* had come to rest on the ledge softly, with no more noise than she was making now, rolling among the boulders. If the US Navy had heard her through their line of coastal hydrophones, they would already have been wheeling above like kites on a dying cow.

Since the Americans had obviously not heard them settle on the ridge, there was no reason to think they would be searching blindly.

Their sub's mission was routine. The US Navy knew that there were Soviet submarines submerged in American waters every day of the year, as their own nuclear subs patrolled off Riga and Murmansk. They would hardly be shocked to find them here—only disappointed later, if they managed a salvage, to find how obsolete they were.

All this the *zampolit* ignored, insisting that the danger of discovery was real, that their secrets were important, that the crew had an enemy to repel. All to give his shipmates a reason—when there was not a valid secret on the ship that could not be destroyed instantly in the code room shredder—to die silently and obediently here below. Next in the idiot's lectures would be reminiscences of the siege of Leningrad.

He was casting himself and all the rest as actors in a patriotic movie. Black and white. No sound. Ten days long and still grinding on.

Garbage.

"The report, comrade?" repeated the *zampolit*.

The captain looked embarrassed at the breach of wardroom etiquette. "Tea first, Peter Rostov?" he murmured, and poured him a cup. Rostov heard the teacup rattle. He hoped the captain's hand was trembling with anger at the *zampolit*'s boorishness, and not fear.

He began his list of passing traffic. At 0300 hours he had heard a freighter, range seventy miles, speed eighteen, course dead west, apparently heading for New York. At 0642 another; at 0934 a third, eastbound, probably departing the United States; and then two more, faster freighters, one at 1040 and another at 1100.

"Freighters?" the *zampolit* murmured. "I have never understood how you can be so sure. Why would merchantmen travel so fast?"

To get where they are going, he almost answered. *Idiot, we should be screaming to them for help, not trying to hide from them!*

Instead he explained the intricacies that gave each ship a sonic signature: propeller cavitation, rpm variation, number of engines. "A destroyer's propeller is a snare drum; a container ship's is a bass violin."

A mistake, that analogy. Rostov knew it as he said it, for he had noticed that the same concert gossip that fascinated the captain and most other officers made the *zampolit*, who had slugged his way from some cultural compost heap, edgy and uncomfortable.

The *zampolit* smiled. "Snare drums and bass viols? To you, Comrade Rostov, life is a big brass band." In the ruddy light his glasses shone warmly, and it was difficult to remember that behind them lay eyes of arctic ice. "Even your whales are musical." In a moment of weakness, when the commissar had come stumbling into the sonar room on one of his inspections of crew morale—which were eroding what was left of it— Peter Rostov had handed him the earphones and let him listen to the humpbacks. He had let the captain listen, too. The *zampolit* had seemed to doubt that what he heard were whales. Perhaps he thought the Americans had developed musical sonar.

"The whales are gone now," Rostov murmured.

"I *envied* the lieutenant," the captain said seriously. "They were beautiful voices."

"Let us not forget something," muttered the *zampolit*. "We all know there are whales—" he paused, rubbed his nose, and said significantly—"*and there are whales.*"

Rostov stared at him. Was he joking or insane? He glanced at the captain. The old man, thank God, seemed equally nonplussed.

"Are you speaking," the captain asked incredulously, "of a kind of *Operation Elsinore?*"

The US Navy's *Operation Elsinore* was famous in the Soviet submarine force. For years the Russian Baltic Fleet had complacently slipped the latest Typhoon nuclear submarines, submerged, from Leningrad to the North Atlantic through the five-mile strait between Hamlet's castle and the Swedish coast. Soviet naval intelligence had discovered last summer, to its horror, that the US Navy was equipping trained pilot whales with underwater movie cameras to film their passage.

"If it happened in the Denmark Straits, why can't it happen here?"

Soviet retaliation, once the whales had been discovered, had been too brutal for Rostov's taste, but he imagined that the *zampolit* gloried in its special flavor and the final outcome.

"That's ridiculous," scoffed Rostov. "If they knew we were here—and even *cared* to film us—they'd hardly bother with trained animals. They'd come with ships and they'd lower TV cameras. Besides, a pilot whale is only a large dolphin. *My* whales, as you put it, are humpbacks. Could they train fifty-foot-long *humpbacks* to be spies? Have you ever *seen* one?" Rostov felt his voice rising. To deal with such dementia was impossible. "And if they could," he finished in exasperation, "surely they'd teach them not to sing while doing it?"

"I am only concerned that one day, while you're listening to their concert, you may miss the sound of a Yankee destroyer. And that an American musical-comedy may start on the surface. And that you will fail to sound the curtain bell in time."

Rostov tensed. "In time for what?"

The captain arose hurriedly, glancing at the ward-room clock. "I'm making my inspection," he told the *zampolit*. "You coming?"

The *zampolit* followed him out. While the captain made his daily round of the creaking, grinding hull, trying to bolster morale, the *zampolit* would follow, destroying it.

When the two had left, Rostov sat swirling the tea in his cup. He had meant to ask the captain what he planned to do when the Latvian admitted defeat and gave up on the engine.

No matter. With the *zampolit* there, the old man would have had nothing to say.

He might not know yet himself.

Rostov finished his tea and headed back to listen for ships.

Or whales.

🌀 15 🌀

The aging sperm lay waiting through the early afternoon, upwind of the herd. It had been a hundred years since the last white-winged whaler had swooped down on the breath of the trade winds to surprise a school, and now modern ships with whirling flukes stalked whales easily from downwind, but still not one male in a hundred posted himself to leeward, so deep was the tradition.

He rested in a trance, one eye open, ears tuned, with half his brain awake. He could hear his half-sister's gentle breathing, a short puff and a long sad sigh, and the higher-pitched, shallower breath of her calf, faster, but in harmony with her own.

His earholes were awash, and as they rose and fell in the water he became aware of a distant roar, not entirely unfamiliar. He dropped his flukes and tilted his body until he was vertical, head raised. With his forehead twenty feet above the surface and his eyes almost six, he turned half-around, his left pupil sweeping one-half the horizon and his right the other.

His vision had evolved for the purpose of searching out the phosphorescent gleam of squid in the midnight void, and he was dazzled for a moment in bright sunlight. But as his vision cleared he could see the mist over the herd from the spumes of their breaths in sleep, and fluffy white clouds racing from windward. He sighted the source of the roaring in the sky: One of the white birds on which men flew, tiny at this distance, trailing a tentacle of vapor as it slid through the blue.

It was far too high for one of the whalers' planes that had harassed his kind, so he lowered himself back into the water.

His movement awakened the calf, who began nuzzling at the cow's ventral slit. She half-rolled to her side until the slit was clear of water. Her upper teat emerged. The calf rolled sidewise, opening his slim lower jaw. His tongue was pink in the dancing sun. He grasped the teat at the side of his lips, made a funnel of the tongue, and adjusted his body so that he was lying half-awash on his mother's flank, his blowhole well clear of the surface.

Only then did she begin to pump milk, thick and fat-laden, floating yellow on the water where it ran down from his lips. For a long while the baby lay, his body parallel to hers, adjusting his position in the heaving swells while her nipple squirted. When she was dry he began to snuffle for the other breast.

He seized it and began again, but long before he was satisfied she heaved him off.

The aging sperm felt a chill of apprehension. He must somehow show the harem master that these waters could kill, through hunger, as surely as harpoons. And that, from all accounts in the northern seas, men's spears off Spain and Portugal were stilled.

He knew that the harem bull had carried human iron in his back since adolescence, and the fear of man in his heart. To dispel his fear might not be easy. The aging sperm himself, who had hardly felt the harpoon blade that scarred him, had just felt a lance of panic at the sound of the passing jet.

When fright had entered the cachalot strain, a madness had infected certain bulls. Man would have called it hatred. It was foreign to the ancient lore, and the old bull had never felt it. He only knew that it existed.

He was sinking into reverie when a crash like the boom of a harpoon gun slammed from the southern horizon. He was certain that no whalers sailed these seas. He had seen clouds racing north, but they bore no thunder. Man's flying squid could make such sounds, but by now the jet was leagues away.

It could only be the jaw-clap of a maddened harem male.

His hopes for peace with the younger bull died instantly. He whirled, began to suck in his breath with heaving, violent gulps. He would need all the air he could get.

Only then did he raise his head to look.

A half-mile away, a great shape rose majestically, hung suspended, framing the sinking sun in flukes grown wider than his own. It twisted in midair and struck the water in a crash of rainbow spray.

Instinctively the aging sperm slammed his own flukes with a clap of thunder that made the cows cry out. He raced toward the younger bull to keep the fight far from the herd.

For there was only battle, now.

Or flight.

And he had come too far with advice too wise for that.

❧ 16 ❧

Of all cetaceans only the sperm had found it necessary to battle his brother for the right to let his seed survive. Dolphins only played at dueling. Even the orca male won his pod, which he might share with another, through hunting skill and swiftness rather than strength of jaw or heart. When a killer attacked another whale, he was not fighting, he was eating.

Baleen whales, of course, had no teeth, disposition, or incentive to fight for females. Most of the gentle grazers simply mated. A male Pacific gray in a Baja lagoon would even steady a mating pair and wait his turn to mount. The giant Atlantic blue males, smaller than their cows, never knew the stress of combat and were faithful to one mate.

This all sperm knew. And they knew why their own bulls, most intelligent of all, were exceptions, forced in primitive times to gamble their lives and teeth and jaws for the herds they loved.

Cachalots alone had been impelled, by their feeding niche, to select huge fighting bulls as the only allowable links to pass massive brains to the unborn young. The deep levels the cachalot had chosen to rule, and the food he pursued, required both size and intelligence. A sperm had to locate speeding giants, faster than he, in a world without light half a mile below. He must calculate his rate of dive, target angle, interception course, the bending of his sonar beam through thermal layers, and his potential caloric gain, before the fight for food even began.

The sperm was the only living creature, including the great white shark, that cared to attack a fifty-foot squid in the squid's own depths. To remain warm in the giant squid's environment required mass. To subdue it required endurance and enormous strength. To match its agility required a brain unsurpassed, so far as the aging sperm knew, in all the world.

The cachalot was uniquely burdened. The gestation period of a sperm cow was sixteen months. If a small bull with a large brain, or a large bull with a small one, was allowed to enter a cow, she might be removed uselessly for the next two years from the breeding chain before her calf was weaned, while the calf, inherently feeble in body or mind, would first grow in her womb and then tug at her teats for milk.

And later, when he lacked the endurance, weight, or mental acuity to hunt large squid, the calf would die.

Lacking enemies of other species to keep his family strong, the bull sperm could compete only with his own kind to prove the potential of his seed.

Male combat before breeding was the only test he knew to keep his strain supreme.

So tested, he was invincible.

Until man.

The aging sperm lunged onward, sounding mighty cracks to pinpoint his adversary and creaking higher frequencies to estimate the younger's present weight.

Astonished, he discovered that his successor had

grown by a good two tons. For a moment he wondered
if it was another giant simply wandering past by chance.

Then he echoed on the harpoon stub that the herd
bull carried. Now he knew that it was he, that he had
simply prospered in the depths while the cows above
him hungered.

He heard the young bull's staccato bursts of sonar
tracking him. Instantly he mimicked the sound to blur
his image in the other's mind. The younger defeated
the tactic by varying his frequencies too swiftly for
him to follow. He had learned new strategies, apparently, in the years since they had fought. But strangely,
he was not yet charging, only computing his elder's
oncoming speed, lying awash in the water less than
half a mile ahead.

For a moment the aging bull had a sparkle of hope.
Perhaps the horrifying challenge had only been in
play. He slowed his headlong charge and glided.

The other did nothing.

Puzzled, the older bull stopped. Almost never, in
recent times, did a big male press for injury. His own
missing teeth had been lost in their previous fight,
but only because of some atavistic stubbornness in the
younger bull. To drown a challenger now would no
longer impassion cows, but anger them into flight. If
a modern harem bull cracked a weaker one's jaw and
doomed him to starvation, he might well lose control
of the herd.

Still, the harem master had clapped his jaw, and
this was the ancient challenge for combat without
mercy, to the death.

He listened. The bull still scanned him curiously.

A truly sagacious harem bull would often beam on
the contender's testicles to see if they were large with
living seed. If not, he might tolerate him as an alter-

nate target for possible whalers until the next breeding season. Then the newcomer would have to fight, at least symbolically, or leave.

Good. His own testes were aged and probably unimpressive, if not dry. If the young bull was not charging, he did not mean to fight. He felt a flood of relief. There could be, if the younger willed it, a simple pact of equals. Over the weeks to come he could picture for the school what he had learned in the north and help the young bull plot its course to other seas.

Then the elder would leave under the full moon, as his sire had left, never to see the herd again.

The harem bull continued to scan, as if they had never met. It was very strange. So the elder whistled his own identity in friendly greeting. The other whale politely stopped his creaks and warbles.

Now the elder heard only the slap of the waves on his own flanks and the faint distant grunts of the cows. They were gathering the babies and adolescents in the age-old crescent of spectators. He heard them snorting and moaning, quieting the young to listen to a struggle that he had hoped would never come to pass.

Slowly he began to swim again. In the cetacean manner he sent pictures of the route he had taken south, the diminishing number of squid he had noticed as he approached the Bermuda Rise, his joy at the fine young calf.

He was suddenly aware of a banging from the herd. It was his half-sister pulsing frantically on the harem bull. He intercepted her returning echoes and swerved, aghast.

The young bull had accelerated silently from dead stop to full charge, and now he was slamming across the water at orca speed, eighty tons of crushing muscle, silent as the deep.

His own salvation was below. With a great heave of flukes he porpoised, twisting into the air, then dove like a startled calf. But his length denied him protection: He was forty feet down, with his flukes still in air, when he felt the other's head-case slam the caudal taper of his tail.

The impact jarred him from tail-root to pectoral fin. He was knocked askew. He heard vertebrae crackling along the full sixty feet of his back.

He sank silently through twinkling blue and into twilight green. He was dazed with the blow, and only dimly conscious of a great black shadow passing above him, soundless as a cloud. Then he was sinking in grateful quiet, afraid to give away his position by echoing either bottom or adversary until he gathered his wits.

His pulse slowed when he dived, and he monitored it now to gauge his endurance, for he had been caught unaware, with no chance to charge his lungs.

He did not yet dare to use sonar: It would give his position away. He began to swim slowly north, helping the current, using precious air to put distance between him and the other. He needed only to ride the Gulf Stream waters until he required air. Then he would surface and escape.

The glancing impact had shown him that to try to stay was useless. He had given his herd to a giant among giants, and could only hope that it thrived.

His half-sister's sonar sounded suddenly with a sad and plaintive note. He felt a flood of love for her, for she was once more deliberately fixing the herd bull's position for him, violating every law of the pod.

He heard the young bull roar in anger. Now the herd master was charging, sounding as he went.

But charging toward the herd, at the cow the aging sperm loved most.

Insane. Against nature. The act of an elephant seal or a mindless shark. No bull could harm a female or the breed was surely doomed.

But the picture sounded clearly and he could not make it leave.

He arched his back, rolled belly-up like a turning wheel to reverse his direction in the fastest way he knew, zeroed his sonar on the distant charging male, and rocketed for the surface. His velocity was such that he breached high in the golden light. Racing toward the bull, he blew a rainbow arch that circled the plummeting sun.

The herd bull had already swerved, and was coming head-on. The move toward the herd had been a feint to draw him up.

The aging sperm clapped his jaws with a crack like a breaking tree-trunk, lowered his head, and charged.

❧ 17 ❧

With eyes set on each side of his head behind the jut of his brow, he was blind dead ahead, and so was his adversary. Closing head-on with a combined speed of almost forty knots, they were using frequencies from every voice box and sounding chamber in their bodies.

Hurling toward impact, each assessed his antagonist's speed, angle of jaw, number of teeth, and present weight.

As they charged they searched for openings in the sperm whale style. Neither could hide fright, for it would show in stomach gases; panic would pulse in the thousand-pound hearts, indecision in the tension of the flukes. The elder saw no fear in the younger and, as usual once battle was joined, felt none in himself.

Each knew the other well. The aging sperm, in their previous contests, had memorized every toothmark on the other's rounded rostrum, each tentacle-slash on his jaw, all of the grating barnacles on his skull. Quickly he groped, from a quarter-mile away, for recent wounds from squid or other bulls that could cause the other pain and give him purchase. He was startled to find an enormous new scar on the young giant's head, as if he had crashed blindly into a coral reef. He scanned it quickly, and found that it was healed and would be of no advantage.

But the foot-high mound on his back where the lance was buried he remembered best of all. He probed it now, hooting out a narrow beam from the very back of his head-case.

He had avoided this hump in their combat three years before, for he had scanned the twisted broken shaft and the blade inside and had known that if he slammed it with his flukes the younger whale would probably die in a frothing plume of blood. Of that he had seen enough in his youth on the whaling grounds.

But he would not avoid the mound today; if he killed the harem master, he would lead the school to richer waters and find the cows another.

And if the bull killed him? He hoped that the female he loved best would not suffer for her love.

* * *

To slam head-on would kill them both. But to swerve too soon was a danger to the one who first turned, for the flank was weaker than the head.

To the aging sperm this initial rush was a test of courage that had served him well before. For he had never been first to turn. He had first learned his tactics from his sire and in play as a calf off Iberian shores. He would hold his charge until the last instant, never swerve, never feint. At his antagonist's panicked last-second turn he would lower his head and crash into the soft underbelly between the hinge of his jaw and his pectoral fins, driving the air from his lungs.

They were a hundred yards apart now, less than five fluke-strokes from combat. He waited for the other to turn. Four, three, two...

The other would not turn.

Startled, the elder ducked. He heaved his flukes high, going for the deep. He felt the rake of barnacles along his back as the younger whale, unswerving and still silent, struck him just behind his head-case, passed over him in a shower of dislodged shells and suckfish, and pounded him once, with his flukes, precisely where the first back-jarring blow had hit.

He seemed not to be fighting the same bull he knew. The silence on meeting, the sneak attack, and now the unswerving charge seemed directed by a different mind.

He was in mortal danger, arched belly-out in pain, with his ventral slit and the penis coiled within it exposed to attack from the other's eight-inch curving teeth. Only ten feet deep, he floundered and straightened, dove for the depths, then arched his spine and tore back for the surface, using his buoyancy to speed his rush.

His target was the other's flukes, for if the half-moon scythes were not weakened now, they might later break his ribs. In the acoustic blind spot behind and below his opponent, he was safe from detection for the moment. He dropped his jaw, and when it was agape, rotated it to the left of his head, tensed, and struck from behind and below.

He clamped the caudal trunk. For an instant he hung on, tasting blood, curved teeth into rock-hard flesh. He felt his body wrenched and torn, and his jaw half-ripped from his skull. He let go, leaving a tooth in the other. A fluke sliced down from above, stunning him.

Now it was he who was blind to the rear. He whirled to meet the charge he knew would come. He had dived the first time; now he leapt. The other bull passed under him and he dropped, as heavily as he could, a full seventy tons from ten feet high, grinding his belly-barnacles into the other for traction.

Another sperm would simply have collapsed under the weight, and the shaft in this one's back should have driven home. It did not. The elder simply felt himself transported across the surface of the water like an ailing calf. Then the other rolled and it was he who was beneath, like a cow being ravaged.

He squirmed free, dove, half-rolled, and returned belly-up with his jaw swinging wide. The younger bull dropped his own jaw and they clamped together, rolling and wrestling a full six cycles, first one on top and then the other.

His heart was pounding, and he felt himself growing weaker. If he did not break away, he was doomed.

At sunset, on the seventh roll, he knew that he must

act. A red mist was forming in his brain, there was no breath, and the immense shape above was holding him below. He had a dim vision of sunny skies off Portugal and found within him a final convulsive twist.

He heard a sound like a breaking ice spire and a chill ran through his body. His jaw, or the other's, had broken and the fight was through. He felt the other relax. He righted himself.

And then came the pain.

His right jawbone, fifteen feet long and as thick as the thigh of a man, had broken five feet from its hinge. His mouth hung slack, immobile. A lance of icy pain struck his jaw again and again as it swung in the unending waves.

He was dimly aware that the other, with methodical, murderous swipes of his flukes, was flailing at his head-case. There was some safety from that below, where water pressure would slow the strokes.

Just before he lost consciousness, he felt a longing for black, quiet depths.

And entered them in his mind.

❧ 18 ❧

She had stationed herself and her baby on the end of the crescent of cows and calves, closest to the struggle but not so near that if one of the bulls fled they would impede his flight, for the child could easily be killed in the rush.

Of all the fights she had heard, none was so silent as this, or so frightening. For she truly believed that if the young bull won, he would kill her for warning the older, and then her calf would starve.

The sun set swiftly, with a dying flash of green.

She called her mind back to listen for sounds of battle. There were none. They must be locked in the final stage, clamped jaw-to-jaw, each wrestling to keep his own blowhole aloft and the other's submerged.

And then she heard a crack and knew that one or the other was doomed to die with a broken jaw. She did not know which until she heard the crashing of the other's flukes on a head-case, and then she knew, for her half-brother would not—and the young bull would—flail at a living brain.

She threw away caution and sounded on them. One vast echo lay blowing on the surface; the other was spiraling helplessly down.

She whistled once, at her oldest daughter, knowing that she would glide to the side of the baby.

Then she sank, silently as a squid, toward the endless depths.

He lay on his side in jet darkness a thousand feet down, half-sunken in primal ooze. A rattailed grenadier flashed by. The remora, sensing death, detached itself from his bloody lip, where it had fastened in arctic waters and feasted for months on scraps of squid. The sperm was as unmoving as the undersea foothills of the Bermuda Rise, half a mile across the plain.

He did not hear the narrow pulses of his half-sister's sonar, probing carefully along the mud, nor would he have, even if he had been awake, for she scanned at a volume so low and a frequency so high that even the bull above could not perceive it.

He lay unconscious, and thus unbreathing. For fifty-nine years, since his mother's cord had broken, a knowing part of him had planned every breath he had taken, awake or in semisleep, alert or entranced. But that part of his brain had failed, with the rest of it, under the pounding flukes. If consciousness returned and he let himself breathe, he would only drown and die more quickly in the end.

He was safe for the moment in the ocean's womb, until his tissues would burn the last of his oxygen against the cold.

His half-sister groped along the bottom at the limit of her diving depth. Her sonar picked him suddenly from among the foothills' mounds. She sensed his heartbeat more than heard it, and swept gently to his side.

She could have lifted a calf, or even a small cow,

squeezing it to her side with a pectoral fin. The unconscious were almost weightless in water. But the aging bull was far too massive. The only purchase she could hope for was his jaw, lying askew and slack, half-buried in bottom slime. She probed it with sound.

It was shattered, and the splintered edges of the fracture had even pierced the skin. To grasp it might trigger him into consciousness. If she awakened him below, and he breathed before he realized where he was, he would die.

He was stirring the mud now, moving the mighty body, and she heard a deepening groan. Quickly she glided to his skull-case, pressed her head against his, and warbled the danger signal. Then, over and over, she groaned a picture of his present plight.

He was dreaming, moaning pictures of surface things. She monitored her own pulse quickly. At a thousand feet she was well beyond her normal depth. Her pulse had slowed for the dive, but it was speeding now, and she had the calf to think of, and her milk. To strain her own heart and her energy store, to go dry, would be against nature and her love for the herd.

She should abandon the aging bull here, and quickly.

She could not.

Frantically she yanked at his jaw. He thrashed violently. She screamed a warning too late. She heard him blow, in a great bubble that flew for the swells above, growing like a monster squid, until at the surface it had increased thirty-fold in size. She heard it burst like a thundercloud directly above.

Then she was tugging, oblivious of his struggles and bellows of pain and the rumble of water pouring into his lungs. She freed him somehow from the bottom slime and pulled him upward, spiraling through squid and plankton and layers of warmth toward the moist night air and moonlight.

As she fought she begged, in sound and mind, for his great heart and brain to help hers.

❧ 19 ❧

He had been dreaming of a cow he had mounted in his youth off Gibraltar, from a pod of Cape Verde whales, while the bull of that pod was fighting another on a warm sunny day long ago. And in the midst of that vision had come another, of himself in the mud at the fringe of the Bermuda Rise, and a megalodon shark, three times as large as himself, twisting at his jaw.

Thus, when consciousness came he was half-prepared for death in the deep. He had been senseless on the bottom for nearly an hour: His pulse had slowed to one beat a minute, but when the nightmare shark struck, his heart began to race. With returning consciousness came the realization that he was near suffocation. His body released his nasal sphincter and he blew instinctively. But the shark shouted a warning that his blowhole was submerged, and he somehow managed to close it against the frigid rush of water. At a thousand feet, with five hundred pounds of pressure on every square inch of his body and his S-shaped blowhole-nostril opened to half a square foot, he had to close his sphincter valve against eighteen tons of water trying to force its way into his lungs.

Somehow he succeeded. He realized that he was being pulled upward by the megalodon shark. As they passed through six hundred feet, he sensed a layer of frigid water. It cleared his brain and he oriented himself. To his shock and fright his half-sister was trying to drag him toward the surface. She should have been with her calf.

With only three hundred feet to rise to the sweet night air, his flukes grew still and he began to sink again. He sensed her moving beneath him, sliding under his body. He had a flash of infant days, buoyed by his mother, and was rising, slowly, to the surface.

He burst into bright moonlight and blew a silvery spume of spray. For long, long moments he lay, wheezing and vomiting fluid from his lungs.

The Antilles current had drifted the herd far north. He could hear the bull sounding, for him or for the missing cow. The *blang* of the herd master, as he searched for him or her, was deafening and frightening, too, but a good ten miles away.

His half-sister keened softly for her calf.

✿ 20 ✿

The moon sped toward the ocean's western rim, drawing a trail of sea-silver like the wake of a frightened seal.

The aging bull lay on the surface, in pain so deep that not even the cow's murmurs of grief could reach him. His thoughts were of how best to die and join the feeding chain.

If he stayed at sea his half-sister might try somehow to feed him, and lose her milk and baby. His mind soared back to Nantucket Sound and the sickly calf they had brought there. Even with the men of the seashore to help, the chain of feeding and Ocean of Thought had captured the baby in the end.

The cow moved closer. He felt her pectoral fin slide over his head to make sure that his blowhole was clear.

He must make her return to her calf. Softly, silently, he pictured for her the storm in the Nantucket cove. He had urged her to sea, to join the other cows, and she had finally obeyed. Now he wanted her back with the cows again, with her sturdy little calf. It was his, he knew suddenly, not the new herd bull's, and the last who could carry his seed. He murmured a note of farewell.

She keened one low bleat of protest. He urged her

again. She pressed closely to him for a full half-hour before she swam away.

He listened to the swirl of her flukes grow fainter until he could hear them no more. Then he lay, a glistening island in a sea of pain, under the pale white moon.

She felt in her heart that her half-brother was doomed.

She had heard the grating of splintered bone in the surge of the ocean, pictured his jaw, swinging pendant in the sea, and grieved softly for the torment he must know. A lesser bull would have been whimpering in pain. She was sure he would never take another squid.

His blubber was thick. She had been sounding it. But she estimated that without food, even if he remained in tepid waters, he would not survive the summer. In a few months the sea would have drained back the last of the heat he had yanked, in squid and cod, from its depths.

He had pictured for her once, lying basking off Gibraltar, the sperm as a living tongue, testing life for the Ocean of Thought. Mammals, he believed, had been created to turn air and light and protein into thought, and then return these things to waters of that communal, ageless Ocean from which all things seemed, to him, to come.

She did not know if he was right, if his mind—or anyone's—was bound for an Ocean she had never seen or sounded. But she was sure that his body would join the feeding chain, and soon.

When he had recalled for her the Nantucket beach

where their calf had beached, she understood that he would travel there to die.

Swimming back to the herd, she could hear the harem bull on the far horizon, searching. Her calf was whining for milk. She suckled him until dawn. Once he squeaked in surprise, and she sensed his sire below, passing north, bound for a thousand miles of pain.

Her half-brother was deliberately hiding from the harem master under a frigid layer. Beneath it lay a different world of sound. Unless there were links she had never believed in, and harmonies unheard, she could not have heard him even if he called.

As the golden squid raised tentacles to feel the eastern sky, she rolled away from her calf and wondered what rages she would endure when the angry bull returned.

PART TWO

North-Northwest

"...waiving all argument, I take the good old fashioned ground that the whale is a fish..."
—Herman Melville,
Moby Dick, 1851

❧ 1 ❧

Lieutenant Peter Rostov slumped in dim ruddy light at the sonar console in the bow of the sunken sub. He watched the second hand of the panel chronometer jerk its way upright. Twelve days down, exactly. He punched his hand calculator: 1,036,800 seconds. A record? What difference now?

He pushed an earphone back so that he could listen to a new and threatening drip, drip, drip of water. It was the latest of many, and it was falling onto the bunk of his senior sonar technician, Olga Ivanova, who lived in the compartment. She had moved her mattress to the passageway outside, where she lay trying to sleep in the glow of a battle lantern.

She was constantly being stumbled over, and complaining of it. But the cursed *zampolit*, who seemed to be rapidly displacing the skipper as captain, had refused to give her permission to move her bedding to the dry deckplates of the Enchanted Forest, where the missilemen slept at the roots of their trunklike silos. The *zampolit* obviously felt that the miserable woman, who had a trim, taut body but one front tooth of bright stainless steel, and whose scratchy voice and unshowered body Rostov found quite unattractive, would prove too alluring for missileman morality. As

usual the commissar had dissembled, ordering Rostov
to remind her simply that the missile area was top
secret.

She had laughed shrilly when he passed the rejec-
tion on. As if she would survive to tell anyone what
she'd seen? Escape, perhaps, from the leaking wreck,
rise like the monster of Loch Ness from water so deep,
swim five hundred miles to New York, defect, and
describe the most obsolete of Soviet missiles to a yawn-
ing US Navy? Let the *zampolit* try it himself!

It was a measure of the fear that was gnawing at
all of them that she trusted Rostov with her sarcasm.
He had better warn her not to talk so in front of the
exec or the communicator. No need, she knew better
than that.

"Use my stateroom," he offered. "Take the navigator's bunk."

"*What?*"

If only she would not screech....

"What difference would it make?" He had shared
a stateroom with the navigator, who would hardly be
returning to his berth. "You and I would not be
together. When *I'm* not here at the console, you *are*."

To his amazement she had reached out in the darkness and squeezed his hand. "*Nyet*," she had whispered. "The *zampolit* would get you court-martialed,
if we ever get out. But thank you, Comrade Rostov,
just the same...."

Her whisper was much sweeter than her voice, and
in light so dim, with the flash of her bright stainless
tooth eclipsed, she looked almost like his wife.

He felt his passion stirring. He was ashamed, for
he had felt that Anna was very close today. But to
yearn first for the ship's surgeon, and now his own

technician, with whom he'd sailed for years without a thought of sex?

Fear of dying? The elemental drive of the doomed to procreate? He had read of this in short stories of the Great War: how men on the lines in the shadow of death, and women, too, grew easily inflamed.

"Thanks? For nothing," he murmured uncomfortably. "At any rate it's there."

He turned back to the console. He missed his symphony tapes, and so did the rest of the crew. He found his throat tightening in anger. The *zampolit* had forced him to end the concerts simply because he hated music. That was the truth of it.

Once he would have pitied such a man. He himself would rather be blind than tone-deaf.

But to deprive this crew of music it loved, steal from it Tchaikovsky's Fifth, which had plucked them again and again from the depths, to soar in starry skies? The act of a Nazi gauleiter.

He toyed with the idea of an appeal to the skipper. It would do no good. He had served under him for three cruises. He had thought himself lucky; the whole crew loved the old man for his thoughtful, gentle ways. But the captain, like himself, was weak; upon the recent death of his wife in Leningrad, he had grown reluctant to make decisions. A lonely man, he wanted only to be liked. In crisis, power had rushed as always into the vacuum of command. The captain's amiable traits had turned his feet to clay. And the *zampolit*'s boots to iron.

Rostov adjusted his earphones. He heard a faint and distant vessel, four-screw by the sound of her, thumping ponderously north on the northeast steamer lanes. He tuned his transducer carefully. The captain or the *zampolit*—who knew?—had forbidden the use of active sonar, because its pings might give away their position. Limited to primitive, passive listening, he felt less sure of his data, though his ear was better for this than anyone's.

He played with his bearing knob, swinging the dish-like ears in the bow. He charted the bearing when the sound peaked, checked it with a null, and estimated the range, longing for the precision of his sonar echoing more than ever. He finally logged the ship as a freighter making nineteen knots, probably heading for Europe.

Southampton, perhaps, with steel? Beef for Le Havre? Baltic-bound grain for Leningrad? A *Russian* ship? They would never know.

His mind flew home. Two blocks from their apartment, on the banks of the Neva, one could see the merchant docks from the Botanical Garden children's park. His mother knitted on a bench in the slanting northern light. His tiny daughter, Marina, bundled in a parka that the skipper's wife had given her, toddled to the river. A merchant ship was docking, its propellers grinding to a stop.

Blue eyes shining, voice rising, Marina pointed to the merchantman, for already she knew he went to sea. Her grandmother beckoned her back to the bench, smiled, and shook her head....

He twisted the knob on the control panel, turning the ears of the sub away from the thump of the screws. His fingers were trembling.

Suppose he was never to see Marina, or Anna, or his mother again?

He heard someone trip and stumble outside, and Olga whining in protest. He heard the *zampolit* curse. He tensed and half-rose.

"Idiot," he muttered. And then: "Watch where you go!"

Miserable, frightened girl, probably even more frightened than he.

Poor Olga....

Poor Nicolai, the navigator, thrashing in his bonds....

Poor Natasha, with the mess steward's death still plucking at her mind....

Poor little leaky submarine, he thought, wrestling the ocean for their lives....

And poor stupid Peter, here by default, whose song of the mourning humpback whales might never be heard at all.

〰 2 〰

The aging sperm swam slowly, and seldom on the surface, because the slapping waves of the Gulf Stream sent maddening pain through his jawbone.

His ability to sound ahead was impaired, for his jaw had evolved as a transmitter to channel the clicks and bangs from his head-case to a useful beam in front. His jawbone, too, was his best receptor, resonating to sounds from around him, for his earholes were tiny and mostly of use in air, when he was surfaced.

So he could neither transmit nor receive at his full capability.

He found his navigation erratic because he could not properly echo the bottom. He began to query other cetaceans for help, though every grunt and croak he emitted vibrated painfully.

Somewhere a single humpback gulped out booming notes to fix his own position for his mate, wherever she was. He questioned the male. The humpback was passing above the Narrows, off Bermuda, almost twenty miles away.

The sperm was far off course. He began to home, as best he could, on the lovely, breathless song, using the echo that followed the notes from below to plumb the depth and estimate bottom contours.

He was making only three knots. For six hours he tracked the sound of the humpback, but the female reached her mate first, and the two departed north and were out of range before he could beg them to wait.

He raised Bermuda visually by dawn, took a bearing on its highest hill, and swung north. He rounded the island wearily and headed east northeast.

By dusk he was confused again. He had somehow missed a ruined city that all Cetacea knew, though man today did not, for it had sunk to the depths when men were children. With his sonar erratic he was almost as blind as a human being in water. He sounded east and west, north and south, and could not find the crumbling walls and mounds of rocks he knew so well.

To strike out across the Gulf Stream without knowing his starting point was useless. He was inclined to turn back to Bermuda and beach himself there. But Nantucket Island beckoned; he plodded northward through the waves.

A pod of porpoises came upon him, bound for waters he had left. They were unreliable navigators, but much concerned with his broken jaw. They gave their position as best they could and continued to the south.

Before they left they pictured a great herd of pilot whales to the north, heading for Georges Bank and Nantucket Sound beyond. The porpoise leaders chirped of hundreds, slowed by newborn calves.

Pilot whales were intelligent, and accurate navigators. If he could overtake them, he would be safely on his way.

Painfully he increased the beat of his flukes.

🌀 3 🌀

She was puzzled by the harem master and did not know what to do.

She had no doubt that he was angry. When she had found the courage to scan his organs from afar, she discovered his bowels tight with rage and his stomach bloated with gas. But he had not so much as bumped her or her calf.

His testicles were heavy with seed after victory. Two of the younger cows were still in heat, and the combat had excited them, but he ignored their gambols and low-pitched, harmonic bleats. Something more than anger at her, or desire for the others, had come to possess his mind.

He was forcing them north, and for a thousand miles, she knew, the waters were thinner with squid than even here.

As always, he stayed to windward. The wind was from the south, so he was following the herd. Prudently she had kept as far from him as possible, and so she was leading on the northern perimeter, with her calf at her pectoral fin.

She disliked the direction in which they were heading, anticipating sparse feeding ahead with a loss of herd energy difficult to replace. But each time she eased her course to the west, thinking of better hunting grounds, he sensed it instantly. From a mile behind the school he would send a boom and rattle like a wave on a graveled beach to command her back on track.

Perhaps he was fleeing his memory of the Florida Straits and the night he had gone berserk.

When he first took over the herd, he had pictured for her his past. His family had been wiped out northwest of Hawaii by killer boats of the tiny men of the western sea. He had fled to the Atlantic through the northwest passage with the harpoon of man in his back.

Once, dozing in a trance, she had imagined that he bore the seed of the Pacific white-scarred bull and awakened terrified, her pulse pounding like the flukes of the mad legend himself.

The young harem master had always feared man: This she understood. The fear had entered him when he was so young and had burrowed so deeply that even her pictures of the Nantucket cove could not destroy it, although he had listened patiently.

There was never any patience in him now. She had seen his fear turn to anger months before, as they hunted squid in the Florida Straits and an unexplainable migration of small boats began to cross from Cuba to the land mass of the north.

He had grown strange, drawing pictures in sound of immense Pacific whales turning on killer boats and thrashing humans to bits in the water. These things had not happened for a hundred years, except in his mind, and he knew it as well as she; but his visions of them, though they fascinated the adolescents, frightened her and the rest of the cows.

When the migration from Cuba grew heavy, he began to shuttle the herd back and forth across the straits, avoiding the boats. But he had become more and more irritable and nervous with every passing day. A hurricane was coming from the south. The day it struck, he became calm, as if he had reached a decision.

She had been hovering that night with her calf at a depth of thirty feet. It was the first hurricane the baby had known. The seas had risen and the calf was frightened by the crash of waves aloft. She scanned the swells above and found them already breaking. She knew that the wind was howling there, and feared for the men and their females and babies, for the migration had not slowed one bit for the storm. Their young must be more alarmed than hers at the great heaving seas.

But their fear of the gale must have been as nothing to their terror later. For long past dark had come the sound of a crash that had startled the hovering herd. The noise was unmistakable. A whale had rammed a boat above. The throb of propellers stopped. She whirled, sent a beam in the direction of the crash, and instantly knew.

The harem bull had struck the leading boat, and not by accident.

The calf was grunting. He needed air. Quickly she surfaced with him. While they blew in the heaving seas, she sounded on the scene ahead.

The echoes she read were incredible, and she heard shock in the bleats of the cows below her. The bull was rampaging among struggling bodies, lashing with his flukes. His head was creased with a streaming wound: He had struck head-on, and the boat was the biggest of the craft above. It was listing, sinking in the sea. She bellowed for the male to stop, but he did not seem to hear. He crashed through mountainous waves at a smaller vessel, demolished it in the night, and pounded the humans who dropped from its sides.

She moved to try to drive him off, but he charged her as if she were a rival male, so she swerved to save her calf. He struck at still another boat, then thrashed the swimming men to death. In the morning there had been only debris and nothing more.

Why he had attacked the boats, she did not understand. Why he would want to kill men in the water passed all cetacean understanding. He would picture for her no reasons afterward. It was as if he did not remember.

Herded north now by the whale who had killed for nothing, she felt his rage behind her: at the bull who had challenged him, at herself, at her calf, and at the men who had wounded him so long ago.

Her stomach and her calf were whining for food. Ahead she sensed starvation. Behind she sensed a madness that could destroy the herd.

She dove blindly and started the evening hunt.

◊ 4 ◊

At the aging sperm's miserable pace it was twenty-four hours before he heard the hoots, whistles, and mewings ahead that told him pilot whales were traveling in enormous numbers north of him. Even after that, though the pilots were slowed by scores of newborn calves, it was half a day before he breasted the rear ranks, and he knew by the snores and bellows ahead that the leading bulls were a good five miles away.

The potheaded pilot whales had joined scores of pods into one, as was their habit for protection from orcas. They were lined in perfect rows traveling on the surface. When one on a flank tossed his flukes to dive, his rank dived too, and each row followed in precise order.

They were intelligent, friendly creatures, and he felt instantly comforted by their presence. They were small whales, less than twenty feet in length, and even the biggest bulls seldom weighed more than seven tons. They were fully as gregarious as his own species, and their ties were so tight that when a leader beached, by accident or design, it was almost impossible for the rest of his herd to refrain from joining him in order to help. Beached bulls, it was thought, had feigned death quietly to save the herd.

He fell in with one of the leaders, a large male with a white belly like an orca's, uncommon in his kind. The pilot whale quickly scanned him and moaned at his shattered jaw, but showed no surprise. The sperm knew that the rear guard had perceived him hours before, while he was still trailing by miles, and sent the news ahead.

Like all cetaceans, the pilot whale communicated in analogs. It was a system simpler than language, understood naturally by all dolphins, porpoises, and whales. In dealing with the concrete, it was more precise and accurate than any speech of man.

Human words, it was thought, bore no physical relation to the images they stood for. So man must somehow have to agree beforehand on the meaning of his sounds. Cetaceans did not. Evolution had agreed for them thirty million years before. The equipment to translate echoes into three-dimensional pictures had existed for aeons in their brains. The accent—sperm, pilot, or even grazing humpback—of the mimicry clouded the picture hardly at all, for since the day of his birth each had a long, continual lesson in the echoes of the sea, from his own species and others.

An arctic narwhal who had never been out of the ice could envision, through the sonar mimicked by an orca passing through the floes, a coral atoll on the equator, just as with man, an Eskimo watching a Norse explorer sketch his king would recognize in the drawing the visual echo of a human being.

The great herd of pilot whales was bound for the continental shelf off Nantucket on its seasonal migration; the leader mimicked for him the echo of a shoal that the sperm recognized as less than half a mile from the strand on which his calf had died. Contentedly he slowed his pace. He was welcome here. With his shattered jaw he would not be competing for squid; even without it, his prey was deeper and larger than that of the pothead, who seldom exceeded a depth of 1,200 feet, so he would not deprive the herd. Pilot whales lived on squid so small that a sperm adolescent would have ignored them as not worth the taking.

He offered security, too, against marauding orcas, who might not notice that he could not fight and thus pass on to other prey.

There were bottlenose dolphins mixed with the pilots, scouting ahead for squid. The pilots repaid them in portions of squid from levels too deep for dolphins to dive.

The sperm settled down for the long passage north. His jaw ached less, though it still dangled helplessly.

A small female bottlenose charged by the white-bellied leader. As she did, she leaped, glittering, and uttered a sound in air.

Astonished, the sperm rolled, freeing an earhole to listen. The pilot whale reared its head and blatted through its blowhole a similar noise, then followed to dive for mackerel.

The aging sperm's heart began to pound. In his fifty-nine years in the ocean he had never heard creatures utter such sounds.

Except man, on the beach at Nantucket.

◈ 5 ◈

The sperm cow's sonar told her that Bermuda was a half-day north, and that the advance front of a herd of southbound dolphin was a mile ahead. A squall lay on the eastern horizon, bubbling cloud forms in the morning sun. She squinted with her right eye over the glint of waves.

Above the eastern skyline, schools of golden minnows raced a whale shark made of clouds. As she watched, it turned into a sperm, and then a whispy fan of coral nodding sleepily in the tide. She eased under her calf to lift him so that he could see it too. He was bored with a steady, unceasing pace that he understood as little as she.

When she knew that he was looking at the cloud form, she grated from deep in her nasal passages the sonar image it would make if it were in the water and could echo. He repeated it as best he could, but he was fretful and not much interested. She eased him back into the water and swam on.

She knew that it was time for sleep, and afterward play, for all the calves were tired of the endless, churning passage. But she still held the lead, and whenever she slowed, the harem bull bellowed. Then, almost without thinking, she would increase the beat of her flukes.

She still had no idea why he was driving the herd north. In past times he had deferred to her experience, as any young harem bull would; she knew the waters better than he, and the energy-state of the younger cows. But now he kept to himself, a mile behind the herd, and would not even deign to sweep through it, as he normally did, to see that there were no laggard calves and that none of the toothless adolescents were molesting the females.

They were all at once in the midst of leaping dolphins flashing in the sun, mock-charging the young harem bulls, skimming a fluke-width away, squeezing at blinding speed between a calf three times their size and a cow of forty tons.

It was always dolphin playtime, for they had little need to conserve fat, and her own little calf waddled away in the wake of the first one who passed.

She piped for her daughter to turn him back, and continued on her way. She could hear the dolphin leader, a mile back, and the sonorous groans of her herd master. She glided, listening.

The big sperm bull was hooting out the image of the aging, broken bull, and as he ended she heard him sound the rising grunt that was, through all Cetacea, known as the sperm whale's request for location.

So all at once she knew.

The herd master was driving them all in pursuit of the dying bull.

She turned and charged back through the herd.

❧ 6 ❧

The aging sperm was filled with excitement at the female dolphin's manlike sounds, and the blatting voice that the pilot pod leader had used in reply. Since his hours near the man on the beach at Nantucket, he had been forever impelled to learn more of the strange, driven human species.

Once, silent in the open ocean, he had lain unseen and unbreathing, watching two humans mating in a small white-winged boat. He treasured a memory of another, sitting like a barnacle with two tentacles astride a four-legged mammal on a beach at Cozumel. He had scanned men swimming by the hundreds, with their females and their young, one summer off Fire Island.

Most cachalots thought them ungainly, especially in the water, all angles, legs, arms, and patches of hair. To him, though, they were no more awkward than crabs or lobsters, and he had never regarded man, as most streamlined cetaceans did, as the ugliest being on earth.

He was awed at the clever uses to which men put their brains, and had studied their works in the seas, but until this moment he had never found, through all his waters and years, a cetacean observer of humans who knew them well enough to mimic their sounds. Now he had apparently come upon two, the dolphin and pilot whale. They may well have lived with man.

All Cetacea had known for years of dolphins and pilots and orcas who had been netted and cared for ashore. Off Fire Island this last spring a five-year-old sperm had lingered in a basin while men pricked him with their strange instruments, trying to clear his ailing lungs. The youngster had survived to rejoin his pod. A baby sperm, beached and lost in a storm on the tip of Maine, had been nursed by humans for weeks until he died, just as men had tried to care for his own little calf on Nantucket for half a day. . . .

In Pacific waters mindless tuna flocked under the herds of dolphins, instinctively using them as guides on the trackless expanse. So when tuna were netted by man, sometimes dolphins were netted too. To release them, men had jumped into swarming seines and been killed by netted sharks.

And there were other tales, of cetaceans captured purposely by man, that gave the big sperm hope. They were seldom harmed, it was said, and well treated, as if man was simply curious about his fellow thinking mammals.

Even orcas had been taken and kept. There were some sperm who did not know why such powerful and intelligent little killers would permit themselves to be captured. The aging bull understood. His own curiosity was such that he would have gone willingly with the man who had tried to save his calf on Nantucket, if there had been a way.

Man was taking more and more cetaceans to his tanks ashore, and it was said that captive cetaceans were returning in larger numbers to the oceans of the world. Some had been released for reasons poorly

understood. Some had taken badly to captivity and
escaped. Some, trusted to the open sea, had tired of
man's game and deserted him.

There had been a report, well believed, that from
the towering islands in the central Pacific, a half-dozen
bottlenose had all been set free at one time. No one,
it was said, including the dolphins themselves, knew
why, any more than anyone knew why the killing of
whales at sea had stopped.

Further west, tiny men had murdered dolphins and
whales for a thousand summers past. Last year, as
always, hundreds of dolphins were waiting for slaughter in a net across a cove. A larger man in a skin of
black blubber had entered and set them free.

It was clear to the aging sperm that man was changing. If humans captured a dolphin or pilot whale and
held him without harm, only as teacher and playmate,
then the eve of prophecy was at hand when whale
would sound to man and man would understand.

These were things he must mull over with the pilot
whale and the dolphin, if he could find them again
in the shifting pattern of their herds.

For the first time in his life he was driven by currents he did not understand. And he had no time to
waste.

⑤ 7 ⑥

Whirling in a swirl of foam, she heard the bottle-nose
dolphins report her half-brother's position to the herd
master and realized that she had been leading a pursuit. The aging bull had been a half-day north of
Bermuda when the dolphins had encountered him.

The harem master heard her coming and tried to
bellow her back on her northward course. Instead she
continued southward, back through the herd, throwing the cows and adolescents who had been following
her into confusion.

She was suddenly very frightened, for her calf more
than herself. She had been almost dry of milk from
the furious pace and the lack of squid: If the harem
bull harmed her, and her teats grew empty, the little
one would starve. But they would all starve anyway if
he was not stopped.

The harem master grew suddenly quiet. His silence
frightened her more than his bellows. And it excited
the curiosity of the dolphins, too, who began to squeal
of conflict and to gather near to listen.

She dove, still heading south, and pictured for him
the hanging gardens of the Sargasso Sea, where they
had always hunted in seasons past and where they
should be feeding now. She heard nothing from above

and continued southward. If he had truly gone insane, he might believe that she would desert her herd and calf for food. He might forget his pursuit of her half-brother to chase her instead.

She turned, hovered five hundred feet below, and sounded on him. Instead of following her, he swam slowly to the herd.

She thought of her baby huddled by her daughter, unknowing and trusting. She could not believe that he would punish a baby so young, but neither could she test his madness to find out.

She swam for the surface. She heard a massive swirl of water where the harem bull had been, an instant of silence as his body cleared the surface, and a crash as he reentered, hurtling toward her.

She froze in the water. He was erecting his penis.

She was long out of estrus, still lactating for her calf. Two other cows were in heat. He could have had them. To enter her now might stop her milk.

Foreplay was essential to her kind, though its males could erect at will. Now his penis was growing beneath him like a five-foot rigid limb. And she flashed on his testes, twenty-five pounds each and bursting with the seed of madness.

She tried to turn to flee, but he was on her like a cloud of thunder; her jaw was locked in his, and he was twisting her over and down, down, down....

The dolphins fled in panic. She was alone with him in a churning, hostile sea. She could not breathe, or think.

She fought.

8

The aging sperm churned stolidly in the first rank of the migrating pilot whales, waiting for the dolphin and the pilot whale leader to return from feeding below. He was impatient to know where they had learned the human sounds.

The dolphin was the first to return. She was very small, even for a bottlenose: hardly over seven feet long and barely five hundred pounds. Man would have credited her with the permanent happy grin that endeared her kind to his; to the sperm the smile meant nothing, but he had always been amused by protruding dolphin snouts and the jaunty melons on their heads, so unlike his own.

This one was troubled by his jaw, and began to picture for him how her own herd and the pilot whales might feed him until it healed.

But that was not the sperm's intention or his interest. He aped the sound she had made above the water, squeezing air through his blowhole as best he could, which was not very well at all. Was this a noise of man's?

He knew from the speeding of her heart that his query excited her. She seemed surprised that he recognized the sound as human.

He pictured for her what he knew of men: the swimmers swarming off Fire Island, the human on the shore clinging to the back of the four-legged animal, and the mating couple in the boat. And finally—reluctantly, for pain clung like a remora to the memory of it still—he painted the picture of the men who had tried to save his calf on the beach at Nantucket.

She moaned in commiseration, moved into his pressure wave to scan him more closely. He felt her sympathy and a certain loneliness that matched his own. She began to picture for him the humans she had known.

She had been taken by man, netted in the Florida Strait from a speeding, howling boat, and then, paralyzed in shock, found herself lifted from the sea, her calf left squealing behind her.

Once taken, she had been gently treated. Men cradled her in softness while they trundled her from the boat. They laid her on the back of a growling beast that rolled over the land on four round claws, later wet her skin while she lay in the belly of a great screaming albatross, and at last put her in a tiny saltwater pool with others of her kind, where they swam and walked with her.

For two full moons she had been anxious, listless, grieving for her calf. But a human female had become her friend, enticing her to eat when she wanted nothing, teasing her into play, swimming with her by the hour.

From the angle of the sun she sensed that she had been taken far from the reefs of her own waters. She knew that her calf would survive in the care of the herd, or would not, and that she could only wait for what the Ocean of Thought would bring.

Meanwhile her portion of man's world, though con-

fined, was a place of color, speed, and action as stim-
ulating as her own. She discovered from observation
of humans by the pool that man's status with others
of his kind occupied him as fully as her own relation-
ship to other dolphins.

She had quickly learned that humans could be
taught by dolphins. She suspected, indeed, that they
had brought her and her companions there to learn
from them.

She and those who shared her tank studied man
carefully. His pectoral fins had evolved into organs
quite different from those of dolphins, or even seals
or manatees. These fins, almost useless for swimming,
were capable of minute and delicate actions: caresses,
pats, scratchings, and groomings that could bring
pleasure to the most insensitive of dolphin skins. With
such fins dolphins, like sea otters, could have used
bottom rocks to crack shellfish. Whales could have
blocked estuaries to trap fish, moved kelp to spur the
growth of plankton, cracked iceholes with boulders,
burrowed channels through tidal bars.

She had more respect for man's dexterity than his
mind. She pictured his brain, though almost as large
as hers, as barely rational, inflexible, incapable of
abstract thinking.

The sperm disagreed silently. He suspected that
aeons ago, man's intellect had simply been set on a
different course. It had evolved to control his strange,
fingered fins and the toys his fingers patterned in a
dry flat world of things, just as cetacean brains had
come to master hearing and sound in a world of depth
and thought. Studying the sound-pictures of her days
with men, he was astonished at the products of human
hands and brains, which seemed to him useful—to

man at least—past all belief. With so practical a creature there was surely hope of mutual understanding.

There was no longer doubt that men communicated among themselves, and not through voice alone. She pictured boxes that talked when men were nowhere near. She had seen other boxes near the pool that showed pictures sent to humans by other humans. Though obviously man *needed* these toys to visualize, while cetaceans needed none, the human mind had cleverly filled the gap with a product of his hand.

The dolphin had not been impressed by these things. Too much of what man did and thought seemed to be centered on his toys, which were sometimes quite angular, with flat sides and edges and corners that bit. Though the ocean's curves were not unknown to him, and he had tossed her balls as round as blowfish to play with, she had decided in her five summers with him that he was a creature of angles and planes, lacking depths and wanting heights. In order to reason at all, he needed a point of departure, a landfall ahead, and a course drawn straight as a cormorant's flight.

Perhaps, offered the sperm, it was in the teaching of his calves that little minds were channeled into narrows too straightly drawn. It was known that man's young, like Cetacea's, grew slowly and had to be taught.

She became silent in thought as they swam slowly north. Perhaps....

She had been petted by children at the side of the pool, had learned all she could of their smooth little brains, and had grown to love them all. Though the piping sounds they made in air sometimes hurt her ears, she always felt sad when they left her at dusk, for they reminded her of her baby calf. Strangely, they understood her, and she them, better even than the woman who swam with her and whom she also had grown to love.

She pictured for the aging sperm many other things, for his curiosity was bottomless. She sent him a vision of her companions in the pool: an orca she learned to trust, seven wild bottlenose like herself, and one young male who had been born in the tank.

The young male knew nothing of dolphin life but what his mother and others had pictured. Until her own arrival he had kept to himself: All of his friends were men.

She had learned what she could from this dolphin, and taught him in turn the dolphin ways of love. He had never dived a coral reef at sunset, or felt the slap of trade-wind waves or the glorious gift of the surf at the bow of a speeding boat far from shore. She would sketch such things for him in pictures by the hour until he grew impatient with her scenes and led her to the surface.

There was beauty in man's world, too, he thought, and in the works of his hands. He drew her attention to the palm trees men had put beside the tank to wave against the sky, and to the tower he had built to feed them from, and the marvelously level roosts from which he watched them at their play.

She found the palm trees skinny compared to those she knew, and the rest quite ugly too. But she had not let him know, for he thought both of them were fortunate to be here, fed and cared for by his friends.

She had pitied him and loved him, for he too reminded her of her calf.

The young dolphin had taught her much of man. She had thought men wore their covering because they lacked blubber for warmth. He knew better: Without their brightly colored clothes they would be

identical. Because no sonar worked in air, they used
vision as dolphins used sound, so detailed scanning
of another was normally impossible for them.
Depending on so unreliable an organ as the eye, he
had decided that they could only distinguish themselves, one from the other, by the covers and colors
they wore.

In the water, apparently using sonar too high or
low for cetaceans to hear, they had no more need for
color and took most of their clothing off.

The sperm whale doubted the theory. Men's *ships*
might echo-sound, but swimming men could not. He
had been near them off Fire Island and had heard
no sonar. But he had too many questions to waste
time in argument. He was interested in the killer whale
in her tank. Orcas, like men, were whale-hunters. What
had the captive orca thought of man?

She thought that the orca's concern had been solely
of survival. She sketched out his story. Stunned in the
Pacific with a strangely tipped harpoon, the killer whale
had awakened in captivity. In the tank, he was tender
with his tiny companions, and their fear of him passed
quickly. For so enormous a being, he was graceful and
quick to learn the dolphin tricks. The orca was sure
that man was keeping all of them for future food, as
orcas played with schools of fish, but he learned swiftly
to please humans, for his appetite was ravenous and
he feared that unless he performed, he would be
starved before he was eaten.

He was never starved and never eaten, and never
free of fear.

The sperm whale's appetite was enormous, too—
hungry for what the dolphin knew of man.

What of man's learning capacity? He sucked oil
from the ocean bottom, pulled rocks from its sands,

dredged tuna from its seas, clanked through antarctic krill fields with ships that ate like great blue whales. Man obviously ruled in the open air: Could he be taught to respect the depths?

Her answer was certain and swift, and tinged with sadness. She and her fellows had been able to teach men only one thing: to feed them fish and squid.

The sperm was shocked. Nothing more?

Nothing. Man seemed only interested in watching them at play.

She seemed to sense his disappointment. He was not to lose heart: There was hope. Rewarded with the most primitive of entertainments, man could be taught to care for cetaceans well. Men were easily amused. The simplest of dolphin games seemed to astonish them: To retrieve a disk or dive through a life ring or leap through a hoop sent them into howls and hoots of joy. They and their young could watch dolphins tirelessly. Long past the time a cetacean would have grown bored with similar human play, crowds of men would perch with their young beside the pool, clapping their flippers like demented seals.

The sperm whale interrupted; his days were short, he had to know. Would the prophecy of communication with man someday perhaps come true?

She hesitated, as if she sensed how much her answer meant. Man, she knew certainly, communicated with other men....

He pressed. But with Cetacea?

She seemed reluctant to answer. Man used all those channels cetaceans used: body, touch, and sight. Mostly, like cetaceans, he used sound....

She had mimicked man's voice. But could she *read* the pictures man spoke? Could man read *hers*?

For a long time she was silent. And when she sounded her answer it was full of pain.

She had learned words of men, but could not read their meanings; not she, nor the dolphin teachers of men she had left behind.

And men saw nothing when she mimicked shapes and forms.

To a dolphin, man's voice was a sound, not a picture.

To a man, a dolphin's squeal was noise.

⚡ 9 ⚡

The sperm cow writhed and struggled. She twisted and tried to dive, but the mad bull's jaw had clamped her own, and his body was as unmoving as a coral reef. She felt as if she had jammed her jawbone between two tidal rocks and would drown alone and unheard.

The passing school of dolphin had sensed the bull's insanity. It was outside the comprehension of cetaceans that a male would take an unwilling, lactating cow. Had they not been frightened, they would certainly have stayed, for sperm copulation in the ocean was an event for all smaller cetaceans, arousing passion in themselves. But now the last of them had gone, shrieking in fear, and she was alone with the harem master, far from her baby and herd.

She could feel his penis snaking toward her ventral slit like a rigid moray eel. She heaved herself sidewise, raised her flukes, and began to pound at his caudal trunk. Surprised, he let his grip on her jaw slip. She wrenched herself free, surfaced for a gasp of air, tossed her flukes toward the morning sun, and dove.

Her endurance, for a cow, was good. But compared to his it was as nothing, for he could slide to a mile's depth and stay for an hour. Her hope for escape was a cold layer to hide beneath, as her half-brother had done.

She whirled and feinted amid the phosphorescent flashes of startled squid, trying to dodge his rush: So long as she was underwater she felt safe from intromission, for sexual activity was always at the surface, lying flat or treading water, never in the breathless depths.

She arched her body, felt him sliding by, and headed deeper. She was out of the dusk into freezing blackness when he caught her, clamping her forward of the flukes and half-breaking her caudal trunk; then, as she writhed, he shifted his grip to her jaw.

She groaned in submission and relaxed, so that he would let her return to the surface. She had lost the struggle and the race, and to drown her below would only waste her life and the little bull calf's too.

To her astonishment the harem master held her. She let out the plaintive bleat that in all the cachalot's world meant distress for air: It was as if he did not hear.

Then, incredibly, at 1,200 feet, she felt his member enter her slit, hard as a spire of coral, grinding, tearing at her uterus, pounding deep inside. She felt his seed pour forth, barely in time, for her body screamed for air. He slammed her away and was gone.

She found herself struggling for the surface, heart wrenching at her chest in huge, rending bursts. She felt consciousness leaving her, knew she was dying, lost all need to breathe....

And suddenly she was in blurred and shimmering sunlight, breathing life into tortured lungs.

When she could, she straggled slowly to the milling herd. Sometime tonight, when she had rested, or tomorrow, when he hunted afar, she must somehow try to escape.

The brain of the little calf would be molded by what he saw of the bull who led them all. To stay with the herd was to see him catch the madness. It could kill him at the hands of man.

֍ 10 ֍

The aging whale listened as the dolphin finished sounding the story of her stay with man.

After months in the tank, she had grown restive. Then a baby had been born to another female, and her longing for her own calf had grown so strong that she decided to join the Ocean of Thought. She ceased to eat.

The female human who cared for her seemed to

resist her decision. She rubbed her ventral slit and tried all the things the dolphin loved, as if to change her mind. But the dolphin saw no reason to live: She had lost her calf, her interest in man, his tricks, his flat and vacant words.

On her first day in the tank, the woman had named her with a sound: Mimi. She mimicked it now for the sperm, in air. At first the sound had of course seemed strange to her—wild dolphins had no names, but only sonic identities they whistled, sending the picture of themselves to others. But she had accepted her label for the woman's convenience, since humans could not translate such calls to pictures.

She also had learned to mimic the name that humans used for her human friend, although to her own ear and brain it did not describe her at all: Susan. Before she decided to die, the dolphin had squeaked it often in open air, using her blowhole lips, which dolphins never did at sea. This had caused great joy for the woman, who learned easily to bring her fish when she repeated these and others of man's calls. But when the dolphin lost her appetite and no longer taught Susan tricks, she could read from the woman's stomach gases and the tension in her muscles that her friend was growing frightened.

Strange men began to enter the water to prick her with needles sharp as a stingray's tail. She was moved to a smaller pool; the water was drained and tubes like branches of kelp were painfully thrust beneath her skin.

She knew that man was trying to make her live. Though her own pod would have tried similarly to save her if she had been accidentally beached, it would never have interfered with the chain of feeding once she decided to die. Man, apparently, would not accept her right to swim back to the Ocean of Thought.

Now she wondered why. She queried the sperm, for cachalots were thought to dive more deeply into that Ocean than other living beings.

The sperm did not believe his wisdom as profound as others thought, but he answered. Perhaps men feared her destination: Perhaps human brains were too young to envision the Ocean of Thought. There were, after all, even sperm whales—his half-sister was one—who doubted its very existence.

This seemed to shock the dolphin, but she continued. One day, as she approached starvation, Susan entered the tank. She was crying like a lonely calf in a most cetacean way; the dolphin scanned her and saw great sadness, as if she grieved for something she would lose.

They lay in the water for hours while the woman rubbed her back. The dolphin towed her several times around the tank, as she used to do in happier days. Then men came and the woman ran away, sobbing; the men lifted the dolphin, trundled her back to the shrieking albatross, and flew her away to the sea.

At nightfall they carried her in and made their noises of farewell. The freshness of the ocean and the singing of the tide, and the sound of sandbars shifting in the Gulf Stream's languid flow, told her that she wanted life, so the humans had been right.

She quickly found her herd and her calf, who was grown to full maturity now and had sired calves of his own.

All that remained for her of the time she had spent with men was the memory of her friend and the children, noisy as dolphin young, and a certain sadness, when the pilot whale leader, who had known less kindly men than she, aped their voices in the air.

She fell silent. The sperm could hear, suddenly, the song of a humpback and his mate resonating with the liquid gurgle that all whales and dolphins loved, adding chorus by chorus to their ageless tale of life and death below.

To better hear the voices, all the pilots and dolphins dove, even the calves. Dolphins and pothead pilot whales gathered and lay in a sound-channel a hundred feet down, listening.

The aging sperm hovered with them, picturing the singers. He saw in his mind their pectoral fins sweeping like great gull wings, as they boomed their incredible tale. For weeks, warbled the distant male, he and his mate had swooped on banks of plankton ahead, listening all the while to man-music. It had come from depths unreachable by them, from among the mindless squid.

The humpbacks had known of the source before they heard it, from the tales that had passed for weeks. It was the first submarine to bottom in years, the first ever known to sing, and Cetacea had guessed already that it was wounded or tired.

For a season the humpbacks would sing the dirge, changing its rhythms until it passed into legend, and then would commence another chant.

At the beginning of each chorus lay the setting for the song.

The sperm grunted in astonishment. The submarine lay in the saddle of the Wallop Seamount, only two short hours ahead. He knew that somehow, before he died himself, he must hear the music coming from the dying submarine.

❧ 11 ❧

Lieutenant Peter Rostov lay propped on the lower bunk in his darkened stateroom, trying to write a letter under the dying gleam of a pocket lantern and the faint red glow of a battle light through his open stateroom door.

The stench from the passageway had him close to retching, but to close the door was to tempt claustrophobia. The toilet in the forward head, not ten feet from his stateroom, had backed up.

The plumbing of a submarine was as complex as that of a spacecraft. Though he had tried to probe its secrets, gagging, his talents were musical, not mechanical. He had failed, and the nuclear engineers and pipefitters aft had told him they had better things to do, and leakages more dangerous than sewage.

He tried to ignore the smell and go on with the letter to his wife, which perhaps no one would read.

"...And so, darling Anna, you know I am not a believer in magic, or ESP and such, but I saw her run to the railing, where the playground overlooks the docks, you know, across the river? And she pointed at that freighter, and Mama called her back and perhaps told her no, her papa was not on *that* one...." He chewed on the pencil. This would never do. She

150

would think that his sanity had broken, and it had not. Yet.

Anna half-believed in the paranormal. He did not, perhaps because he lacked her sensitivity. Still, the vision had been so clear, and his little Marina so vivid, that he was certain the scene had occurred, four thousand miles away.

The pencil hovered. He would leave the paragraph in.

No one would ever read it.

Suddenly, shattering his mood, the image of the doctor intruded. He had an almost unmanageable desire to seek her out and bring her here, to fold her into his arms...

With a force of will, he penciled on: "And sometimes, Anna, you see, I can hear *you* in my mind, through those hydrophones, before you leave for the opera house, telling the story to Marina of the elves in the snow to make her eat her porridge. That tape I love so much—of your solo last October—I was saving, in case things became worse, and now that they are worse, I am forbidden to play any tapes at all, although I think they would raise the spirits of my comrades here. The goddamn *zampolit*..."

He carefully blotted out the last three words. If they ever escaped to anyplace he could post the letter, it would be subject to censorship anyway. Besides, his failure in music—and her success—had burdened her with guilt. If he whined of the comrades fate had chosen him, it would only sadden her further.

He chewed his pencil. What else was there to say?

Suddenly he slashed musical staffs across the page and inserted the notes of the prelude to what might be his final composition.

"This is the opening theme of a movement for you

and Marina. I call it in my mind 'Cetacea,' and it comes not from that record we heard at the University— remember?—but no, from real humpbacks here below.... You should hear them; live, their voices are so much more beautiful. But I suppose you never will...." Nor would she hear his own *Unfinished Symphony*. He crumpled the letter and hurled it from the bunk.

The hull shuddered and clanked. His berth trembled strangely. He stared into darkness, wide-eyed. The sub was balanced on a razor's edge. He sensed that the current was nudging them closer to the brink.

Ridiculous. They were solidly down, displaced almost ten thousand tons.

A drip began in the stateroom, ticking the time away. He could not see it and probed with his flashlight, which flickered suddenly and went out. The drip went on.

The stench closed in with the darkness. He was sweating, and the air seemed quilted. When he panted, he needed even more.

The navigator was right. They were trapped in a sewer pipe a hundred fathoms down. A wail of despair welled up in his chest. He tried to hold it back.

He heard the navigator bellowing in his chains, ten yards away, in sick bay.

His own screaming began with a groan; he could no more stop it than his heart—

The springs on the bunk above him squealed. "Lieutenant? Comrade Rostov?"

He froze into silence. His wife? The surgeon? No: hard, nasal. His technician, Olga. He jerked up, banging his head. "What—?" A lithe, slender form slid from above, stood silhouetted in the ruddy light from his doorway, then dropped to its knees by his bunk. He stared at her in the gloom.

"Are you all right?" she whispered. "You yelled, I think dreaming; I was too. I'm here because... the leak... you were right, my own spot was impossible...."

He wanted her, suddenly, very much. "I'm glad."

"Oh, Rostov..."

She took his hand, clung to it for a moment, then drew it away.

"No," she murmured. "We can't."

She did not mean it, not at all: Her body must be crying as loudly for release from the grave as his own.

Anna would understand if he filled out her ghost with flesh. But he had never cheated on her yet. He took a deep breath, swung his feet out of his bunk, and somehow managed the words, "You're right, Olga, we can't."

In the dim light her eyes flashed in surprise. "I am?" she asked wryly. "Would I be right if I were an officer, I wonder? The doctor?"

He could not answer.

"The hell with it. And with you. *And* your quack. And this miserable hunk of iron." She stood, smoothing her skirt. "Jesus, I'm so scared. Are we really going to die?"

"I don't know. Look, you're no more scared than I am."

"Thank you, Peter Rostov."

"And you're braver than I thought, to come here."

She touched his lips with her fingers and grinned. Her stainless tooth flashed faintly. "You are less."

He watched her as she left. He was in prison with them all.

But her appearance out of the dripping dark had saved him from the chains.

🐚 12 🐚

She was trying to wean her calf. The rape at 1,200 feet had not dried her milk, as she had feared, but the scarcity of large squid as they churned north of Bermuda had turned her skin soft and her teats flabby.

She knew that she must escape and that she must take her calf, for soon her daughter, twelve years old and gravid for the last sixteen months by the harem master's seed, would give birth to her own calf, and could not care for an orphaned little bull.

The cow dove often and slowly, so that he could keep up, and found him young squid. He would not touch them yet: He wanted milk. She ground them to bits with her teeth. He rejected the pieces, and nuzzled her slit. She shrugged him off and found him cod. She crushed these and slid them into his jaw. He coughed them out.

Finally her patience expired. She took a squid and dismembered it for him, shaking it until its tentacles fell and spiraled down below. She tore off its beak. She presented the rest to the calf. He rolled and dove, babylike, hanging suspended, head down, twenty feet below the surface. She circled him, the squid's body in her jaw, searching for a chance to jam it into his mouth. He rotated, squealing in delight.

The time for the ultimate lesson had come. She returned to the world of air, and when he tired of teasing her and tried to surface, she caught his head under her left pectoral fin and forced him down.

Now his squeals were of rage, and finally of fright, and when she let him up he was like another calf. He accepted the squid and dove with her, and by nightfall was killing his own. The next day her milk was gone.

She began to make plans. A night's swimming dead north toward Nantucket, at the calf's full speed, could give them a start. For the bull to leave his whole harem in pursuit of a cow and a calf seemed unthinkable, no matter what madness he carried.

She began to fuel their bodies for flight. She dove often and deeply, teaching the calf to take ever larger squid and fish. When he tired and became full, she forced him to dive again, to hunt, to eat. She was waiting for a cold layer below that could hide them while they fled; in the meantime they would lay on blubber for the escape.

Now she had a new problem: Her daughter was lagging behind. She was very near term, and the older cow feared that her infant would be born in waters so cold that it might not survive.

All the cows had scanned the baby in her womb. It was female.

Since the rape, the older cow had tried repeatedly to divert the bull and turn him south. He was unyielding, although he did not attack her again.

One night, sixty miles north of Bermuda, diving with her calf in waters colder and deeper than any he had dived before, she heard the harem master, miles away, *blang*ing on a vessel. From the echoes she read, she envisioned a small fishing boat. She had a vague picture of him charging at its keel; then she lost the sound in a layer of plankton.

The next morning, when he returned, his blunt snout was cut and bleeding steadily, and she knew he had struck again.

That afternoon they came upon the wreckage of the boat. Near it, wearing only a floating vest, bobbed the broken body of a tiny human female hanging lifeless in the water.

The shock of it staggered the herd. All had known in the Straits of Florida what their harem master had wrought, but the storm had hidden the evidence. None had seen a dead human child before, much less one killed by a whale: In the dissonance of their cries and squeals the cow read panic.

Her calf became restless and left her side, which he had seldom done before. Two adolescent males began to fight, although the season for this was over. An ancient female with stomach trouble began to vomit and strangle, and for half an hour the cow supported her as she writhed and coughed.

When the hunting cries of a passing orca pod were heard, the herd bolted, each member in a different direction, rather than bunching. The bull was too preoccupied to notice. When the killer whales grew silent, the cows and calves back, but she sensed that the orcas were nearby, waiting to see what other surprises this strange sperm pod would show.

The bull swam implacably onward through the chaos he had caused.

The cow's daughter began to defecate continually. She was about to give birth.

❧ 13 ❧

The aging sperm knew that pilot whales were lethargic when the sun was high in the sky. But he was surprised by the indifference of the young pod leader to the news from the humpback whales that the submarine was so close. A sperm whale herd would have been sounding the hulk within hours. The pothead leader seemed actually to slow his pace, though the Wallop Seamount, where the submarine lay, was directly in his path.

And the young leader had lived with man.

The pain that remained in the sperm whale's jaw was becoming bearable, but his curiosity was not. He must learn more about the contact the pilot whale had had with humans, for the dolphin had pictured him as having played with man in his games at sea, as she had played in the tank ashore.

The pilot whale was a sturdy young bull. His rare white belly was taken among his kind to be a sign of fortune, since the flash of it in the darkness below was said to attract more squid.

He seemed confused and surprised at the sperm whale's interest in his life with man at sea. He was silent for a moment, then began to mew and whistle, in his singsong cadences, a montage of his life among men.

Seven summers before, when he was young, his herd had been attacked by starving orcas off Iceland working silently and efficiently in fog. The herd master, his sire, directed the pod shoreward while the bulls, bringing up the rear, flailed at the killers with their scythelike tails.

They escaped the orcas, who failed even to kill a calf. But the bulls had followed the pod toward shore and found themselves beached as the tide ran out. His sire, heaviest of all of them, was most seriously grounded. Despite his entreaties to be left to die, the herd refused to leave.

The next morning men landed from a boat that beached with gaping jaws, like a bowhead washed ashore. Each man wore clothes of jungle green. The boat vomited vehicles with six round legs. Those pilot whales closest to the tideline were carefully dragged to the water and released.

They had even managed to save his sire. But the pilot whale himself, and two other adolescent bulls, had been left high on the beach. The men made no effort to help them to join the rest. Instead, they washed them with salt water while others dug beneath them in the sand, slowly working slings beneath their bodies. Then they were lifted with long-legged machines like giant beach birds. They were swung into the boat, which closed its jaws and carried them across the ocean, all the time under the care of humans who sloshed their burning skins. They were lifted to a dock on America's eastern shore and put into a tank.

Man, in releasing the rest of the herd, had earned the affection and caught the interest of the three he had taken.

They began to play man's games. The three young
pilot whales had found the sounds of man incompre-
hensible, impossible to mimic underwater, and difficult to duplicate with their blowholes even in air. So
the three taught man to whistle as a dolphin might.
Soon the men had built a device with musical tones,
pleasant to cetacean ears, which they sounded loudly
underwater to make their wishes known.

Together, man and the three pilot whales devised
many games. All three learned to hunt man's toys
when they sank to the bottom. Some of these toys,
swift as hunting orcas, were built like tiny submarines,
hardly longer than a dolphin, with whirling flukes in
back.

Of the words men spoke, which were clumsy and
vague, the pilot had learned very few. But he rose
reluctantly to the surface when the sperm whale
begged him to, and blew laboriously:

"Tor...peed...oh..."

The sperm tried to copy the word with his own
blowhole but failed. The two cartwheeled back to the
depths, and the pilot continued to picture his life with
the men by the sea.

Man in his play had sent the torpedoes to race after
ships, sometimes thudding against them and falling,
sometimes passing below. Of this humans never
seemed to tire, tracking their path with a pinging
sonar like the sound of a baby sperm. When the torpedoes themselves grew weary, they often sank.

To retrieve them men built each of the three pilot
whales a mouthpiece to grasp, and clamps that closed
when they were placed around a torpedo on the bottom. The whales would echo-locate the torpedo, dive,
attach the clamp, and let man tug his prize to the
surface.

But this was only one of the games. Others he liked more. He had guarded his human friends, who dove with bubbling tanks, and he would drive away sharks and other men who pretended they would harm them. He carried men's burdens below when the humans themselves could not. He helped them to enter chambers they had strewed along the bottom, in which they tried to live. Once he had saved one from drowning when depth made him silly and careless, carrying him and his tank slowly, level by level, from the ocean floor, because to rocket upward made men writhe in agony and would kill them. He had carried slates on which divers made marks, and he sounded this picture to the sperm: A human wearing the strange black blubber that they donned in the sea, with bubbles rising to the surface like a humpback netting fish, was scratching on a slate with a stick in his hand and placing it between the pilot whale's jaws. He pictured then another man taking it and peering at it and *knowing* what the first man wished him to know....

Excited, the sperm asked how this could be, unless men, like whales, *did* think in pictures.

The pilot whale grew silent. Surprised, the sperm scanned his body carefully. The pilot's stomach was knotted with anger and his muscles tense with rage. His bowels were churning gases, and when he sounded in reply, his voice chambers vibrated with grief.

He grunted that he knew nothing of how man thought, or of his scratchings on slates below, or why his games were played. And he cared much less. For men he had loved had tricked and tried to kill him, and that was why he was back with his herd in the sea. If the men in the submarine ahead had died, it was no concern of his. For him all men had died one afternoon in the Straits of Denmark, long ago. Silent and morose, he surfaced to blow, and swam solidly north through the chop.

The sperm whale was saddened. He might never know the story. He would have told his tale of Nantucket, but the pilot had swum away.

The seamount was on their route, and the sperm knew that he would never see another submarine if he ignored the one ahead. And so he pushed on alone.

✹ 14 ✹

Lieutenant Peter Rostov flicked on the light that illuminated the sonar console. He blinked in its glare. An icy trickle had begun to work its way down the bulkhead behind it. It would not be many days before it seeped behind the circuit boards, shorted out the transducers, and stilled the sonar's pings forever.

No matter. He was permitted only to listen for surface targets: To search with sonar was forbidden.

Everything else was forbidden, too: the light he had just turned on, and that over his stateroom washbasin. Even new batteries for his dead flashlight were denied, saved for the engineers. His face was stubbled because he could not shave.

Fourteen days, fourteen hours, fifty minutes on the bottom, at dark of noon today.

He sniffed deliberately, testing the air. The oxygen

scrubbers would not last forever, but he could hear them whirring faintly. The air conditioning was shut down when they had grounded, to save power and silence the ship.

The smell of the submarine was fecal, but no one could die from that. The humidity was almost unbearable, and getting worse, but it was unlikely that anyone would live long enough to die of dehydration. When the shaft-seals on the turbines gave way, the ship would be contaminated with radioactive plutonium. This would be unfortunate for bottom fish and those who ate them, from the beginning of the feeding chain to man, but of no concern, he imagined, to him or the rest of the crew if they were dead.

It was anoxia that he had to fear.

Like all submarine officers, he had fair knowledge of the effects of oxygen deprivation. Insidiously, as the oxygen content dropped from twenty percent to nineteen, eighteen, seventeen percent, he would become happy, lightheaded, as if he had been sipping vodka. Merriment, it was said, would reign below. Mistakes in judgment would be made. Great delusions of power would come to them all. Stories of trapped U-boat crews in World War II, singing lustily on the bottom, were legion in the fleet. Then would come a swift and lethal hangover. When the oxygen content dropped to fourteen percent, foreheads would throb. Men would become irritable and combative. A task undertaken would become a monstrous problem, and even the wrong technique in solving it would become sacrosanct, not to be changed at any cost. They would begin to pant. Vision would suffer, and hearing next. Nausea and vomiting, extreme weakness, and convulsions would come. And finally, irreversibly, blood pressure would drop and the heart would flutter. They would die flopping like fish in a trawler's hold.

He forced his mind back to the present. There were plenty of discomforts now without dreaming of those to come. There were no more warm meals in either mess; rock-hard rye and moldy cheese was piled on the wardroom table, and one groped for food as best one could.

Better than starving in rubble, said the *zampolit*, who wore the ribbon of the Leningrad Siege.

Perhaps better, perhaps worse. The toilet in the forward head was still clogged. When he had complained about it, the engineer proposed that those who lived forward bucket their excrement into the torpedo tubes, so that it could be discharged in the manner of the Lithuanian steward. No one had accepted the suggestion.

He had long ago assigned himself a double stint of duty at his console, to escape from thought and to avoid the stench in his stateroom. He wore earphones twelves hours a day, and his ears itched. He removed the phones to scratch. Someone was standing behind him. He swung on his swivel chair. It was the surgeon. He had not seen her in full light since her lecture about the *Glomar Explorer*. Washing was forbidden, and her hair hung lifelessly.

As if reading his mind, she ran her fingers through the strands. Her dark eyes were breathtaking, but shadowed with fatigue. Because he knew she was embarrassed at her appearance, he turned off the light and adjusted a panel rheostat until the rosy glow flattered her skin.

"You've got Nicolai quieted, Natasha," he observed, referring to the navigator.

"Sleeping. Sedated. I wish *I* were." The *zampolit* had

found her with nothing to do and put her to work with Phase I of the Destruction Bill. "I have to destroy everyone's handbooks, so the Yankees can't read them if they find us and salvage the boat."

Bad news. The captain, or the *zampolit*, had perhaps given up on the Latvian's engines.

"Salvage?" he murmured, shaking his head in wonder. "Six hundred feet under the sea?"

"It seems possible to the *zampolit*." She looked into his eyes. "Is it, Peter?"

He shrugged and began to twist the dial on the sonar-room safe. "I suppose. You were there when their *Glomar Explorer* went to work. We're close to New York, and not nearly as deep as the *Baku*."

"If they find us before we die... will they kill us, Peter? Or try to save us?"

The submarine writhed in the current, and a deck frame squealed in agony. Forward, one of his sonar men moaned. He heard the navigator awaken and begin to chant what seemed like a prayer from aft.

"They'd try to *save* us, Natasha," he murmured, although if the CIA became involved, he was not sure at all. "We're in international waters. We're not at war. Why would they kill us?"

"I don't know, I don't *know.*" Tears glittered in her eyes. "I only know that I haven't even lived! My whole damn life has been school! And hospitals! I've had *one* man, a dental student, I can hardly remember his face, it was too close to finals! I've never had a child! Or a picnic on the beach!"

They should never have sent her to this hulk; the only other female doctor he had seen on a sub was forty and looked sixty. "Why'd they post you here?" he asked angrily.

"The admiral on that flagship. And also his chief of staff."

"For not sleeping with them?" he muttered.

"I doubt there was much sleep involved. Now I wish I had."

"*Bastards!*" he grated. "They ought to be shot!"

"Am I wrong to want to live?" she gulped. "The *only* one? I *want* to be rescued! I don't care by whom! Am I some kind of traitor?"

Dangerous grounds. "We'll get her moving again, Natasha." He'd admitted his fears to Olga, but to Natasha he could not: She needed strength and comfort. "If not, I'll talk to the captain about releasing another buoy."

He drew his restricted documents from the safe. In his view there was nothing in any of them that would have surprised a U-boat commander from the First World War, but at least feeding them into the shredder in the crypto room would give her something to do. He stacked them on her arms. When they touched, he felt a warmth from his belly to his groin. God, he wanted this woman pressed close. He almost dashed the handbooks to the floor to take her into his arms.

"You don't really think he will, though?" she persisted. "Release another buoy?"

"If I talk to him..."

She looked into his eyes. "You're frightened too, Peter."

He smiled. "It shows?"

"To me." She squeezed his hand. "But thanks for trying."

Olga had thanked him for admitting his fear; Natasha thanked him for trying to hide it. Neither knew that the fear was for Anna, not himself.

Anna, it's you I want. It's my body that doesn't know it.

He took a deep breath, piled the last of the hand-books on top, and sat down, trembling. She regarded him for a moment, then started out, avoiding a shimmering puddle on the deckplates.

"No," he called softly. "Wait."

She turned in the bloodred light.

"Natasha," he murmured, "about rescue. You should *not* care by whom, but hope only that it happens. I am hoping—praying—for rescue too. By anyone at all."

She returned, kissed him lightly on the lips, and left.

He became aware that Olga had stepped through the green curtain from the bunkroom forward. She looked after the departing doctor and turned to Rostov. Her stainless tooth glittered with what he took to be a smile.

"With so many heroes in your wardroom, a girl is grateful to a man who wants to survive. We line up for your favors."

He felt his face flaming. "Not exactly."

He caught the glint of tears. She jerked her thumb toward the forward bunkroom, where the steward had slept. "Her last patient's bunk is quite dry. Blood-stained, but I think I'll take to using *it*. You'll need your privacy aft."

"I won't, really," he muttered.

"Well, you can always hope." She glanced at the clock. "Shall I eat before I relieve you?"

He nodded, turned back to his console, and retuned the ears of the ship.

A nearby frame cracked, this time like a rifle shot. He held his breath and listened. He knew every drip and dribble in his darkened world, and he heard nothing new.

The navigator, jolted perhaps by the same bolt of panic, began to shriek from forward, warbling like an ambulance threading the Leningrad streets.

And the *zampolit* was worried about surface vessels picking up the sound of muted tapes? In terms of decibels the poor man was Caruso in *I Paggliacci* running wild.

Rostov pulled down his earphones and began to listen to the ocean, from which man and every living thing, they said, had come. Now that the grieving whales had left, crackling shrimp and croakers and scurrying crabs owned the world outside.

When the hull collapsed, they would own his world, too, and flesh and bones and brain.

〰 15 〰

The birth of a sperm whale calf had never been a thing taken lightly in the cetacean world. The cachalot was king, and his calf was a prince or a princess.

Cetacea had always recognized the sperm's primacy, not alone in strength and courage, but in brain and spirit too. The dolphin and the porpoise were welcomed everywhere for their cheer, and the humpback and beluga for their songs beneath the waves;

even the orca were respected by potential prey for their efficiency in the hunt.

But sperm whales had earned love and a kind of fealty from every species in the sea for their patience and their wisdom. In waters where sperm gave birth, smaller whales and dolphins would gather like courtiers when they heard the moans of a female in labor, and within hours of a successful delivery, the word spread far and wide.

The cow knew by dusk that today there would be no dolphin spectators when her daughter gave birth to the mad bull's calf. The sire had already led them too far from their normal waters, into an ocean too cold, and the dolphins had long ago fled from the strange doings of this pod. Only fearless, starving orcas remained nearby, silent as floating ice. And the pod bull was ignoring them.

As she listened to the groans of her frightened daughter, who had never given birth before, she became more and more concerned for mother and unborn calf. She had been scanning the womb of the younger cow for sixteen months, since almost the moment of conception. The initial signs had been reasonably good.

Sperm cows ovulated more actively with the left than the right ovary, though it was not known why. Like all mammals but man and his brother primates, the cachalot female's uterus consisted of two horn-shaped chambers, like conch shells connected mouth-to-mouth. Each had an ovary connected by a Fallopian tube at its smaller end. It was to the left one of these cornucopian chambers, rather than to the right, that the egg most frequently clung to be fertilized, and here the fetus grew; and it was thought that the left-horn pregnancy was more often successful than the right.

The cow had noted instantly that the egg had lodged normally in the left of the two uterine chambers, and that fortunately it was single. Of a hundred copulations only one might result in twins, but since the normal sperm whale baby weighed two full tons at birth, the mother and twin babies almost always died.

She had continued to scan her daughter almost every day. By the end of the second month, when the fetus was hardly three inches long, gull-like with a tiny beak and fingers that would change to fins, she and the other cows had already perceived that the embryo was healthy. With ultrasonic precision they had inspected it organ by organ: It had had eight tiny nipples, six of which would disappear before birth; this was universally thought to mean that in ancient days on land her ancestors had borne litters, as it was thought that land animals still did.

By the fifth month the embryo had grown to two hundred pounds and the uterine chamber sagged with its weight. If born normally, the tail must lead the body out the birth canal. For unlike its ungulate cousins, such as ancestral cattle and pigs it had left on land, sperm babies survived best in a breech birth.

The reason was one of timing. Sperm cows gave birth five fathoms down. The umbilical cord was short, so that it would break whether head or tail emerged first, since there was no way for the mother to bite it. When it broke, all oxygen to the baby stopped. Head out or tail out, the baby was in danger of taking its first breath in a liquid, whether salt water or amniotic fluid, unless it was carried quickly to the surface. There was a critical instant, after the umbilical cord snapped, when the baby was half-in, half-out of the womb, holding its breath.

The remainder of parturition was touch and go. But tail-first births were swifter, for the sperm body was essentially wedge-shaped, and the baby's blunt head gave better purchase for uterine contractions than its tiny flukes, hardly three feet across. Only a baby born tail first was assured freedom in time to be brought up for air.

At nine months the cow had worriedly noted that the head was leading in the birth canal, and that the cord was wrapped tightly around the body, which already weighed a thousand pounds.

At ten months, off Yucatán, the young mother had been diving at a thousand feet when the squid she was chasing squirted ink from its jet and climbed. She soared violently after it. The embryo had tumbled, the cord had unwrapped, and all had seemed well to the mother of the pregnant cow.

But today, with the birth approaching, orcas lurking, and the harem master swimming in some private world of madness, she was anxious. Her half-brother believed that to pour good hopes into the Ocean of Thought could change events. She did not agree, but wished he were here to try.

Of all times for disarray, birthing was the worst. For cetacean ancestors had fled from land, which was full of surprises, to an environment that was, a fathom or two below storms and gales, benign and unchanging. And so—except for killer whales, who thrived on disruption—they had never evolved to deal well with confusion.

The silent orcas began to sound again, in the chilling secret code of hunting that other whales or dolphins could not read. The cow knew that they used it only near cetaceans they intended to attack.

She trusted orcas well enough in waters rich with fish. She was grateful to them for the swift messengers they were. But she instinctively avoided them when her scanning showed them hungry.

She was not scanning them now. She had no wish to attract attention to her calf. Her daughter was swimming far to the rear, and more and more slowly. Forced by the bull to take the lead herself, the older cow was torn between fear for her daughter and fear for her own little calf.

With a bolt of panic she heard the orcas closing on her daughter, as if their leader realized that the big sperm bull was mad. The cow grunted once, imperiously, for her calf to close on her flank. Then she turned, ignoring a warning from the harem master, and hurtled back under the pod.

The orca leader sent a sudden barrage of messages from half a mile away. He was directing his adolescents from afar; only when the assault seemed failing would the adults take a part. Swift stubby forms were quickly everywhere, circling her daughter like sharks in the sonic shadows.

She slammed her jaws together like a bull. Startled, the orcas grew silent. She slanted down for the nearest echo, a sleek young killer male, thirty feet long and almost as heavy as she. Astounded, he slid for the depths. Her calf, in echelon at her right flank, was uttering little cries, which she took to be of defiance, at another orca three times bigger than himself.

She dove and slipped beneath her baby, blocking the new assailant. The orca feinted once and went for her caudal trunk. With a sidewise slice of her flukes she caught him, crushing his ribs and sending him spinning toward dim sunlight above.

The orcas regrouped, conferring. She could not read their hunting code, but she could almost read their minds. When the newborn infant was half from the mother's womb, the cord taut and ready to break, they would close and resume the attack.

She shrieked one hopeless call of distress after the departing harem master, and swam to her daughter.

Defecation had stopped. At a depth of thirty feet, the laboring mother floated helplessly, waving her fins. She grunted in agony. Tiny flukes emerged and began to beckon from her bleeding ventral slit.

❧ 16 ❧

The sperm bore the pain of sounding as well as he could and began to echo-locate, searching for the spire of Wallop Seamount.

Cetacea's knowledge of submarines was limited. Whales did not really understand why man would dive at all, since he caught no food from his undersea vessels. When the explosive plagues of thunder and lightning struck his ships, submarines seemed to suffer worst of all, and were forever being sunk to rust below. The mystery was insoluble, since the interiors of submarines were impervious to sonar; they remained as obscure inside to the acoustical observer as to the visual, and of course the submarine he was hunting now lay in depths far past any remnants of light.

He knew that he would learn little, but he wanted to hear it singing. He felt that finding it would somehow close the circle of his life.

Thirty summers had passed since he had dived on a shattered submarine in the Florida Strait. It had been lying on its side. Close to it was the twisted carcass of the surface ship that, it was said, had struck it.

But his interest had been in the submarine, the first he had heard of that lay open to the sea. It lay less than six hundred feet deep. And indeed, it had been cut almost in half. Sidling up to it, he had been able to peer with his sonar inside its jagged wound, frightening a hammerhead shark and a school of barracuda from its guts.

He sounded on its inward workings for an hour, lying in sand by the hull, his head too big to enter the hole and probe more closely inside. But he stayed, clicking, squealing, squeaking, fingering echoes of the jagged and wonderful things within.

He had scanned for a time a skeleton lying in a niche, picked bare of flesh a decade before by barracudas, perhaps, or crabs. Finally, unable to understand the devices inside or their use to man, he had left, but the mystery and puzzlement had lived with him for thirty years.

It was then that the first glimmer of hope that the prophecy would come true had flickered in his mind. It was as though he had encountered a pod of river dolphins who had dived as deeply as he into the Ocean of Thought. He had wondered then how so small a brain as man's could bring to birth so complex and wondrous a thing.

Animals so clever seemed surely ready: Only the channels seemed closed.

He quit *blang*ing for the sake of his tortured jaw, but continued on course toward the seamount. At a range of one mile, swimming at fifty feet below the surface, he heard a distant clinking from its ridge. He steeled his jaw against the pain and sent out a train of pulses. He waited.

All at once he visualized the submarine, clearly and distinctly, rocking gently on the saddle of the mountain crest a quarter-mile below. It was so carefully balanced, on the only peak within five hundred miles, that it could only have been placed there by some conscious effort of man.

All whales had listened to man's feeble echo-locaters; indeed, sperm had been hunted by them from surface ships in recent times. Man's undersea vessels apparently used echoes exactly as cetaceans had for thirty million years; to hunt for other ships and subs and to grope their way across the bottom. To find the seamount, this one must have used its sonar. Living men had guided it here.

There was no more music from it, only the clang it made on rocks.

He *blang*ed loudly to awaken it and listened for the song that the humpbacks had mimicked. It remained silent. Again and again he sounded and heard nothing in return.

The men must be dead from lack of air.

A hundred feet below the surface, he trailed his flukes and glided. He would never hear man's music now, or hear the prophecy come true. He suddenly felt very old and very much alone.

Of a dozen brothers born off Spain, only he had survived. Nine had been lanced to death by man; one, driven from good feeding grounds by whalers, had weakened and died of pneumonia; another, like their sire, had drowned under northern ice.

His jaw was shattered, his lungs were tired, and his heart was weary too. He should push on to Nantucket, or he would die at sea.

The submarine was already dead. He would never hear it sing.

Then he heard a bang from below, as if something had broken within it. A strange warm current from the Ocean of Thought caught him and made him stay.

〽 17 〽

Lieutenant Peter Rostov, sitting at his sonar console, was losing track of time again. He could hear one of his men, a giant farm boy from the Ukraine, crying in his bunk at the forward end of the sonar compartment. He could not remember whether the sobbing had been going on for minutes or for hours. Or for days....

If *that* one, who stood six feet two and weighed a

good two hundred pounds, had to be restrained, it would take half the ship to handle him.

In the pitch darkness, at his console, he had the sudden sense of an alien presence. He swiveled and switched on the light.

The *zampolit* loomed above him. His glasses glittered. Rostov's first guilty reaction was to turn off the light. The *zampolit* clutched his arm. If he had really fought at Leningrad, he must now be well past sixty, but he was amazingly strong.

"Leave it," he growled. "It is not the first time."

Rostov shrugged. "To what do we owe this honor, comrade?" he asked.

"We were destroying your handbooks in the crypto room. I heard a sharp report. Was that from your compartment?"

Rostov regarded him in astonishment. The old soldier must actually suspect he was trying to signal for help: Why else would he come all this way?

"Another frame cracking from the pressure," Rostov explained. "You're in the wrong department, comrade. Speak to Damage Control."

The *zampolit* nodded. "It seemed to set the navigator off. Tell me, could a ship on the surface hear his yells?"

"He is quiet now," muttered Rostov.

"She's sedated him. But that wasn't my question."

For all Rostov knew, to admit such a thing might tempt him to put his ex-roommate to sleep forever. "From a hundred fathoms? Never!"

The *zampolit* glanced at him narrowly, then pulled a pack of cigarettes from his pocket. He offered one to Rostov, who shook his head. The eyes behind the thick, steel-framed glasses had always intimidated him, but still, this domain of sound was his own. "Not in this compartment, comrade. The air is bad enough."

The *zampolit* hesitated, then replaced the pack unused. The young man forward began to sob again. "What's wrong with *him*?"

"Dreaming," Rostov said.

"Or cracking. Like your frame, or your friend the navigator. Perhaps it's contagious."

"Asleep," insisted Rostov.

"What's his name?"

"There are three who bunk there, how should I know? Comrade, he is all right!"

"When pressure cracks a weak frame, that's the problem of Damage Control. And when pressure cracks a weak mind, it's *my* problem."

Rostov shrugged. "All right, but leave *that* one to me."

"Watch him, whoever he is. He could panic my crew."

Rostov stared at him. "*Your—*"

"*Ours*, then." He paused. "Rostov, you're too restless yourself. We both know what we must do if the engineers fail. You're a man of intelligence. Why do you resist this?"

Rostov's throat was tight. "*What* must we do?"

The *zampolit*'s eyeglasses glittered. Behind them the eyes were diamond hard. He patted Rostov's shoulder. "*Nothing*, my young friend. Absolutely nothing. Please do not suggest otherwise, to the captain or anyone else."

He turned and left.

Rostov found that his mouth had gone dry. His pulse pounded. Again he felt the tension rising in his body, the sense of the hull pushing in, of the air growing heavier. It was crushing him. He began to pant. He felt a screech of agony welling deep inside.

No! He jammed his fist into his mouth, bit his knuckle, drawing blood. He switched off the light, swiveled quickly back to the console, jammed his earphones tight.

Escape lay through his ears, and he groped for the familiar way through the midnight black to sapphire blue above, and sunshine. He turned up the sensitivity, searching for the slap of waves six hundred feet above, the sound of a passing vessel, anything to break the *zampolit*'s freezing grip on mind and soul.

He turned the dial on the console. Forward, he could hear the grinding of the electronic ears as he listened west, toward the shores of America, then north, east....

Nothing....

More slowly, hopelessly, he listened to the south.

In the distant background he heard it approaching slowly, fading, returning.

"*Blang...blang...blang...*"

He recognized the sound instantly. The humpbacks had left, but a single *kashalot*, a whale of another species-*catodon*, genus *Physeter*, family *Physeteridae*—had come to take their place. The distant banging was metallic, like a hammer beating a sickle of iron.

The sperm whale was echo-locating, probably hunting squid. Rostov had often listened to their voices on tapes in Sonic Officer's School in Moscow, and then on the long Atlantic passages out of Kiev, and when he had served out of Vladivostok too.

"*Blang, blang, blang...*"

No beauty there, no melody. But perfect, meticulous rhythm, like an enormous metronome clanging in the water.

Soon the animal would doubtless speed up the beat. Rostov knew from experience that it would become allegro as he closed in on the squid, in an ever-increasing tempo that would turn it a ratchety clicking, then a croak. In any waters Rostov had monitored, the voice of the *kashalot*, clashing or clicking, remained under tight and conscious control.

He sat back, feeling much better, and began to work the gonging rhythm into his mental symphony, leading the orchestra in the dark.

All was not hopeless. Perhaps the humpbacks would return and join their lovely basses to the beat of the cymbalist above. He thought already that he could hear dolphin noises in the background, or pilot whales, or both.

But the *kashalot* easily dominated: *"Blang, blang, blang..."*

The sonar officer hummed a key: *"Ta dum, ta dum ...Now the bass, and the clarion call of a trumpet, clarissimo..."*

His spirits rose further.

They might die at the bottom of the sea. But they were not dead yet. And not alone.

He had once promised to call the medical officer when he heard another whale. He called sick bay, then the crypto room on the ship's telephone. She sounded excited, but the *zampolit* had her shredding documents, and so she could not come.

Too bad. In the clanging of the *kashalot*'s cymbals there was discord, to be sure.

But also, for some reason he did not quite understand, he heard a note of hope.

⚙ 18 ⚙

Her daughter groaned in the birthing, maintaining her depth at twenty feet. She was free of the glittering surface chop that the cow could see above her, but she would be within reach of air when the baby was born.

The tiny flukes, hardly three feet wide, had emerged first, bent almost double; they had waved and were trying already to straighten. The newborn calf was half out of the womb now, and the cow below could already see that her dorsal hump was perfectly formed.

But there was more to be done than to watch. The siren squeals of the orcas were everywhere, direction-less and impossible to decipher: a cacophony of noise that was meant to dizzy and confuse her, to freeze her where she was.

Her little calf huddled in the shelter of her fin. She could not bring herself to nudge him away, though she wanted freedom to act when the orca leader sig-naled another attack. They were exposed from below, and the newborn would be the first victim when the two cows tried to shove it to the surface for its first breath.

Above her, the little flukes popped suddenly straight

and began to tremble as uterine contractions squeezed at the body and head. She tried to comfort her daughter with a picture of the emerging baby, but the new mother was so frightened that she only moaned.

She felt her calf nudging at her. He squealed as a white-bellied orca flashed by, grating a chain of pulses. She clapped her jaws in warning and the orca rolled, breaking his secret code to chatter her a sound-picture of bloody waters and floating flesh. The picture was a threat, meant to frighten them, and her calf shrieked in terror. But the cow whirled and caught the killer with a downward stroke of flukes as wide as he was long. She heard bone shatter beneath the blubber of his chest, and a mighty explosion of air five fathoms below as his breath left his body. A curtain of diamond bubbles rose, engulfing them and shielding them all from the sonar of the circling predators.

The cow moved up, caressing her daughter's body as the tiny fetus wriggled to be free. Its cord, taut as a kelp stalk, broke too soon. It would drown in amniotic fluid with its blowhole still in the womb. Ignoring the howling orcas, the cow clasped the tiny body in her jaws as gently as she could and backed her flukes.

A young female orca slammed past, whining and squeaking, apparently reporting to the leaders outside the attack circle. A young bull, jaws gaping and rows of teeth glittering, grabbed for the newborn's tail, two feet from the cow's own jaw. The cow yanked the tiny flukes away, and the orca missed.

All at once the baby popped free. She drew it swiftly from the womb in a cloud of amber liquid. The cord snaked after it.

She tossed the tiny body, not ten feet long, from her jaws, cartwheeled backward to clasp it to her chest in her pectoral fins. It struggled for air, confused and clumsy, slipped loose, and headed downward. She heard an orca scream below, in triumph or in hunger. She lunged and grabbed the newborn in her fins again.

All at once, from a hundred yards away, there was a thunderous crash of flukes. It was the harem bull, sounding a challenge that nothing in the sea could face. In an instant the orcas were silent and fleeing.

The cow rocketed through shards of sapphire light. She was suddenly floating on waves tipped with gold under the setting sun. With a puff and an explosive little suck, the infant in her fins began to breathe. Air whistled down the tiny windpipe, life poured into little arteries and veins. In a few moments she could ease her body from beneath the tiny one, let it float alone, let it try to swim. For now, she preferred simply to lie with it cradled on her belly.

The orcas were far away. Sated someday, in waters richer with fish and squid, the same pod might swim to her with messages and play with the infant calf.

Such was the way of the orca, as unfathomable to her mind as man, who killed and nurtured, harmed and helped, slaughtered and tried to save.

She caressed the newborn infant as her own calf nudged her, squealing for attention. Her daughter rose, blew, passed a fin over her baby, moaning in delight, then sank, and hovered, resting.

The cow caught the whine of a distant propeller, westward-bound. The harem master was homing on it, *blang*ing mighty peals. He had not charged in to save them, but passed in pursuit of yet another boat.

She was much too tired to care. She judged the boat to be moving too fast for him to catch, a measure of his madness. She wished the men in it well, but hoped that he would chase them to where the sun had sunk.

His pursuit was her chance, and she would not fail. Tonight she would escape.

〽 19 〽

The aging sperm had always marveled at the treasures the Sea of Thought had alloted the cachalot strain. No creature in all the seas occupied so deep a vertical niche. No other animal had access to so many levels of marine environment. That part of the oceanic abyss that he could not penetrate was useless to him anyway, and to most other forms of life.

His ancestors had first earned domination—undisputed for thirty million years—over the rich and essential interface between surface and air. Even man had discovered that he must keep this interface empty for a rising whale. Oarsmen had learned quickly that to drift over the spot where a sounding cachalot intended to blow was to end up floundering in the whale's own sea.

But the sperm ruled more than this golden level of sunshine and wind. He swam unchallenged through layers almost as desirable just below the surface, where successful predators like sharks and tuna had earned a place. Deeper still, he penetrated without risk the twilight green between light and dark, where lantern fish and plankton had learned to survive. Finally, he ruled the midnight deep, where the losers—deep-sea grenadiers, hatchetfish, and sablefish—lived on detritus from above, and giant squid tried to hide.

Not until the day of undersea telegraph transmission, when sperm, dragging their jaws along the bottom for buried skates and rays, began to tangle and suffocate in marine cables four thousand feet below, did man's world interfere with the sperm whale in a dive.

A healthy young bull in good condition could dive seven thousand feet. He could survive with a ton and a half of pressure on every square inch of his skin, when each cubic foot of air he had breathed on the surface had become a bubble two inches in diameter.

A helmeted diver at a depth one-twentieth the sperm whale's maximum was known to lose his senses. Sperm had echo-sounded on divers, hauled too quickly to the surface, whose blood had begun to froth and boil. They had known humans, diving too deep and staying too long, to double in agony and die as the bubbles reached their joints and brains.

A sperm whale a mile deep could operate with all his mental faculties and rise without harm as swiftly as he wished. Sperm had scanned their fellows and knew the reason why.

To increase his diving endurance, the sperm had a labyrinth of blood vessels that restricted unnecessary circulation and caloric expenditure when below. When he dived, his heart rate halved to save him energy. His nervous system ignored the carbon dioxide in his blood that ultimately forced land mammals to take a breath. He absorbed life from his air three times more efficiently than a human, and his tolerance for the surge of body acids that forced a tiring man's muscles to fail was immense.

The emperor whale could sink a mile beneath the surface and stay for an hour and a half. At a depth where man's steel-ribbed submarines collapsed, his sixteen-foot-long ribs of bone hardly began to bend.

His evolution had endowed him with lungs seven feet long. From the size of a tiger shark on the surface, each lung compressed to the size of a cod by the time he reached his maximum depth. The sperm was naturally buoyant, unlike most whales, and depended on forward motion and pectoral fins like dive brakes to send him down. He always dived with half-filled lungs, because when he forced himself below against the added buoyancy of full lungs, it cost him more calories than the protein he chased.

So instead of depending on great volumes trapped at the surface, he hyperventilated, as human pearl-divers did, but exchanging stale for fresh air four times more efficiently. He charged his lungs on the surface, breathing deeply in a sleepy trance that renewed mental energies depleted by the previous dive. He blew ten minutes for every hour he dived, sending his slanted exhalations skyward and forward, each breath a minute long. When his blood was fully charged with oxygen, he exhaled half a breath, tossed his flukes, and plummeted.

His breathing habits, any sperm knew, had spelled his doom with whalers, who had learned his formula quickly and drew closer each time he surfaced. They forced him to dive at shorter and shorter intervals until he lacked the breath to dive at all. But his respiration was a product of thirty million years in a world free of surface enemies. He could no more stop his fatal exhalations than a hiding man could hold a sneeze.

The emperor whale held high ground in the ocean chain of feeding. But man had seized ground higher still.

❧ 20 ❧

A hundred feet below the surface, in waters dimly green, the aging sperm rested silently. His jaw tormented him, and to echo-sound was torture, for his normal sonic explosion, which could stun a fifty-foot squid into immobility, jarred the right jawbone like an impact with a reef.

Like all Atlantic whales he had had an accurate picture of the Wallop Seamount in his mind since adolescence, so he needed no sonic map of the terrain below. When he had gritted his teeth, blatted painfully, and located the submarine, he perceived that it was teetering on the saddle between the highest peak and a castellated spire. If it had indeed been put there consciously, then men had picked a very precarious place for it.

He had no idea what depths a submarine could withstand. Every one he had sounded had been in shallower water than this. When he had studied the submarine off Florida he had tried to compare it to the living things he knew.

The girths of whales and sea lions and walruses were flexible, and diminished as pressure squeezed their ribs and lungs. But he had noticed that a submarine on the bottom retained its normal diameter. Therefore, its ribs and skin were rigid, like the shell of a crab. But nothing inflexible could resist forever the pressure of increasing depth: Consequently, a submarine would probably collapse suddenly if it went too deep, as a kelp bulb drawn in play by a diving calf would implode with a satisfying pop.

Now he was curious to see if the one below him had buckled. He cooled the oil in his head-case and sank slowly to four hundred feet. In darkness, two hundred feet above the submarine, he scanned it with a long-drawn, ratchety stream of sound.

It appeared intact.

He wondered how long the men had survived as the air in its lungs was used up. The noisy submarines of his youth had surfaced often, but the silent undersea craft of today stayed down longer. Twenty-five summers ago he had marveled to hear of one that had dived in the Atlantic under the northern icecap. All Cetacea had followed the reports, sounded by arctic beluga whales and narwhals, of its progress. Unlike a bowhead or even a sperm, the submarine had whined its way under the ice all the way to the Pacific without stopping at a single blowhole to breathe.

Man's toys seemed to evolve much faster than living things. The new submarines must have enormous lungs. Perhaps men had somehow learned to extract the gases of life from the water around them, as gilled creatures could do and whales could not. If so, he envied them. For to hide, never breathing above, had been the dream of hunted whales since man had first laid siege to the surface. Perhaps whale lungs would someday evolve to do this. Whales had come so far already that the final metamorphosis to true creatures of the sea seemed not so long a leap. First came the need, then the thought, then the long sure aeons of change.

Archaic ancestors had sensed a dark and peaceful world below, where they might hide from blazing heat and stinging gales. Their mammalian eyes were too feeble for it, but ten million years of desire had given them instead the voice and hearing to hunt blindly in the blackness that they craved. They had grown eyes of sound: They could grow lungs like gills.

Only man could prevent it by murdering them all. Man made the years move faster with his hands. His time was a flash of lightning against the iceberg of cetacean evolution. In this flash he had learned to breathe where whales might not for a hundred thousand years.

But man had so recently entered the Ocean of Thought that he did not seem to know that another thinking creature swam there with him. Unless he could be told, then one day he would swim there all alone.

The aging sperm emerged from his trance, hovering in the set of the warming current, tasting waters from a thousand miles south. His kind had long ago lost the sense of smell, but evolution had replaced it with receptors under his tongue so sensitive that they could identify a pod member's urine a hundred miles upcurrent.

Now, in the flow of the Gulf Stream, he thought

of his half-sister and the calf, but surely this could not be taste, only imagination, for by now the herd would be southbound, east of Cuba, heading for the line.

He should continue north, if he was to make Nantucket by the rounding of the moon. He wanted to arrive at full high tide. His dying calf had been beached while the moon was round, and at the end had entered peacefully into the Ocean of Thought. He wanted the same for himself.

But something held him here. His heart was pounding oddly, although he was hardly six hundred feet deep and had hung there less than half a hour.

He was noticing a strange and wondrous thing: There were no vessels on the surface.

Around every other newly-wounded submarine, around every diving vessel that was drowning, man's herds had gathered above like pilot whales at the side of a dying leader. Like any thinking creature, man tried to rescue his kind. Sometimes, like a grieving cow with a dead calf, he would bring the victims to the surface even after they had died.

Why were other men ignoring this submarine?

There was only one answer. They did not even know it was here.

Suppose they were shown? They had tried to help his dying calf; he would try to help them find their dead.

How?

The pilot whale and the little dolphin knew man well.

He turned suddenly and drove back toward the pilot herd and the dolphin pods, which were feeding to the south. He pierced the darkness at a hundred fathoms, each stroke of his fifteen-foot flukes swirling a thousand gallons of water into the depths behind.

Since children had ridden dolphins in Europe's inland sea, sperm had swum with the prophecy. Perhaps the Ocean of Thought had carried him here to make that dream come true. He hoped that it was not too late for him to try.

PART THREE

Soundings

"Rain, with a silver flail;
   Sun, with a golden ball;
Ocean, wherein the whale
   Swims minnow-small."
      —William Rose Benét,
      "*Whale*," 1933

❖ 1 ❖

The submarine shuddered on the Wallop Seamount. An eddy of the current flowing around it had set up a humming vibration in the rudder, which must have been jarred loose in the impact of bottoming almost two weeks before.

Peter Rostov, feeling the console tremble, found the drumming more frightening than the leaks that were so terrifying to his sonarmen, and to Olga, his leading technician. He kept his own fears to himself, for the poor girl had somehow set her hopes on the bulletins issuing from the nuclear propulsion compartment, where the black-gang sweated in a clammy hell of oil and turbine blades and, for all he knew, unshielded plutonium fuel.

Rostov was afraid that slack in the rudder was academic: It would never be used again. The bullheaded Latvian chief engineer would never repair the turbines, and was probably the only officer on the ship who truly thought he could.

A sullen anger burned in Rostov's gut. Let the cursed *zampolit* hope for his Red Star in heaven or in hell. Let the navigator escape to madness and the Lithuanian steward to oblivion. He himself loved music and sunlight too much to spend his final moment fighting

his mates for the last molecule of oxygen as water
crept to the overhead and the air grew foul with fear.

But to dwell on that now, while air remained and
the hull stayed rigid, would soon have him screaming
like the navigator. He slipped back to the pitch-black
world outside. To shut out the thrumming and remove
the hand of fear, he cupped his earphones more closely.
Olga had tried to relieve him a few minutes ago, and
he had told her that he was tracking a passing tanker:
Actually, for the last half hour he had been listening
to the *kashalot* hovering somewhere in the midnight
wastes above. Because the sperm whale was free and
alive and could surface when it pleased, it gave him
a contact with wind and sun and stars that he had
longed for.

Like all sonar officers, he knew a great deal about
sperm, and finbacks, and sei whales too. Whales often
cluttered the sonar screen, infuriating Olga. The echo
of an approaching sperm or a blue on his screen was
so similar to that of a NATO attack submarine that it
was difficult to tell that the blip on the video was
harmless.

So one learned all one could of whales and their
habitats. For two vast sonic worlds—the western and
the Soviet—lay glowering at each other in the depths
of the planet's seas. "*Ex scientia tridens*—From knowledge, sea power" was the primary rule of the game.

Until last year, the Russian whaling fleet had stalked
the ocean, and naval reports of whale contacts, sonic
and visual, helped build a data base for the annual
hunting plan. But no more, if *Pravda* and *Red Star*
could be believed. He had read and welcomed the
news that at last the Russian whaling armada had
retired ashore, along with the Japanese.

Once, in a Vladivostok waterfront restaurant, he

had shared a table with a huge Mongol flenser off the whaler *Vostok*. The giant had spoken of crazy young Canadian hippies, and Americans, too, trying to stop the killing from rubber boats. The Mongol butcher of whalemeat had laughed at their foolhardiness— they had actually managed to *board* the factory ship— but the sonar officer thought he understood, deep inside, their need to try.

In a Leningrad cinema house as a child, he had seen a movie of whalers harpooning. He had been sickened by the reddened seas and laughing men.

Now that legal slaughter had stopped, *Pravda* and *Red Star* were claiming that the laying up of the Russian whalers was a sacrifice Soviet industry was making for the ecology of the seas. More lies, more dissembling. He suspected from the rarity of sperm whale sounds that the animals had been hounded almost to extinction. If capitalistic Japanese, Norwegians, Portuguese, Australians, and South Africans had quit whaling from factory ships, it could only be because they had killed too many of the geese that laid their golden eggs. He saw no reason to credit his motherland with a less cynical motive.

Whales had become so scarce that whaling, by corporations or Soviet cooperatives, had simply ceased to pay.

He strained to hear the *kashalot* above.

Now he heard nothing. Too bad. Natasha had never got to hear him. He had had a mighty voice, too, that one, with a strange broken ring to its peals of sound, like a drum with a damaged case.

The flenser had told him of surprising such *bogodooly*, irascible and lonely in old age, and how they would twist a good harpoon and carry it halfway to hell.

This one remained silent. Perhaps it had scanned their hull, found it boring, and moved on to more interesting things. How long could a thinking creature occupy itself with a hunk of sunken metal?

At the Leninskiy Higher Naval School of Submarine Navigation he had taken the standard course in biosonics—"sound-garbage" the officer-students called it. It encompassed all the living voices of the sea, from pistol shrimp and croakers to Wedell seals and humpback whales. The class was meant to teach sonar operators the background noises of the oceans, so that their ears could pick from it the whirr of NATO subs.

He had puzzled over the sperm whale's massive brain, wondered what an animal, doomed forever to live in an undemanding sea, would do with such an instrument. He had asked the professor, a chain-smoking civilian with jagged teeth and breath like a Siberian musk ox.

"Large bodies," the instructor had coughed, "*require* large brains. Listen, comrade, *kashalot* is nothing more than a pig who dove below, belched, heard an echo, found food, and got fat. No more intelligent than the swine he left on shore. Else why does he get caught?"

For the same reason that a submarine got caught, he had thought. Or a swimmer diving to escape red Indians in a canoe. Both had eventually to surface for air.

And *pig*? Perhaps, perhaps not. He wondered now if the professor had ever really listened to the tapes he played in class. No musician in the hearing of an echo-sounding sperm could confuse him with a pig, or fail to sense the working of a calculating mind. Perhaps the *instructor* had been the pig, tone-deaf to a genius in the undersea orchestra he had gathered for the class.

Rostov turned up the console light and studied the marching peaks and valleys on his sonograph of the sperm whale's peals that the pen had traced. A mighty voice indeed, from the height of the sawtoothed rows. And the shape of the valleys between showed that the whale was of tremendous size: over sixty feet, he estimated, from the spacing between the primary burst at the nose of the beast and the echo from the after-end of his head-case.

Where was the *kashalot* now? He wished he could entice it back for the doctor. He longed for Natasha's form close to his, fantasized the touch of her arm as they listened together, the softness of her breast against his shoulder.

He was tempted to flick on his own sonar to prick the beast's curiosity. Sometimes a submarine's pings drew answering *blang*'s from sperms: point, counterpoint; always exactly the same number: *ping, ping, ping; blang, blang, blang*. They mimicked the rhythm precisely and never missed a beat, as if the animals were eager to prove they could count or join a duet.

So much for the theory of deep-diving pigs.

If he started the sonar the *zampolit* would hear it through the steel of the hull. Mutiny...

He ripped the sonograph from its roll, crumpled the paper, and tossed it away. Who cared anymore for sonic signatures for Leningrad's naval pigeonholes, or field observations for Fleet Intelligence in Riga? The data would only drown here below, with the man who compiled it.

He was removing his headset when his ear caught the faintest of chimes from the departing monster,

ringing down some endless valley in the ebony void
below.

Good-bye, old fellow. Enjoy your respite, may your
tribe increase. Do not breed too fast, or man will return
to kill your young and the calves of young to come.

Farewell, *bogodoo*.

Suddenly lonely, frightened, and chilled, he called
for Olga to take her watch and rose from the console
at last. It was time to report to the *zampolit* on the
ships that had passed in the night.

❧ 2 ❧

She floated on her back, clasping her daughter's newborn baby between her pectoral fins, listening to the
eager wheeze of the tiny female's breathing.

Deliberately, with the tip of her fin, she splashed a
few drops of water onto the S-shaped opening of the
blowhole at the top of the head. The lips sealed
instantly, quivered, and opened again when they felt
no more spray. Good. The baby was small, less than
twelve feet long, but seemed perfectly formed and
already alert. She hugged it gently, and tried to make
it relax.

Only occasionally could she hear the distant whine
of the fast-moving boat over the slap of the waves,
and the clanging echoes of the mad whale chasing it.

Very quickly, while the harem bull was off rampaging, she must leave the infant with her daughter and escape from the herd with her calf.

Her own little bull jostled for attention at her flank, still shaken by the killer whale attack. Every now and then he would tread water to sneak an envious glance at the baby on her chest.

She sensed her daughter moving twenty feet below her, swirling away the afterbirth. When finally the new mother surfaced again beside her, it was time for her baby's first lesson.

The cow eased her own bulk below the waves. The infant floated free and began to pump its flukes. Soon it was moving through the water, but simply to paddle was not enough. Bulls on the move disliked straggling; to dawdle and overhunt an area was to starve. This herd's bull, now that his senses had left him, might leave cow and infant behind.

So the older cow and the new mother moved away, testing the baby. It bleated, cried, and turned in confusion. They forced themselves to wait until it somehow located them and waddled to their side. By sundown it would have to swim two miles an hour, perhaps more, if the mad bull demanded. And it must learn to dive.

The cow moved to the baby's side and placed a pectoral fin on its head. When it inhaled, secure and sheltered, she slid the fin over its blowhole and pressed the tiny body down. The baby thrashed for a moment, resisting, then relaxed and stayed below. The cow moved away and let it bob to the surface. By tomorrow, if the mother was to feed herself and make her milk, the baby at her side must plunge a hundred feet and last for a quarter-hour.

It was crying for food now, and the cow felt her

own teats straining. But this lesson was her daughter's
to teach and to learn herself.

Her daughter rolled correctly to her left side.
Mother and infant must lie belly to belly, tail to tail,
mother on her left flank, calf on its right, so that the
infant's off-centered blowhole would be raised and
clear of the surface chop.

Her daughter whistled softly at the infant. The
baby fluttered its little flukes and struggled to the
mother's belly. Hidden in two mammary slits, one on
each side of the three-foot genital cleft, lay her daughter's teats, four feet in length, carrying two gallons
each of butter-thick milk so rich that the baby would
gain a pound an hour for the next full year.

Now the teats were peeping for the first time from
the slits, though protruding only four inches beyond
the surface of her belly to keep the contents warm.
They were tipped with gleaming white nipples to guide
the infant to its food.

The baby approached from the wrong direction,
her little head toward the mother's tail. When it rolled
to seize a nipple, its blowhole would submerge.

This would not do, and the cow could not wait for
mother and daughter to sort the matter out. She eased
under the baby, rolled belly up, and turned it end to
end in the arms of her pectoral fins. She worked the
infant into position until its toothless jaw was nuzzling
the mother's teat. Left side up now, belly to belly with
her mother, its blowhole was well clear of the water.
In a sudden, solid stream, the milk gushed forth
untasted, wasted on the sea.

The cow forced the baby's mouth to the yellow
fountain of fluid. Its immobile narrow jaw, shaped
like a slim trap door, prevented sucking; it must learn
to clamp the teat, form its tongue into a feeding tube,

and let its mother pump. Patiently the cow guided the jaw, again and again, to the flow of milk. The baby whined in hunger and the mother in despair.

Miles away, ricocheting from the depths, came the *blang*'s of the bull returning. With a last effort the older cow jammed the little head against the mother's belly, holding it while the infant struggled. She heard a groan of satisfaction from the mother and the child.

She trailed a pectoral along her daughter's side in farewell, and touched the infant with the tip of her fin. She swam through the herd and nuzzled each adolescent and cow in turn, then called her calf to her side. She headed north toward Nantucket with the little bull, who kept up as best he could.

By dawn they were off Cape Hatteras. The harem master, she estimated, was one full night behind.

§ 3 §

The aging sperm closed quickly on the sleeping pilot whales. They were, of all cetaceans, the only species that slumbered deeply, for the potheads' light, bulbous head-cases, like buoys, allowed them to float erect, flukes hanging, water slashing well below the blowholes near the end of their rounded snouts. And so they dangled now, heads bobbing in the surface chop, flukes relaxed and waving in currents twenty feet below.

As always, the pod leader held the upwind position. The sperm had no wish to disturb the herd. The men in the submarine were dead; there was no hurry. So he basked nearby, waiting.

A gull swooped and soared, cawing, then landed softly twenty feet from his left eye. Entranced, he watched it. It would never have set down so close to a killer whale, which might gobble it. How such tiny-brained creatures knew that they were safe with sperm but not with orcas, he did not know.

The Ocean of Thought reached the sky that gulls flew in as it flooded the lands of man. Perhaps their little gull-brains, which somehow drew from the Ocean the skill to navigate and the lore of weather, drank other knowledge from that Ocean too.

The sperm fell into a mystic trance and thought he saw it all: sky, ocean, and islands of earth washed with the waters of Thought. Bird, whale, and man were simply three of many tentacles through which Thought was gathering knowledge. Fish and krill and seaweed sounded for knowledge, too, and trees above and coral below, and clouds and rocks and tides. All were like the trembling antennae of rock lobsters testing and feeling the seas. All gave to the Ocean's store of thought, changed it, fed from it, were changed by it as well.

It was very strange. For most of his fifty-nine years he had sounded the Ocean as deeply as any being in its waters, or probably on its shores. He would soon die and know all or nothing. But though the gull, with its tiny brain, could only skim its surface, if an orca or shark took it this instant, in the very next moment the bird would know more of the Ocean than he.

The gull floated closer. It sat preening arrogantly not three feet from his head. He sank until his blow-hole lay a foot below the surface. With a flick of his tail he glided beneath the bird. He drifted six inches higher. Casting his left eye upward, he could see the oval white of its breast, a bubble trapped in feathers like a tiny silver sun, a drop of water glittering on the shimmering beak above, the dangling, lazy legs. He blew enormously and surfaced.

The gull thrashing on the geyser, screamed in terror, upside-down and twelve feet high. It fell back into the water, righted and shook itself, squawked indignantly, and took off in a flurry of white flashing wings and spray.

The sperm rolled to his back to warm his belly in the sun.

But the pilot whale awoke.

They remained quite near the surface, the pilot whale and he, moving northward with the current as the dolphins fed below. The sperm pictured for the pothead the submarine as he had scanned it, teetering on the ridge. And he tried to picture, as well as he could, his vision of oneness if the prophecy came true.

If whales led man to his submarine, they would show that trust had returned with the end of the harpooning. The means to beckon man was here, in the pilot whale and dolphin.

On an island in a sound, five hundred miles from there, humans were known to be packed like lobsters. They lived in holes in spires of rock between a river and the ocean. It was thought that they communicated with those who sailed the sea. If they could be told of the submarine, they would come to get their dead.

The pilot whale and dolphin must somehow regain contact with man. Such a chance might never return. Perhaps, the aging sperm enthused, the memory of porpoises and human young, playing together in Europe's inland sea, still lived in human lore.

The pilot whale groaned as if saddened by the innocence of a calf. He had learned in a single morning in the Danish Straits that men were quite insane. If any cetacean lived in human history, it would be the mad Pacific sperm, not dolphins who had swum with children off ancient isles of Greece.

And the pilot whale began to sound a story he had never told before.

$$\text{❋ 4 ❋}$$

Lieutenant Peter Rostov found the captain sitting shirtless on his bunk in his tiny cabin. Rivulets of sweat wound through the hair on his chest and glistened on the rolls of his belly. The shadows from a feeble reading lamp etched his jowls with more strength than they deserved, but as he angled the light to read the daily report of sound contacts, the sonar officer saw that he was pale and very tired.

He scanned the paper and handed it back, smiling faintly. "No warships, then? No *Glomar Explorer* today to raise us from the dead?"

"No, Captain."

The submarine shivered. A grinding noise amidships told them that another boulder was trying to work its way into the hull. At last he had the captain alone, and he knew he must waste no time.

"One can feel it, Captain. The Gulf Stream is moving faster. Perhaps a storm to the south?"

"Perhaps," the captain murmured. He seemed suddenly guarded. He must sense what is coming, thought Rostov, and it could be a mistake to press him. Still, there might never be another chance, away from the *zampolit.* "Even at this depth, Captain, the current is flowing faster than yesterday."

"Well, I doubt it will roll us off."

"That isn't what I mean."

The captain stiffened. "What *do* you mean, Lieutenant?"

"That on the surface it fairly races. I can hear it through the hydrophones, in the chop of the waves."

"So?"

Rostov's palms grew moist and his voice sounded squeaky in his ears. "If you are going to release another buoy—"

"Who said I am?"

"No one. But if you do—"

"That's a command decision. I've said this before."

"Yes, sir." He had committed himself now, and he went on in a rush: "If another buoy is released now, in that current—perhaps three knots, four—it will be a hundred miles safely northeast tomorrow, two hundred on the next day—"

The captain's lips compressed. "I can multiply, Peter."

"In a week," Rostov rushed on blindly, "it would

be well under the track of our polar satellites, which listen for it—"

"And what of *their* satellites?" The captain quoted the *zampolit* and communicator, both of whom doubted the distress codes were secure. And suppose, by chance, the transmitter-buoy was seen as it surfaced? It was, unfortunately, painted international orange for greater visibility in home waters. It nestled on deck to be released remotely, from the crypto room, and could not be repainted below.

In waters so close to the United States the last thing the captain wanted was a bright flashing buoy floating on the surface, emblazoned in giant cyrillic letters with a plea to notify the nearest Soviet naval base. There were ships passing nearby, three, four a day. He tapped Rostov's logs of Asdic contacts. "It is all in your own reports."

Rostov was struck with a dishonorable thought: He should have lied and listed nothing. No, he had not fallen so low. "The first buoy obviously was *not* seen," he countered weakly.

"And its message not heard at Havana, either. Or Riga. So why risk another?"

"But another might be heard, carried further north. The current today—"

"Perhaps we were only lucky the first one wasn't sighted. I think the *zampolit* was right and I was wrong." The captain pointed out that the ship was perched in open ocean, on the only shallow seamount within five hundred miles. She could not have bottomed anywhere else short of the continental shelf of America without being crushed by the pressure, and any American fisherman with a set of hydrographic charts would know this. He reminded Rostov that any Russian buoy found from Bermuda to Cap Cod would bring US destroyers to the seamount like hornets to a picnic. "There's no place else to look! We're lucky they don't patrol this ridge routinely!"

"Too far offshore," Rostov muttered. "We're in international waters!"

"Like poor little *Baku*? Listen Peter! We are loaded with nuclear missiles. And we're *not* in the Baltic! They're perhaps less tolerant than you think."

"The buoys are issued for *use*!"

"Not five hundred miles from New York!" The captain was growing angry. "Next you'll suggest a *tethered* buoy. Or a mayday call on low-frequency undersea channels."

Rostov knew that the captain liked him. And behind the tightened jaw and bloodshot eyes he still sensed uncertainty and vacillation. So it would be a mistake to fuel his rising petulance. All was not lost yet. He must not push so hard that the captain silenced him. He owed this to his wife, Anna, and his daughter, Marina, and to the doctor and the rest of the crew as well. If he seemed hysterical, or a traitor to the state, the captain would never listen. "No," Rostov murmured. "Low freq is out of the question. Or a *tethered* buoy. I have never suggested those."

The captain softened. "Peter, we've sailed too many miles together for words like these. It's I who must decide, and no one else."

"I hope so, Captain," Rostov murmured. "*No* one else."

"The *zampolit*?" The captain regarded him for a long moment. "Be careful what you say of him. Or *to* him. We may yet get this ship home. You have a naval career and a lovely wife and daughter. He won his first Star at Leningrad. I assume his arm is very long."

Rostov could hear hammering in the main propulsion plant, and someone cursing loudly. The ship's clock chimed from the wardroom, resounding down the central passage. Its dings were funereal. Rostov's moment with the captain seemed over, but the old man was reluctant to dismiss him. Now he was glancing at the sound-log. "No more humpback whales?"

"Not since we stopped the music. Only a *kashalot* banging away."

"Too bad," sighed the captain. "You understood, Peter, about the tapes?"

He understood too well. The skipper, in silencing them, had shrunk in his eyes, though in fairness he had to admit that, if they survived, it would be the captain, not himself, whom the *zampolit* would criticize to the Party for not keeping a quiet ship. The commissar, in port, spewed paper like a teletype gone mad.

"I understood, Captain," Rostov said sadly.

"I wonder if you did," the captain murmured. To Rostov's astonishment, the old man's eyes turned suddenly wet. He reached to his desk, took a framed photograph from it, passed it to Rostov.

"You knew her, but not my son."

They had returned from their last cruise to find that the captain's wife had died of a heart attack. Rostov had liked her. She was a cheerful white-haired lady who had sent Marina on her first birthday a blue parka that exactly matched her eyes.

In the photo, mother and son stood, arms linked, before an ancient cannon: In the background were the ramparts of the Frunze Higher Naval School. The boy was perhaps eighteen, a chubby, smiling naval cadet squinting at the camera. Rostov again expressed his regret at the passing of the captain's wife.

The captain shrugged. "Pain fades." He waved his hand. "It makes this seem less important."

For you, perhaps, old friend, Rostov thought. *But do not forget the rest of us, please.*

"You bring my son to mind," the captain said—not in looks, his son being more "robust." But he thought their movements, their steady gaze, and their soft manner of speaking very much the same.

"I'm flattered, sir."

"He hasn't *your* talent, of course, but he plays the accordion quite well." For a long while he sat studying the photo. Finally he smiled: "He graduates in June. To submarines. I hope to get him orders to this ship."

Good, Rostov thought. *He can be the new sonar officer. It is still a military secret, but the present one has just retired at twenty-eight.* "That would be pleasant," he mumbled.

The captain arose and stretched. "I am glad we talked, Peter. As for the buoys, you may be right or wrong, who knows?" He put the photo back on the desk, picked it up, and put it down again. "I know one thing. My career is ending. I may make admiral, or I may sit in the park and watch boats on the Neva. Or die here on this ridge. But *his* career lies ahead. He's all I've left. Whether he gets orders to this ship or she disappears without a trace, there's one claim that he will never hear."

"What is that?" asked Rostov softly.

The captain looked deeply into his eyes. "That his father," he murmured, "put her into Yankee hands."

The old man opened the door politely; Rostov stumbled out as the submarine lurched in the current. There would be no more buoys. He'd lost.

⚡ 5 ⚡

The aging sperm hovered with the pilot whale and listened to the last of his days with men. It was easy to perceive that his grief had smoldered too long.

The pilot had long given up trying to understand man's motives. If the sperm could, good: He did not care.

Some of the games he had played with humans were diverting—to rescue a diver or find men's toys below. There was one that puzzled and bored him and his mates, but they played it patiently just the same, curious to find out why man would waste his time.

In this game man fastened to the pilot whales' harnesses a device with a round gleaming eye, its pupil as large as a sperm's. Men sent submarines from their base not far from where they swam today, and the submarines would dive. Then the pilot whales practiced swimming by, pointing the eyes at the submarine, and returned to the base to be fed.

Only that, and nothing more, the sperm whale wondered?

Only that.

A device, the sperm suggested, to show other men the diving submarine? As orca pods used adolescents to scout the salmon schools?

Orca pods *ate* salmon, the pilot pointed out. Man ate no submarines. Orcas had one rule: survival. This they never tried to hide. Man had no rules in the games he played.

And he murdered trusting whales.

The pilot and his two herd mates and the men who cared for them had played this last boring game for weeks, in waters not far from there. Then they had been carried northeast in a tank on a great slab-sided ship. When finally they anchored in shallow waters, it was in the shadow of an ancient structure known for centuries to Cetacea. The castle was a landmark of the Straits of Denmark, where the fingers of the Baltic groped for the great North Sea. Here they resumed the game that so amused the men. When a submarine passed through the straits, men would harness the one-eyed toys to the pilot whales' backs and open a gate in their floating home. The three whales would pass into the sea, start the toys by pressing their pectoral fins to their sides, and swim close by the submarines.

Over the months the play became so dull that they yearned to leave. They could easily bite through one another's harnesses, abandon the toys, and return to the open sea. They had learned less than they wanted of man and his ways, but when the days lengthened and the sun shone longer, they knew the time had come, for they had been without sex, except between themselves, for over a year. Female bodies ripened as days grew long, and would be heavy with desire in Iceland's sheltered coves.

The decision was made as they closed on a submarine which was leaving the straits just fifty feet below the surface, quite close to the Danish coast. They would play the game once more, return to the ship to fatten on man's squid and cod, and on the next mission depart forever.

That day they had noticed, not far from the path of the submarine, another ship with a gate astern, much like their own. To their astonishment, as they made their passes by the submarine, the gate on this new craft opened with a metallic grinding, and they heard the mewings of female pilots squealing with desire. Quickly they swerved toward the cows. There were three....

The pilot whale grew silent, reluctant to go on. The sperm moved closer, touching his gnarled pectoral to the younger's rubbery body.

The pilot's voice began again, high-pitched and taut with pain.

He had answered the females' crying with joy with his own happy guttural moans. He had been last in line. When they swerved to pair in couples, his two herd mates were far ahead. There would be hours of foreplay, days of delight.

His brother, two years older than he, was rolling beneath the leading female, excited and playful, running his pectoral the length of her fine little body. His other herd mate and his cow were close behind. The four passed under a sound-layer. In his own excitement he lost contact.

He remembered, from their direction, a faint explosion and then another. But he had heard explosions before in waters close to man. Unconcerned, he doubled back, sounding on the little cow.

She hovered, frozen in what seemed like shock, a hundred yards away. He raced toward her, mewing the ancient song of love. But suddenly she whirled and raced for her ship.

Females often played such tricks to inflame their

consorts more. He rolled and raced behind her, deliberately slowing his rush to prolong the excitement of the chase. But then he heard her shrilling the rising, frightened whistle of a pilot sensing danger.

Swiftly and instinctively he scanned for orcas, sharks, or shoals ahead. There was nothing: The submarine by now was miles away; his own ship nestled silently on the coast. Hers lay dead ahead, its anchor chain thrumming in the wash of the Danish Straits.

Against all the laws of all his kind, he listened to his body, not her warning. She twisted and squirmed as if he were a killer whale and she a baby seal. He was puzzled, but still rigid with desire. When she dove, he dove, too, and when she wheeled and dodged and doubled back, he followed every move.

She was trying to echo something for which there was no sound. When he could not see her meaning, she raced for her ship. Caught by surprise, he followed.

At the waterline she swerved and rolled. At the very last moment he saw that she wore, around her body and ventral slit, a harness of her own.

Man's trickery was suddenly as clear to him as to her, but the truth had come a lightning flash too late. He banked away, squealing understanding, but not in time. She skidded in and struck the ship. There came an orange flash and a boom like summer thunder. He was hurled to the surface. He glimpsed the ship. Its rails were crowded with white-faced, waving men. He dove and passed a bloody swirl where the little whale had been.

He sounded for the bottom and headed northnorthwest. In daylight he raced toward the summer sun and at night toward the Northern Shark. In his angry flight he braved the tidal rips of Scapa Flow, where no whales went, and where lightning long ago had struck the ships of man.

The enormous sunken carcasses lay rusting in streaming tides. He wondered if some trickery of man had put them there, and wished he had seen them die.

Ten days later he had rejoined his old herd in the floe-packed inlets of Iceland, not far from the beach from which he had been taken years before.

The mind of man was a maelstrom in the Ocean of Thought. The pilot had come nowhere near him or his devices since. And never would.

The sperm whale had listened, astonished and sad, for he had felt the prophecy close at hand, and now it was slipping away. He was puzzled at the story. He felt helpless and ashamed. Among Cetacea, he was emperor: All other whales, from tiny dolphins to the great-bodied blues, deferred to the wisdom of any aging sperm. But he had no more understanding of man's motives in the Denmark Straits than a Ganges River dolphin, blind in the river mud, had for the myriads of humans washing daily in the flow. He could only answer with the story of another face of man, on the beach at Nantucket, years ago. And so he began.

All Cetacea loved the tales sperm told, and his echoes were so sharply etched and his memories so clear that the pilots and the dolphins gathered in a circle to listen and live the saga for themselves. The eldest had heard it before, in the tales the humpbacks sang, but to hear it from the sire of the baby sperm silenced even the restless young.

⚘ 6 ⚘

The morning that the aging sperm's half-sister would spend in mortal combat was mild and golden, with mackerel clouds in ranks above and shoals of codfish slithering below. At her passage depth of fifty feet, the water was sapphire blue.

She was slowed by her calf, though he seemed to sense her need for haste. He had somehow come to realize that if he continued, babylike, to ride the pressure wave just off her pectoral fin, he produced invisible drag on her own progress. So, valiantly, he would slide away, stroking three little fluke-beats to her one, always to her left, where she could better glance back at him with the larger and more sensitive of her eyes. But by noon he would be flailing, and almost against his will, would resume the position he was trying to outgrow too quickly. Then she could feel the drag of his ten-ton body, bound to her own in a swirling network of suction.

She had grown very hungry. As they reached colder water, her energy requirements grew.

A day north of Cape Hatteras, she was sounding the bottom for an undersea hill she remembered from the herd's hopeful journey to Nantucket. Almost two thousand feet below her, deep in the abyss off the

continental shelf, she echoed on eight giant squid, the
largest she had scanned for years. They were swimming slowly on a northeast course.

They were near her depth limit. Though she was
forty feet long, the smallest squid's two largest tentacles almost equaled the length of her body. Its eight
sessile members, the shorter arms with which it grasped
its food, were a good ten feet in length. The seven
other squid were out of the question. Squid so large
might easily cap her blowhole and drown her below.

She had a half-hour supply of air in her lungs. She
blatted three peals with her sonar and calculated an
angle of dive and pursuit curve that would bring her
above and ahead of the school. She arched down,
leaving the level of aquamarine for dark and chilling
depths.

She plummeted through a school of herring, which
shifted direction, ten thousand fish acting as a single
organism. Driving herself downward with huge, eco-
nomical strokes of her flukes, she was quickly blind,
except to the flash of lantern fish and anglers.

Any giant squid at its own depth had advantages
in speed and eyesight over the sperm whale. It carried
a gleam of luminescence that, though primarily for
prey attraction, enabled it sometimes to glimpse a
sperm by reflected light. The squid itself was a murderous carnivore. Its ten arms were dappled with
tightly gripping suckers, each with a sawtooth edge
that could cut through whale blubber like a flenser's
blade. The two longer of these arms hugged the victim
to the shorter ones, which were studded with suckers
from tip to base and as strong as tempered steel. A
thousand-pound squid in normal feeding could latch
its longer members to an arctic shark, draw it struggling to the shorter arms, and squeeze it immobile as

it tore it to bits with its parrot beak and devoured it under cover of its mantle. No adult sperm of either sex was without the scars of battle with squid on head-case, jaw, or thorax.

Squid eyesight was famous: Its eyes, enormous glaring saucers, found remnants of sunlight in the deep mesopelagic zone, at depths that, to whales, seemed pitch black.

Squid, jetting in panic, were infinitely faster than sperm, squid eyes superior, squid intelligence not to be underestimated. But the cow carrying the battle to the squid's own depths had a weapon that, if properly utilized, could provide the ultimate striking tool of the hunt.

The weapon was her explosive, concentrated sound. The enormous *blang* of her inner lips, focused by her head-case and beamed precisely at short range, could stun the squid into an instant of incredulous immobility. It was at this moment that she must clamp some portion of his body with her jaw. To fail was to lose the prey.

She continued downward, increasing the beat of her silent flukes, ratcheting sound-pulses to check the squid's location. At last she was perfectly positioned. A thousand yards ahead of the group, she leveled, turned, and waited, motionless as the depths.

Somewhere from high above, she heard her calf's questioning bleat. He was safe on the surface.

An angler flashed by. She ignored it, hoping the light from its antenna would not reflect from her own head-case. She ratcheted again softly.

The eight squid were approaching, still unaware, but closer than she had thought, and the lead had changed to a larger squid.

She had no time to change her plan. She shifted

her focus to the leading squid, *blang*ed mightily, dropped her jaw, and lurched at the bulk of his body.

She stunned him, but not enough. He slithered half-free, and she felt his long suckered tentacles groping for her eyes and his beak probing for her blowhole.

She had erred badly. Her only salvation lay in air, two thousand feet above. She heaved for the surface, burdened by eight hundred pounds of grasping, slicing squid.

🜨 7 🜨

Peter Rostov lurched along the dark central passageway heading forward from the captain's cabin. It was hot, but his hands were suddenly freezing, his skin shivering in clammy warmth. His lungs strained in weighty, stinking air. The walls of the passageway seemed narrower than on his useless journey aft.

He stumbled as the passageway trembled under him. He envisioned himself alone on a Moscow subway, driven by demented motormen toward a rushing wall of human waste spilling down the track ahead. He needed light more than air.

He grabbed for a handrail leading to the engine room hatch. The main propulsion chamber was the only fully lighted compartment on the ship. He squinted down into its glare. He had avoided the chamber since the grounding, fearing radioactive leakage from the turbines. But now, like a moth to a flame, he was drawn to the source. He swung down the ladder. On the bottom rung he paused.

There were massive engine parts strewn everywhere, dripping with condensation. Three naked men slumped against a bulkhead. Their stubbled faces were smeared with grease: One of them, a petty officer who had worked in the oil fields at Baku, seemed to have turned to a black African since he had seen him last.

The three were a perfect tableau of defeat, but one was giggling. Anoxia?

He had a great desire to talk to the engineer—alone. When he asked where he was, the petty officer glowered at him.

"Try the wardroom, comrade. Where else would an officer hide?"

Rostov had served for seven years in the navy. Never had he heard a petty officer speak so. There was no doubt now: He was seeing the first stages of oxygen starvation. The boat might well turn into a madhouse before they were through. He climbed into the dark above and made his way to the wardroom.

The Latvian was seated alone at the table, in the red light of a battle lantern. He scowled at Rostov like a cornered bear. "Thank you, Comrade Rostov, for bringing us here."

"You were glad enough I found bottom," said Rostov. He could not resent the engineer: For weeks, while the pulse of the ship slowed elsewhere to a stop, he had tinkered with her open heart, working twenty hours a day.

Rostov found tepid tea in the pot and poured some.

He looked at the Latvian questioningly. "Tea, comrade? A piece of bread?"

Two weeks ago the engineer had been a ruddy, red-cheeked man with an athlete's flat slitted eyes and a weight lifter's arms. Now his face was grey and his body cadaverous. "It's piss. The food's shit. I'd rather die of thirst. Or starve. He'll blow us up anyway, the idiot!"

"Blow us *up*? The *zampolit*?" He almost dropped his tea. "What do you mean?"

"He's got the Destruction Bill, doesn't he? Well, he knows where the charges are, and how to set them out, and how to arm them. One of my petty officers saw him in the engine room, checking them already." He managed a ghoulish grin. "If he can get help doing it, *boom*! Kaput! He'll do it, all right."

"Have you told the captain?"

"Who *is* captain, comrade? Tell me that!"

It didn't make sense. If they had to die, why not in silence? Why advertise their position with an explosion, a rerun of poor *Baku*?

"Your turbines—"

"They're *dead*, comrade. They were dying when you put us on this rock. I just didn't have the guts to bury them."

"What in hell do we *do*?"

"It's not our problem, yours or mine," shrugged the engineer. "The *zampolit* knows we've failed." He got heavily to his feet. "It's time to tell the captain." He left.

Peter Rostov was staring blindly into his teacup when he sensed the *zampolit* looming in the doorway. Slowly, deliberately, the old soldier sat down across the table and lit a cigarette. The match flared in the darkness, hurting Rostov's eyes.

"Is it permitted *here*?" The commissar smiled, shaking out the flame. "Or does it still offend your nose?"

"It's not the *cigarette* that offends my nose." He could not remember, even as a schoolboy on the streets of Leningrad, having said a thing so crude to an older man. He heard himself blurt, "Why do you want to blow us up?"

The *zampolit* stiffened. For a moment Rostov thought the commissar would lash out at him, hoped he would, longed for the first time in his life to smash another's face, to splatter his strong sharp nose, shatter the glasses, splinter his yellowing teeth.

But the commissar smiled suddenly. "Who says I do?" he asked softly. "The surgeon?"

"No! But...I heard you inspected the destruct charges."

For a long moment the *zampolit* looked into his eyes. "You're a threat to morale. If you repeat that to another soul, I'll have you chained in sick bay. Alongside your friend the navigator. He can scream to his stars above, you can sing to your whales."

"But it's true?"

The *zampolit* carefully reached across the table, flicked his cigarette in Rostov's teacup. "Only if we're discovered. We once blew up half of Russia to save her. We can surely blow up a sub."

"Are you *insane*?"

The commissar shrugged. "Old."

He *was* insane. "*Old*?" whispered Rostov.

"The oldest on the boat." He took off his glasses, inhaled largely on his cigarette, and sat back, eyes half-closed. "I was not much younger than you, and just as unwilling to die, at Leningrad." He exhaled a cloud of smoke tinged bloodred from the light. "Where do you live in Leningrad, Rostov?"

Shocked, Rostov heard himself answer, as to a policeman: "Number 8 Kirovski Prospect, across from the botanical gardens."

"Near the naval school?"

Rostov nodded.

The *zampolit* replaced his glasses. "Our regiment *held* the naval school. Though we were only militia, chased all the way north from the Don." He sucked on his cigarette, eyes distant. "Von Manstein bivouacked panzers in the gardens, opposite your apartment. It's a pity that—" His voice trailed off.

Rostov waited. When the commissar remained silent, he asked: "What's a pity?"

"That you and I look on this so differently. That you feel about me as you do, and about the Party."

"I'm a Party member," Rostov said mechanically, "and I love Russia as much as any man." He felt himself blushing. Damned if he would weasel. "It's true," he conceded, "I'm not political."

"Too bad." The commissar took a deep drag. "We saved your home, Peter Rostov. Before you were even born."

Rostov shivered, listening to a ghost from another age, and one who could apparently fill him with guilt. "I am grateful, of course," he said quietly. "But what's that to do with—"

"*And* saved the motherland. And the Party. And the Revolution."

Rostov toyed with his teacup. "What's that to do with destroying this ship?"

"You would not understand." The *zampolit's* face hardened. "Eight of us fought from the rubble of a locker room where the soccer field is now." He began to count on his fingers. "Mikhail Ivanovitch, Boris Sak—"

"Comrade! You have not answered!"

"*Comrade?*" The commissar snorted. "*Those* were comrades! We ate rats and drank our own piss. Five died there, and two later, and then there was me—" He stood suddenly, ripped open his shirt, and jerked the battle lantern to shine on his parchment belly. A ridge of scar, two feet long, slashed diagonally across the skin. "I was left there to die."

"Yes," muttered Rostov, "I have heard that."

"Then hear this," the *zampolit* said, rebuttoning his shirt. "I did not die. So I'm the oldest aboard. It's perhaps easier for me. Look on me as your opportunity to depart this world in good conscience. For when we are discovered—"

"There's no reason to think we'll be discovered."

"Fine. Can I trust you to tell me if we are?"

The *zampolit*'s eyes probed his own. Peter Rostov's mouth went dry. He forced himself to hold to the glittering gaze. "Do you think I'm some kind of goddamn traitor? I'll tell the captain, of course!"

"The captain. Yes." The commissar drew on his cigarette. "Good. I'll accept that." He stretched like a cat. He seemed bored by their danger, and contemptuous: Rostov knew that the *zampolit* must sense his growing panic, which surely gleamed from every pore. The commissar droned on. He said that if ships came, Rostov must steel himself to go in an instant, as the men of the crew were steeled. "To surrender is a characteristic of officers. I've been trapped in the rubble, I *know*. Even your captain's guts have turned to shit."

Rostov began to rise. "He commands this ship! To destroy her or not is *his* decision. It is time he was told—"

The commissar grabbed his arm. "You have tried to tell him enough, I think..." The engineer's stubby shape blocked the light from the doorway as the Latvian returned to the wardroom. "...and I think the comrade engineer has just told him a little more."

The engineer sat down. He rubbed his eyes. "The captain says to waste no more oxygen working on the turbines." He stared at Rostov. "It's strange, comrade. He said he hoped *you'd* understand. Why you alone?"

Rostov tensed. "He *what*?" His hands began to tremble.

"The old man thinks him talented," the *zampolit* chuckled. "You have only to go to the opera to see: It's more painful for artists to die."

The clock on the wardroom bulkhead chimed six bells: *ding-ding, ding-ding, ding-ding.* The captain's message gave him an awful premonition. He lunged to his feet, started for the door.

There was a shattering gun blast from aft, where the captain's quarters lay. He knew instantly what it was. The engineer half-rose, white-faced and shaking. But if the *zampolit* even blinked his glasses hid it. He drowned his cigarette in Rostov's teacup, stepped to the intercom on the bulkhead, and depressed the switch.

"*Ship's surgeon, ship's surgeon!*" he called. His voice reverberated down the corridor outside. "*Captain's quarters! On the double!*" He let the switch flip back. "She'll find a mess, I think. You going to help her, Rostov?"

"Yes," he croaked.

"Good," grinned the commissar. "He hoped you'd understand."

Rostov, leaping from the wardroom, almost crashed into Natasha stumbling down the passageway.

Together they headed aft.

🔥 8 🔥

The sperm cow finally brought the struggling squid to the surface. All the long dark climb from two thousand feet to the levels where green-filtered sunlight began to reach, she had torn at his slithering arms with her teeth, clamping his beak in her jaw with all her strength. As she had broken surface, she felt the hooked beak break with a snap, but still the arms grappled at her head-case.

She blew mightly once and felt one of the squid's two longest arms groping for her blowhole, its sucker-studded tentacle clamping to her skull. Desperately she breached in high, arching flight, twisting belly-up at its peak to smack head-down into the unyielding chop.

The squid only shifted for a better hold. She could taste its blood, and she felt the sharp edges of its broken beak tearing at her lips and tongue. Then its mantle covered one eye and she was half-blind. She became disoriented and had no idea where her calf was, or whether the sun was to her left or her right. She caught brief glimpses of flashing waves and knew a great desire for air, which she could not get with the sessile tentacle blocking her airhole. Instinctively she grunted a call for aid, although there were none of her kind, save her little calf, for miles around.

She breached again, shaking her body violently in the air, and crashed once, twice, and again into the water. She had not inhaled since before the dive, almost half an hour ago, and her heart was pounding.

All at once she sensed the pressure easing on her head-case, and felt a rubbery, smooth-skinned body next to hers. It was the little bull, yanking with his toothless jaws at the writhing sessile limb that was shutting off her air. She rolled, using his body for leverage, and felt the squid peeling from her skull. She sucked air in a slurping, liquid sigh, blew, and inhaled again.

She was free of the squid now, and it was struggling on the surface, torn and bleeding darkly, blinded in the sunlight, with its tissues bloated from the release of a lifetime's pressure below. She clamped it, crushed the writhing body in her jaws, and shook it until its limbs fell free. She tore the squid to bits and watched as her calf gulped the flesh. Sated, he wanted to sleep.

There was a male taste to the flowing Gulf Stream that spoke of a bull to the south. So she dove to a hundred feet, where a blanket of warm water lay, to listen for channeled sound. For ten minutes she hovered, alert to the voice of the young harem bull.

She heard no sonar to the south, though she could hear the mewings and squeals of dolphins and pilots to the north. If the herd master was pursuing, he was running silently. She let the calf sleep until the sun was three flukes high, and then resumed their course.

❧ 9 ❧

Peter Rostov reluctantly took his seat at the listening console in the sonar chamber. The captain's body was waiting forward, on a slipway in the torpedo room. The *zampolit* had refused to eject the corpse, with its attendant explosion of air, without another sonic scan for ships.

With the *zampolit* standing behind him, Rostov swept the electronic ears in a slow semicircle. He hesitated on a southeast bearing when he heard the faint thump of a vessel's screws, tracked her patiently for a moment, and evaluated her as a supertanker bound west for New York Harbor. She was churning properly along the right-hand lane of the shipping route, and would approach the seamount nowhere closer than ten nautical miles.

He continued his sweep, pausing again to the south, where he heard the mewings of echo-ranging pilot whales, the chirp of dolphins, and an occasional *blang* from his friend the *kashalot*, who seemed to be returning.

He swung in his swivel chair and reported all this to the *zampolit*. To his surprise the commissar seemed as much concerned with the pilot whales as with the ship.

"Come now, comrade," said Rostov, arising to hand the earphones to Olga. "You don't really *fear* the pilots?"

The commissar pointed out sourly that the Soviet sub skippers off Elsinore had not feared pilot whales, either, until one wearing a camera had been spotted on the surface; in the meantime, for a year every nuclear submarine leaving Baltic waters had been filmed from bow to stern.

That was certainly true enough, and unanswerable. He followed the commissar to the torpedo room. Of the officers, only the exec, communicator, engineer, and surgeon had bothered to crowd their way to the bow of the boat, where torpedo men's bunks were jammed between the gleaming cylinders of death and the chains on the hatch to the pressure lock mocked them all, and the stench of Torpex sickened one, and the air was as heavy as lead.

More could and should have come, despite the foul air forward. But it was becoming an act of will to move about the boat, with the air so dead that to leave one's bunk was an effort.

Rostov looked down at the captain's canvas-covered body, trying to remember him as he had been before, and not as he had last seen him, with the shattered skull that lay beneath the shroud.

But the last view erased the rest. The captain had been slumped over his desk when Rostov burst in with Natasha. In the old man's hand was clutched an ancient Luger, which Rostov had never seen before. The photo of his wife and son had tipped and lay on the desk in a pool of blood. Rostov had wiped it clean and stood it up. The commissar had viewed the scene, picked up the gun, and had the body removed. All else was left as it was and the door, for all eternity, simply closed.

Now the captain lay nude, already weighted, on a rolling torpedo pallet on rails, ready to slide into the number 6 tube. In a few moments he would be fired from the ship in a blast of compressed air. Rostov could hear the accumulators whirring, gathering pressure now.

All this had been done on the *zampolit*'s orders. The corpse had been stripped naked, even of its wedding band. The *zampolit* had insisted that the old man's dental bridgework and fillings be chiseled from his mouth by the carpenter's mate, probably on the good Party assumption that if the body was somehow found, Soviet dentistry would be recognizably superior to American.

This time, thank God, there were no tattoos for the surgeon to peel. The doctor, who had held up so bravely at the steward's death, had looked on the captain with affection, for his preening, when she was about, had amused and flattered her.

The captain had been a father figure to the crew, too, but they felt that he had deserted them—as he certainly had—and turned morose and bitter at his death.

And now the communicator had failed to bring the ship's ensign to cover the body while it lay on the pallet.

"Where's the flag?" demanded Rostov.

"Code room," said the communications officer. "We decided—"

"Forget the flag," growled the *zampolit*. "I want to get this done."

"No!" barked Rostov. He glanced at the doctor. Her eyes misted. "Please, Lieutenant Poplova?"

She left to get it. The commissar glared. "It's a *worker's* flag. He doesn't deserve it. He did damn little work in his life, and he deserted his post."

"So did the steward."

"The steward was a Lithuanian cretin who knew no better. This bourgeois clown was a naval commander. But he risked giving away our position once, and might damn well have done it again."

Rostov peered at the *zampolit*. A strong suspicion was growing. He had never seen the Luger until the suicide, and it was certainly not navy issue. In his training he had learned as little of guns as possible, but the pistol had had the look of World War II. "Where did he *get* that gun?"

The *zampolit* grinned. For a strange moment his face seemed to expand in Rostov's sight and his yellowing teeth to grow longer. Rostov shuddered. Into his mind flashed Marina, on his knee, shivering delightedly at the wolf in grandma's bonnet in a picture book. He felt himself shivering, too, but without delight.

"My fault," said the *zampolit*. "I forgot it in his cabin."

Rostov came back to reality. "*You forgot it in his cabin?*"

"Too bad, *nyet*? I took it off a dead Nazi not a hundred yards from where you live. A small world?" The commissar lit a cigarette. "I was showing it to the captain. He fretted for the young men here. I told him how we had fought like half-grown rats, and how young were those who died, some younger than any on this ship."

"You bastard!" breathed Rostov.

"Steady," murmured the commissar. "Steady, Rostov!" His thick glasses caught the light, and behind them the eyes were slits of stone, yellow as Kremlin walls. The Luger was suddenly lying in his hand. He hefted it tenderly. "I showed him this, with the clip nearly empty. The kraut I killed with a grenade. Here, you can see on the grip..."

Rostov became aware that Natasha had returned, was staring at the commissar. Rostov took the red naval flag, with its hammer and sickle, and began gently to drape it over the shrouded form. With the girl watching he tried to hide the shaking of his hands, and she helped him smooth the folds.

The *zampolit* exhaled a cloud of smoke. "You can see on the grip where a piece of the shrapnel struck." He presented the gun to Rostov, grip first. "I think there's another round inside. Would you like me to leave it with *you*?"

"I'd like," said Rostov quietly, "to jam it up your ass."

For a long while the *zampolit* studied him. The compressor whirred. Forward, a torpedo man coughed in his bunk. A nearby deckframe squealed.

The commissar slipped the gun into his pocket and suddenly ripped the flag from the body. He reached for the loading lever on the bulkhead which would slam the corpse into the tube on its rolling pallet, spin the breech closed, charge the tube with high pressure air, and open the outer torpedo hatch. Rostov lunged for his wrist and clutched it.

Frozen, arms up, the two faced each other. Peter Rostov summoned strength he had not known he had, braced himself, and yanked. The older man's arm came down.

"*After* you've spoken, Comrade *Zampolit*. As you did for the steward."

"He'll rot first," said the *zampolit*, "and I speak for the crew."

"You, Commander?" Rostov challenged the exec.

"No," said the exec. "And *I* speak for the ward-room."

"Then why are we here?" demanded Natasha.

"To see he gets off," growled the commissar. His voice seemed slurred. He rocked on his heels, recovered himself. "Before he starts to smell."

"That's not why *I'm* here!" Natasha's eyes flashed. "He was a kind man and cared for us. He simply broke. We'll *all* break soon when the oxygen goes; *you're* closer than you think!" Her lip was quivering. "To me he's no traitor!"

"Or me," Rostov said gently. He touched the canvas shroud. "Good-bye, friend. And comrade."

He reached up and pulled the pallet lever. The pallet with its burden rolled into the shining tunnel. The hatch clanged shut and spun. A roar of water invading the tube told him that the outer door had opened. He yanked the red firing lever above the switch.

Three hundred pounds of air pressure filled the tube, there was an explosive boom as the bubble tore the body from its womb, the submarine shuddered once, and the captain was gone.

As they passed together down the passageway, he took Natasha's hand. She pressed his palm for an instant, but her fingers slipped to his wrist. She was feeling his pulse.

"Are you all right, Peter?"

"Of course. Why?"

The navigator, who had been roaring all day with laughter, began to scream with rage. She went forward to give him a shot.

Rostov poked his head into the sonar chamber. Olga reported that the tanker was no closer. She had heard the burial's empty bubble breaking surface far above.

The *kashalot* was back, hunting squid. She offered him the earphones if he wanted to hear him.

He told her he did not need earphones: The old *bogodoo* was so close and his voice so strong he was sure he could hear it through the hull. He felt at peace with all mankind and could not imagine why. To his amazement he found himself patting her affectionately on the shoulder. He had never done such a thing before. She glanced at him strangely, shrugged, and returned to her listening.

He headed for his stateroom. He felt all at once lightheaded and elated. He found himself humming the anvil chorus from *Il Trovatore* in time with the faint distant *blam*'s. How stupid to grieve for a friend who had, after all, so brilliantly escaped! He would somehow find release himself. A joyous certainty of good things to come went surging through his veins.

"Dum, dum, de-dum, da-dum, de-dum, da-dum, de-dum-dum," he bellowed, moving down the passageway. The engineering officer emerged from the stench of the befouled forward head, cinching up his belt. He was grinning stupidly. Rostov had not seen him smile in weeks. The engineer reached out, tousled Rostov's scalp, and staggered down the passageway.

Anoxia? wondered Rostov. Ridiculous, or he would be feeling it himself. Simply drunk. Not a bad idea.

He stumbled toward his stateroom. Two years ago they had shown the flag in Helsinki. He had a bottle of Finnish vodka, bought extravagantly as a souvenir, and in his desk the revolver they had made him wear to play policeman on shore patrol.

He would need all the courage he could find in the bottle if he decided to use the gun.

❦ 10 ❦

When the aging sperm had finished sounding his tale of the kindly men of Nantucket to the ring of pilot whales and dolphins, the pilot whale leader seemed angry and confused. He sounded a question to the wisest of them all.

Were there then two species of men? Orcas and dolphins? Bad and good? Those who murdered and those who helped the dying?

The sperm whale could not answer. Men seemed of one species, wherever he was found.

Then, the pilot whale decided, his herd would avoid them all, and the things he put into the sea, and his cities by the shore. He cartwheeled into the depths to begin his afternoon hunting, and his pod dove with him.

Only the sperm and the dolphin were left. They swam to the seamount and hovered a hundred feet deep, in a shimmering world of jade. Together they tired to think of a way to inform a passing ship, or the hordes of men crammed into the city to the east, that their dead lay waiting below. But the dolphin knew no signal that would lead them back. In the tanks, when she had played her games, it had been for man's amusement and hers: There was no message in her actions or in theirs.

Perhaps, he thought, if they swam to the path of the passing ships, and she breached and whirled and danced and did the tricks she had learned with men ...

Gently she reminded him that all dolphins played with ships at sea: How was man to know he was to follow them?

He had no answer. He could hear a great clanking from the submarine on the rocks and began to sound on it. The great southern current would roll it from the ridge within weeks or months. If humans did not find it soon they would never know it had died.

The dolphin became restless. The men below were dead; to lead other men to find them would not bring them back to life. She would go with him to Nantucket and catch him cod and halibut and soon his jaw would heal....

He would go to Nantucket, but alone, to die himself. He felt no desire to heal his jaw if the prophecy had died.

He let a fin trail over her body in farewell, *blang*ed one last beam at the submarine, and was about to swing north when he felt a quiet, concussive jolt, as if from a flatulent herd mate below. Astonished, he sounded again.

A huge and growing bubble was speeding toward him from the sub. He dove instantly, blatting a train of signals, for he perceived something below it very much like the body of a man. He passed through the bubble as it sped for sunlight, expanding as it rose, and heard it break the surface above in a crash of hissing spray. He spiraled down a cylindrical net of tiny comets, trailing in its wake a sparkling mesh exactly like that which humpbacks blew to confuse and trap their fish.

Along the undersea ridge, bounding north in the current and heading for the cliff, was a human corpse. The sperm half-rolled, swung open his aching jaw, and grabbed it as it bounced over the brink. Clamping it as best he could, he rose. In golden beams of sunlight at two hundred feet, the dolphin waited. She had no more idea than he how or why the submarine had ejected one of its dead. But she perceived instantly what was in his mind.

She had heard a vessel to the south, a half-hour's swim away. He listened, scanning it with his *blang*'s. It was enormous, heading east, and traveling slowly enough to intercept.

The message was in his mouth. He would somehow bear the agony, for the prophecy was at hand. If man could understand.

❧ 11 ❧

The sperm whale cow plowed north, her calf sometimes at her flank, but more often making little forays to investigate echoes he made and noises he heard.

She heard the song of humpbacks from the sapphire depths ahead. Weeks before, she knew, they had blared of a submarine singing on a ridge she soon would pass; now they groaned and warbled that the submarine was dead.

Her half-brother had always wondered why men would take their vessels to the depths. But such puzzles bored her. Her thoughts had always been of the young, and of adolescents learning sperm whale ways, and of how to mediate the gentle conflicts of females in the pod. Now she felt an emptiness, even with her calf.

She would swim parallel to the continental shelf until she reached Nantucket. If her half-brother, who knew the oceans of the world as she knew the lives of her herd mates, had not already died in passage, he could picture for her another herd and advise her where to join it. She had need to shelter in the lee of his body and mind for she was tired from the battle with the squid and had never been so long without others of her kind.

Today she had been hearing squeals of hunting dolphins and mewing pilot whales near the seamount where the submarine was said to lie. She veered east now to ask them if the aging bull had passed.

Upwind of the pilot whales she encountered their white-bellied leader. She passed to him the information she had of salinity down the Gulf Stream, and of opalescent squid, which pilot whales loved to eat, drifting near the seamount she had passed. From him she learned that the big bull sperm with the injured jaw had departed westward to that same seamount with a dolphin who had known man. She was joyful that her half-brother was near but puzzled that she had not met him when she passed the ridge. She reversed her course and the pilot whale drew his herd after her to the undersea peak to feed on the squid she had reported.

The squid were still feeding near the seamount but her half-brother was gone. The dolphins and the pilots began to dive. She sounded the submarine, and her calf caught her echo. She and the pilot whale listened with amusement while the little one tried to dive to it.

This was how young learned their limits, and it was good to let them do it when time was slow and food was near and the sun, filtered by rolling fog, was turning orange in the west.

Tomorrow, she would head for Nantucket again. For tonight she felt secure and she would rest.

✹ 12 ✹

The chief mate of the ultralarge crude carrier *Star of Texas* stood braced against a gentle wind of passage, far aft on the starboard wing of her bridge. He was two hundred feet above the water. He was looking for a whale his bow lookout had reported.

The mate was searching with binoculars past the bulwark of the starboard bow, which rose across a quarter-mile wasteland of rusting deckplates and hoses snaking from their cranes. He was a massive, red-bearded man with twenty years at sea. He had once commanded a Navy tanker, and later the jewel of a passenger line, but his personal disaster was easy to read in an alcoholic network of capillaries scampering down his cheeks and a certain yellowing glitter in the whites of his pale blue eyes.

It was well past cocktail hour in the officers' lounge. As always, when delayed at such times, an inward rage glowed like a bunker fire in the pit of his stomach. Directed at the ship, the young Greek captain, the owners, and himself, it flared and crackled with his longing for a drink.

He hated every foot of the enormous hull beneath him, from her bulbous bow to the giant stern swaying behind him like the buttocks of a fat New Orleans whore. The supertanker was virtually unmanageable in any kind of heavy weather. Even now, in the minuscule Gulf Stream chop, she was visibly heaving and flexing, like some volcanic island rumbling with terrestrial problems far below.

She was very new, with eggshell plates. She was more a mobile reservoir than a ship, built as a portable oilfield to last only some seven years before she would be sold for scrap or quietly scuttled for insurance. Her top speed was said to be eighteen knots, but even her erratic little skipper, as unpredictable, untried, and unstable as the ship herself, had never risked testing it. Slogging at her present normal pace, logging only twelve knots even with this fair wind on her quarter, she would still take almost twenty-five minutes to stop.

She represented the end of the nautical road for the mate and every officer aboard. Her draft was so deep that she seldom docked, pumping oil instead to buoyed hoses or smaller tankers offshore. Some of her forty-man crew had not walked on land for a year. She was a long, flimsy city in which bicycles were used as transportation from bow to stern, a traveling industrial community full of garish urban comforts to keep her crew amused. She had a swimming pool, movie theater, bar and grill, gymnasium, library, and a population of malcontents and misfits. Half her officers' wives lived aboard, grappling at each other's throats while their children thronged the TV room. Though most of her crew was American, her skipper was a five-foot-tall young Greek, nephew of the owner. She sailed this year under the flag of Liberia, which she had never visited and never would.

Every reasonable design criteria that bore on seaworthiness had been sacrificed to give her a capacity of four million barrels of oil. She could swallow, and often did, half the daily output of certain oil states on the Gulf of Oman, and depart with it to wallow in harm's way. She was, in her chief mate's eyes, a worldwide oil spill asking to be loosed.

But at this moment, with his gut rumbling for a drink as he humored the anonymous bow-lookout a quarter of a mile away, he could hardly have cared less. His binoculars trembled wildly. This morning he had avoided, in deference to increasing Manhattan-bound maritime traffic, even a beer for breakfast and his martini at lunch. He decided now that the ship would have been safer if he'd steadied himself with a blast. Okay, traffic or not, he was damned if he would miss cocktail hour.

He braced his arms on the cold metal rail and scanned the far horizon off the bow where the lookout had asked him to search. Into the shimmer of the afternoon sun, he could at first distinguish nothing. Glasses still to his eyes, he reached for the switch on the intercom linking him to the disembodied voice of the bow.

"I don't see him, lookout.... No! Wait...."

His voice trailed off as he caught the glint of a spout dancing a mile ahead. A plume of golden spray hovered, then descended to dimple the water below.

"Yeah," he said, trying to hide his impatience. But any lookout who was not asleep on watch, or stoned on pot, was deserving of instruction. "'Thar she blows,' all right, son. He's 'sparm.'"

"Jesus," the anonymous voice crackled, "he's big! What's he doing?"

"Spouting. They got to breathe, you know. They're not like fish."

To presume the lookout didn't know this was an insult to any real seaman. But there were no seamen on this hulk, only farmboys and urban cowboys putting in time to get papers, rejects and maritime failures like himself.

He lowered the glasses. He had no need to stay there. He was in fact hindering the operation of the bridge. Lulled by his comforting presence, the watch officer was dozing in the skipper's chair. The mulatto pirate who farted in Spanish was at the helm, scowling in concentration and enthusiastically writing his name in their wake, wasting fifty dollars' worth of fuel with every unnecessary yank of the wheel.

The chief mate was slipping the binoculars into their case when the lookout's voice grated back. "You suppose he's the one, sir?"

"What 'one'?" He wished the kid would go back to his comic book. But the "sir" stirred memories of better days in Navy blues: The lad up forward, whoever he was, could not simply be ignored.

"On CBS Evening News. That whale that sank the sailboat off Virginia Beach?"

He grinned. "If he attacks *us*, give me a call."

He turned away, but the intercom box persisted. "He's got Flipper with him, or something. *Hey!*"

The pure astonishment in the boy's voice held the chief mate where he was. Reluctantly he pulled the glasses out again and trained them on the whale.

The animal was enormous, and swimming on the surface very fast. Moving beside him in the most incredible manner was a sleek black porpoise. Or dolphin? He had never been sure which was which.

It was not the dolphin's presence that surprised him—for all he knew, they followed whales as pilot fish followed sharks. It was the dolphin's actions.

The chief mate was childless and had never been to Sea World or Marineland, but he had lately spent long lonely hours with children, drink in hand, staring with blank eyes at the TV tube that the brats aboard preempted. Half the programs that mesmerized them seemed to deal with dolphins pirouetting in a pool. He had watched them until his eyeballs turned to stone.

Nothing he had seen on the screen compared with the waltz the whale's little partner was performing, approaching the starboard bow.

He felt his pulse quicken. He forgot the drink he longed for. He stared as the dolphin leaped, spinning on its tail in the glittering sun, fell in a wide-flung sheet of water, then began to vault the sperm whale's head, right to left, left to right, in great soaring arcs as the whale churned steadily toward them on a careful collision course.

"What the hell..." he breathed softly.

The sperm whale's head was rising as if he was checking his course. The mate's hands began to tremble again. He refocused. "What's that in his *mouth*?"

Static snapped from the speaker. The intercom itself seemed choking with excitement.

"A man!" screamed the lookout. "He's got a fucking *man!*"

"Stop all engines!" yelled the mate. "All engines back. *Full!*"

He lurched into the pilot house. The helmsman had not moved; the watch officer gaped, blinking from his nap. The mate grabbed the handles of the engine-room telegraph, jammed them forward and then aft in a jangle of startled bells. The watch officer came to life, grabbed for the general alarm, and pulled the whistle instead. The foghorn bellowed, making the deckplates dance. The helmsman deserted the wheel and bolted for the starboard wing to look. The captain stumbled from his sea cabin. His wife, half a foot taller than he, padded out behind him in a swirl of crumpled nylon, squawking in Greek.

The mate yanked the mike from the radiotelephone, dropped it, picked it up again.

"Coast Guard Radio Montauk! *Star of Texas* here! Inbound, five hundred miles east. *We got that killer whale in sight!*"

🕭 13 🕭

To Lieutenant Peter Rostov his stateroom seemed darker. He had been taught that this was a symptom of oxygen deprivation: Anoxia would dim vision first, then his ears would go—he would become an instant Beethoven, hearing only his inward songs. Asphyxia would follow shortly, and then the end in strangled convulsions.

There was a better way, and his captain had shown it. He groped in his locker for the bottle of vodka. He found it and placed it on his desk. He opened a drawer and grubbed through musical scores and paperback novels until he found the pistol.

In the ruddy light from the passageway he discovered that he had, as required by regulations, removed the bullets. Somewhere in the drawer should be a plastic box of ammunition. He felt for it, found something, and moved back into the light.

His heart lurched. It was not the case of bullets, but a tape of Mozart's *Prague* recorded by the Leningrad Symphony Orchestra. He cherished it above all the others. In the rousing second movement his wife's cool flute stirred the woodwinds like a breeze off Lake Ladoga on a long hot summer's day.

This tape he had kept in the stateroom for himself

and never played for the crew. He had listened to it nightly on his portable recorder until a million years ago when its batteries had finally died. He longed to hear it just once more.

His pulse was racing. His head began to ache. He pressed the cassette to his forehead. Its coolness subdued the pain.

He heard someone retching from forward, where the smell of sewage was worst, and the navigator in sick bay yelling for the doctor, and the *zampolit*'s voice echoing over the PA system. His words were garbled and oddly strangled. Dazedly Rostov tried to concentrate and catch their meaning.

The commissar was ordering all hands who bunked forward to move aft to the messing compartment: The engineer had determined that fecal gases in the bow were nearing lethal levels; the commissar intended to empty the forward torpedo room and sonar chamber and close the forward collision hatch.

It would be better to leave the crew where it was. Already Rostov could hear a growling of dissent. Men who had been lying days in their berths to save oxygen were lethargic and drugged: They would rather die in the fetid gases than waste energy moving to better air.

He had the gun, and somewhere the bullets. He found them in the drawer and fumbled with the cylinder. His hands shook. He finally loaded a single shell and turned the cylinder to place it into the firing position.

"Anna," he murmured. "Marina, mother..."

He cocked the gun and reached for the vodka.

He stopped.

The *zampolit*, who had offered him a gun himself,

would be amused. Olga would think him a coward. He would be leaving Natasha to face death alone.

He could not.

He hurled the bottle to the passageway. He heard it shatter on a pipe. Stumbling shapes flitted past his door, grinding the broken glass under their feet. Two men collided, there was an animal explosion of profanity; someone was shoved roughly against the bulkhead.

The crew had been a happy one for years, true comrades, afloat or ashore. Now lack of oxygen was turning them all to animals, a heartbeat from anarchy.

He was suddenly enraged. They were fine men and women, too good for their fate. The buoys should have been released, every one. The *zampolit* had betrayed them.

Maniac....

Murderer....

He would not use the gun, but he was damned if he would die on command, fighting his comrades for air, with the commissar's voice probably croaking of Party and state as the last sound he would hear on earth.

He shoved the tape into his pocket, left the gun on his bunk, and staggered forward against the stream of men. In his womb in the bow he found Olga hanging up her earphones.

"We should be aft," she gasped. "He said we'll die here, from..."

"From our own shit," he muttered. "Better that than his!"

"He's going to close the collision door! He's *ordered* us aft!"

He took her hand and squeezed it. He looked into her eyes. "Then go."

For a moment she hesitated. Then she nodded, turned, and stumbled from the room. He moved to the tape deck, groped for the panel, slammed the cassette into the magazine. A silhouette blocked the door.

"Peter?"

He froze. It was Natasha. "Yes?"

"I couldn't find you." Her voice was gentle, as if she were talking to a patient or a child. "And I thought you hadn't heard."

"I heard," he muttered. "But he's not going to get me to die back there."

"Then I want to stay with you." She was suddenly in his arms. Her firm strong back was willowy and warm. He pressed her close and kissed her and her lips had the taste of salt.

Someone called from the collision door, checking to see if anyone forward was left. When it slammed and squeaked as its dogs spun home, Rostov jammed a fire axe into the wheel that set them, to isolate the forward chambers from the aft.

They were alone now, with torpedoes sleeping in the bow and Mozart waiting with his Anna on the tape, and perhaps the whales outside, and the sound of the seas above if they wished to listen.

He flicked the switch on the ship's PA system and turned the volume up so that the rest of the crew could hear.

Prague. . . .

The prelude slammed through the submarine like the crash of breakers on a beach. Three mighty chords flew into eternity, there was silence, he heard Natasha draw in her breath; then cosmic brasses thundered, percussions pounded, and his Anna's flute took wing.

Her notes flashed over the rest, like a tern wheeling over the surf.

Once he heard banging on the collision door and the *zampolit* screaming at him to turn off the music. But in a while the hammering and the yelling ceased and Natasha was in his arms.

She nestled there on a soggy mattress on the deck, and he soared over Baltic waters and lakes and mountains far away.

❧ 14 ❧

The sperm cow mother lolled with the pilot whale leader echo-sounding on her calf to keep him in hearing while he dove. She heard, as well, the clank of the submarine's hull plates on the seamount far below.

She was suddenly aware of an eerie, mounting harmony, as rhythmic as her own, in a higher, shriller octave than the songs that humpbacks sang.

The music came from the submarine, far below.

As she listened, amazed, it turned to a booming, thumping crescendo, then died and was replaced by a thin, melodious trilling, like the wail of a lost beluga whale anxious for his herd. There was life inside the submarine, then, despite what the humpbacks

had thought. She was surprised at that, but astonished at the effect of the trills on the white-bellied pilot leader.

At a depth of three hundred feet he lay shocked
for a moment, immobile as a basking shark. He suddenly squealed, checking the submarine for movement. There was none. The music resumed, now a
high, melodious fluting, like a dolphin seeking help.

The pilot whale exploded into action. He dove
abruptly, spiraling down, down, down, deeper by far
than her calf had dived, to the very limits of his lungs.
She perceived him now, alongside the submarine,
swimming in the black void and mewing in a frequency as high as a dolphin's—too high, almost, for
her to read.

He seemed to be searching purposefully. Once he
paused at a circular wart, rising like a barnacle from
the top of the hull, as if he expected to find something;
then he continued along the hull, nosing curiously.

He rose slowly from the depths, rumbling to her a
sonic picture of men he had once played with, who
would summon him with whistles and harmonies like
the submarine's and had tricked him in the end.

She paid him no attention. A sperm whale was
*blang*ing somewhere to the south. It was a bull.

For a moment she feared the harem master. Then
she recognized the voice, and the sidetone that spoke
of the fractured jaw. It was her half-brother, hardly
a mile from her now.

She bleated joyfully and beamed a train of sound
to trace his passage. But when the returning echo
reached her, she circled with her baby exactly where
she was.

She did not understand the picture, and she would
not risk her calf. The bull was swimming slowly toward

them. From his jaw there hung a man. Beside him played a dolphin.

And behind him crawled the largest vessel she had ever seen or heard.

❡ 15 ❡

Lieutenant Peter Rostov traced his finger across Natasha's cheek. In the light from the sonar panel he could see that her eyes had opened.

The symphony had risen to a crescendo as their bodies merged; ended in kettledrums as they parted. Now he heard only the eternal clanging of the rocks against the hull, and the faint *blang*ing of a *kashalot* as if it had picked up the rhythm of Mozart and would not let it go.

"Peter?" She pressed the back of her hand to his lips. "When I saw on your health record that you were married, I almost cried."

"I wanted you from the night you came aboard," he murmured. "With your silly little bear."

"I left him in my stateroom. I chose you."

"I'm honored."

"And I almost cried again that night I heard you play." She kissed his finger. "You were cheated. You should be in that orchestra, not here."

"Cheated? What about you?" She should have been assigned to a Naval Hospital or a submarine tender.

Monsters, idiots, apes in ribbons and gold braid! "We were all cheated. We should have sent up every buoy we had."

A trip-hammer *blang* made the hull plates shiver. "My God!" she murmured. "What's that?"

"A friend of mine." He stumbled to the console, flicked on the sonar for the first time since their grounding to echo-range on whatever monster was knocking at their door. Olga would doubtless be stationed by the *zampolit* at the sonar monitor in the periscope compartment. He wondered if she would report him when she saw her sonar screen light up. It didn't matter: The *zampolit* would hear the pinging anyway through the steel plates of the hull.

The chamber came alive.

Ping . . . ping . . . ping . . .

He hoped the commissar liked the sound. He knew that the sperm whale would. And if no one cared where they were but a great ugly whale, why deny the beast his fun?

The whale seemed to answer: "*Bl . . . a . . . n . . . g . . .*"

The animal was playing their game with them.

Ping-blang . . . ping-blang . . . ping-blang.

Rostov had never seen a live sperm whale. In Vladivostok he had shuddered at the dead ones streaming vapor on the docks, and at the movie of the whale hunt as a child. At sea he had seen their spoutings and heard their crashing echoes from depths no man could reach.

But now he had a vision of a great blunt-headed beast groping, probing, trying to understand the submarine and him. All of this was as clear and sharp as the fantasy of his daughter hop-skip-jumping in the park.

His mind joined the mighty *kashalot*'s and he swam

with him in an ocean warm as summer, as sapphire-blue as Anna's eyes. Wordlessly he told the whale of his terrors and his fears. The great beast murmured back to him of waters far away....

"Peter?" called a woman's voice. "*Peter!*"

He heard his own voice answer: "Anna...Natasha?"

He was back in the chamber, confused but strangely comforted by the vision. She was smiling. "'Natasha,' please."

"Did you see him?" he mumbled. "Why didn't you come with us?"

She felt his brow. "Oh, Peter. It's the air...."

She was right, of course. He was breathing too fast and his heart was drumming too. The scent of stale CO_2 was everywhere, and the smell of other men.

"Rostov," crackled the *zampolit* on the intercom. "Get that sonar *off*!"

Rostov groped for a pipe wrench in the tool locker and battered the loudspeaker off the bulkhead. So much for the voice of the Soviet state.

He lurched to the console. There were whale echoes everywhere, pilots and dolphins. He searched for the bigger blip of a sperm.

Four hundred yards southeast, eight hundred feet deep now, a whale descended. But it was too small for a sperm: It was a pilot. He heard its unmistakable squeal.

His heart jumped. A pilot whale? Trained to scout for the Americans? Who knew? And now, who cared?

The sonar swept around. He stared at its screen.

Southwest, a thousand yards away, lay the blip of the big sperm whale. Behind it lay a target too large to be believed. He shifted the sonar's gain, changed its beat and frequency, finally tapped the screen. The blip remained.

"Natasha!" he yelled.

She was at his side. "What is it?"

"How big was the *Glomar Explorer*?"

She stared at the screen. He swung her to him and looked into her face. His heart was pounding and his eyes were hot.

"How *big* was she?" he repeated.

"Thirty-six thousand tons, I think," she whispered. "Very, very big."

Behind the whale, dead in the water, lay the largest vessel he had seen since they had cruised the Persian Gulf.

〽 16 〽

The aging sperm had calculated that the monster ship was feeble for its size, as slow to react as a blue-whale cow with a broken fluke. So when he led it back he slowed a mile short of the undersea mountain to give it time to stop.

A sperm cow was scanning somewhere ahead.

Gliding silently, he listened in astonishment. Her voice, recognizable over the thrashing of the giant propellers behind him, was his half-sister's. Instantly he realized that she had deserted the herd to follow him, for the new baby whales in the pod could never have made the long trip north so quickly.

He blatted joyfully, though he could not speed his pace, for he did not want to outdistance the ship. He did not know why she had come, but whatever the reason, it seemed straight from the Ocean of Thought.

Now that she would share his last days he accepted her presence happily. These ancestral shoals, now that man had ceased to kill, should be as safe for cow and calf as any in the world.

When the ship's whirling flukes had at last brought it to a standstill, he presented the body to the men he could see peering down from its side. He hoped that they could devise some means to accept it. When they did not, he left the dolphin on the surface to mark the place to which he would return, and dove.

Echo-sounding all the while, he plummeted with the body through blue waters and green, aqua, and finally black. He placed it gently in the cloudy silt, downcurrent of the submarine, where it might be sheltered for a time by the clanking hull. He stretched his aching jaw.

The submarine burst suddenly into voices.

Ping...

Astonished, he froze. Men inside *were* alive!

He answered: "*Blang*..."

Ping...Man had caught his rhythm, or he had caught man's.

"*Blang-ping*...*blang-ping*...*blang-ping*..."

What he heard must be one of the toys of man, like those he had scanned in the shattered submarine so many summers past. Or perhaps it was like the whistle that the pilot whale had known. Whatever it was, a living being was causing the toy to speak; the man was sounding to him in the only way he knew. The *ping* was empty of pictures, but it seemed a cry for help.

Perhaps, despite what the dolphin and pilot whale thought, man *could* understand with his curious toys, and only could not speak.

Be calm, the sperm murmured, as if to a frightened calf.

He painted a picture with waves of sound to comfort the man inside. He pealed of lagoons under starry skies in the distant Ocean of Thought. He led the man through arctic fjords, where the bases of bergs were blue and the voices of life were everywhere, in the seals and diving terns. He carried him to great sea trenches into which no living creature dove, where the thoughts of men and whales and starfish glittered in the night.

Men surely knew that the Ocean washed over them when their chain of feeding closed. But they thought of the Ocean as a sea of storms, and were frightened of its depths.

Be calm. Our thoughts are twined like kelp in the surge of the Ocean's tides.

Be calm. Together we order the stars, and the tides will always run.

❦ 17 ❦

The chief mate of *Star of Texas* smelled fog on the
breeze from the distant coast. He stood sweating in
the sinking sun outside the pilothouse.

The ship lay dead in the water for the second time
that day. He was dimly aware that the tubby Jamaican
radioman was offering him the latest of a half-dozen
Coast Guard messages.

He could hardly tear his attention from the starboard quarter. The dolphin was circling the spot near
the stern where the whale had dived.

The whale had first moved alongside, very close.
His hideous body, covered with barnacles, had risen
higher and higher, as if he were trying to climb from
the water: The flukes that kept him aloft must be
powerful as the *Star*'s own screws. For a good ten
seconds, as the tail churned blisters on the calm blue
surface, the monster hung suspended, two-thirds of
his length clear of the water, the corpse hanging like
a limp rag doll. The effect was exactly as if he was
offering his victim to the ship.

Jesus, he wished they'd had a five-inch gun mounted
aft, or one of the forty-millimeter quads he had known
in Korean waters long ago. . . .

"Did you *see* that?" he muttered to the radioman.

He was beginning to doubt his own sanity. Maybe he could bribe the steward into bringing him a drink on the bridge. No, like everyone else, the idiot would be topside with his camera, lost in the crowd on the starboard bulwark, staring at the footprint the whale had left in the water.

"I wonder if we're doing right?" asked the radioman.

The mate tore his eyes from the water. "*Right*? My God, did you see that poor bastard?"

"*Something's* bloody crazy. They're peaceful animals!"

The black had an accent like a Limey professor. The mate regarded him coldly. Like most radio officers he was the token freak, a recluse who stayed in his shack for days, was never seen at the bar, and seemed to feed himself on midnight snacks like the cockroaches in the galley.

"Peaceful?" He took the message. "Okay, he does that again, you ride down on a cargo net and get the poor fucker he killed!"

He squinted at the message. The armed Coast Guard cutter that was to eliminate this particular menace to navigation would afterward try to pick up the corpse. She reported her position as just over the eastern horizon, steaming in fog at flank speed.

The cutter and half the US Coast Guard, he had been told, had been hunting the monster for weeks. The whale had sunk a thirty-foot sailboat and killed another yachtsman north of Cape Hatteras three days before. The yachtsman's wife had miraculously survived to tell the tale to fishermen off the cape.

He handed the message back to the radio officer. "Show it to the skipper, Sparks," he said. Everything in English was Greek to the captain, but in his present explosive condition, he had said that he wanted to see it all. "You better *read* it to him. Slow."

He leaned on the rail. The crazy dolphin was still marking the spot where the whale had dived, pirouetting in the sun.

He heard the radiotelephone crackling from the pilothouse. He stepped inside.

"*Star of Texas*," the receiver squealed, "this is Coast Guard cutter *Sand Island*. We have you in sight. You got the whale?"

"Just dove. But they can't stay down forever. Load up everything you got. He'll be back."

"Maintain station. We're on our way!"

"No! We go, *now*!" barked the captain, sliding from his chair toward the engineroom telegraph. "Long enough!"

The mate grabbed his arm. "They'll inspect us if you do!" Safety inspections were the Hooligan Navy's ultimate weapon. "We better hang in."

Reluctantly the captain returned to his seat. The mate stepped back to the wing. He could see the slim cutter knifing east out of the fog banks, five minutes away, with a gleaming white bone in her teeth. On her bow, men were clustering around what looked like a three-inch gun.

Good. He had missed cocktail hour to see the bastard killed. The captain could damn well wait too.

⚉ 18 ⚉

To Peter Rostov the sonar screen had become a great shimmering pool of green water, with the range circles stretching to infinity from a pebble dropped into the center. The pebble was the giant echo of the *Glomar Explorer*, which now hung directly above them and would save them all. For the CIA would surely carry a diving bell to mate with a Soviet escape-hatch. He himself would hacksaw through the *zampolit*'s chain and unclog the door.

To the east another blip on the screen was closing at thirty knots. This he took to be a US destroyer charging in to reinforce the salvage vessel's sonar with her own. God knew how many helicopters, deep-sea submersibles, rescue subs, diving bells, and undersea TV cameras the Yankees had on their way.

He began to hum the march from *Aida*.

He felt Natasha's hand on his brow. "You are feverish, Peter Rostov," she said from the dark above his head.

"Perhaps. But we'll *live*, Natasha. You'll see...."

Pilot whales were everywhere above: Perhaps it was they who had found the sub, or perhaps the Yanks had trained even sperm. Maybe the *kashalot* was a lieutenant in their navy, like himself. Anything seemed possible since their swim in the sapphire sea.

Ping ... blang ... ping ...
Ping-blang ... ping-blang ... ping-blang ...

Thank you, comrade *bogodoo*, for coming to the party. You have turned it from a funeral to a fête.

Rostov was Neptune, welcoming them all below to his iron castle under the sea. He wished he had not smashed the vodka bottle and could toast their saviors, one and all.

The light on his console phone was flashing. It would be Olga manning the sonar monitor near the periscope in the control room.

"Yes, my dear?" he said grandly.

Her voice was slurred. "Lieutenant Rostov, we're dying back here, and you're ... what? Drunk?"

"You shall not die, I promise. Do you see on the screen?"

"*Da!*" Her voice dropped to a whisper. "Is it the *Glomar*?"

"Of course," he blurted. "Or something like it." His mind raced. "Switch off your screen. And tell *only* the engineer. He knows where the buoys are released."

"Idiot!" she screamed suddenly. "The *zampolit* has a gun on me!"

The *zampolit*'s voice came on the line. It was slurred and sounded strangled, a symptom of high CO_2 level in the blood. "Thank you, Comrade Rostov, for sounding the curtain bell. For that is what you've done. I'm setting the charges out."

"There's help above, you idiot!"

"And with your goddamned sonar, you've told them we are here."

The phone went dead, as if ripped from the panel. Rostov groaned and beat his fist on the console.

He'd failed in music, failed in life. He had failed here. He had been the captain's favorite, failed to sway him, failed even to try to sway the crew. He'd failed Natasha, Olga, the navigator, his sonar men, all who wanted sunshine and to hear birds sing again.

He had failed once more, and this time had killed them all.

And Anna, and his mother, and Marina, who would soon forget his face.

Unless...

He leaped to his feet. With the *zampolit* groggy and his helpers, if he found any, dying breath by breath, it would take an hour or more to move the charges into place, set them, wire them up. If a signal could be sent above to hurry...

A *living* signal? Why shouldn't he try?

The escape-hatch chain would take a half an hour to hacksaw, but Natasha could do that while he soared through the waters of cobalt blue. Then, if he could survive the bends, just long enough to tell...

She was watching him. "Peter?"

His body surged with energy and strength he thought he had lost. He yanked a hacksaw from the tool bin.

"Come on," he barked. "There's just a chance..."

He grabbed her hand and pulled her forward to the torpedo room. He lurched past the sleeping stainless fish to the locker where the Pavlovitch rescue lungs were kept. He hurled open the door and hauled one out.

"No!" she cried. "You can't!"

"It'll get me to the surface."

"And you'll die! Screaming! Have you ever seen the bends?"

"There'll be time to tell them you're alive! And where to find the hatch!"

He pulled on the vest, which would raise him, and the transparent face mask, which, like a hangman's hood, was supposed to give one courage. He checked the pressure in the helium-oxygen tank that was supposed to minimize bends and let him survive to the surface.

"It's insane!"

"To let him kill *you* is insane! *This* is common sense!"

He shrugged into the vest.

"He's chained the hatch! It'll take us half an hour to cut it!"

"I'll go out the tube." He nodded at the hacksaw. "You'll cut the chain while I'm gone. And wait for three bangs on the hull, I'll tell them that. The moment I'm gone, start cutting."

"I don't know how to charge the tube!"

He showed her. "You've seen us shoot two bodies out. You can do it." He was in the gear now, with only the mask to pull down. He looked into her eyes.

"Good-bye, Natasha."

Her lips trembled, and she could not speak. The *kashalot* pealed faintly, and his mind went calm.

"Good-bye," he said again, and pulled down the mask. He slithered into the tube. He heard her close the breech.

He lay freezing in the cylinder. His fear began to build. But before panic clutched him he heard the drum of the pressure pump, the rush of water, and a great hand pressed him into the steel. Then, in an enormous *bloom* of air, he was hurled from the submarine into the ebony void.

* * *

He did not know how long he had been unconscious or where he was, for in his world there was no up, no down, no sideways, and all was midnight black.

He concentrated on breathing, behind the mask, for to hold one's breath was instant death. This they taught in the deep-water tank at submarine school, where scuba instructors clung to every level and one eased hand-over-hand up a buoyed and marked line, with interminable equalizing stops at every fifteen feet.

But now there were no teachers, or lines to slow him, and he sped toward the surface unchecked. He knew that his blood was foaming, for his joints squeezed tight in pain. His back cramped and he twisted in agony. He became dizzy and nauseous: for an instant returned to the elation he had felt aboard: then his spirits crashed; he knew vaguely that he was in the grip of narcosis, seducer of divers, that to surrender to the rapture of the deep would be fatal. Breathe...breathe...never forget to breathe. He had an urge to swallow, and fought it, because to close his Eustachian tubes for even an instant would blow out his eardrums. He gagged and spat, almost dislodging his mouthpiece.

The squeeze was becoming enormous. He must somehow slow his ascent....

Suddenly he sensed a presence moving above. For an instant he knew panic. Then he heard the mewing of a pilot whale, felt skin like a tightly inflated rubber tire pressing him down. He bounced along a smooth belly, caught the faintest gleam of white, and discovered himself in the tight embrace of two small pectoral fins. He heard a distant *blang* from the mighty *kashalot*.

The pilot whale incredibly leveled, hovering, waiting, as if he knew the price of a rapid ascent. The mewing grew softer and more comforting, and he felt his limbs relax. They rose a few feet and leveled, hovered, rose again, and stayed. And again, and still once more.

In less than five minutes, in the pilot whale's embrace, he had climbed two hundred feet. The freezing waters around him had turned from ebony into green.

A calm descended on his mind. He would save Natasha and the rest, see Anna and Marina once again.

And then he felt the great concussion far below. The grip relaxed, the pilot whale was gone, and he was flailing in a jumbled world of bubbles.

When the first great mass of air churned past he was tumbled upward like a doll. In an instant he was floating on a foggy placid sea. All were dead below, he knew, and he had failed again.

The world he had left in sunshine, weeks before, was hung with shrouds.

Pain struck again, lancing joints and temples.

His body curled in agony. He heard himself shrieking. He began to thrash water, knees and elbows twisting under pressures no man could endure.

He heard distant shouts. A demented foghorn bellowed somewhere in the mist.

He did not care. He hoped only to die quickly, please God, quickly, quickly, quickly...

He stared across at a baby whale, a hundred times his size.

He tried to move, could not.

For the mother clasped him to her breast and moved swiftly through the sea.

◊ 19 ◊

When the aging sperm felt the shock wave he reacted instantly. He had tracked the pilot whale's trajectory as it plummeted, sounded on the meeting between man and cetacean, noted carefully how the pilot leader enfolded the man and the gradual ascent of the two, climbing, leveling, hovering, climbing again.

He was trumpeting joyfully to his half-sister the meaning of it all when the explosion ripped the dream. It jolted his body, jarred his ears, slammed shut his aching jaw. It hurled him a hundred feet toward the surface, flukes thrashing, before he could catch his balance.

The pilot whale dropped his burden. Whistling warnings to his herd, he fled angrily to the east.

He had been right. Man was mad. There was no hope.

The human the whales were trying to save was tumbling to the surface in the enormous bubble from below.

The water tasted suddenly of oil and human things. Debris began to wobble past from inside the shattered hull. He scanned the seamount below: Fragments were scattered from peak to cliff. But whatever man had done—to destroy the whales?—had killed the men as well, had hurled the bulk of the submarine into the abyss, where not even sperm could dive. He would see to it before he died that no sperm would ever try.

Human bodies rolling in the silt below showed the depths of men's strange hatred for brains larger than their own. Man would kill himself to kill cetaceans: All was clear. The prophecy was a lie. His own place was now between his half-sister, her calf, and danger.

He scanned the ocean above. He grunted in amazement. She had swum with her little one to the center of the boiling sea, and was clasping the human to her chest as if he were an infant calf.

She knew nothing of the story of the Denmark Straits. She was trying to complete the rescue to please *him*, and for no other reason at all. She gathered speed and sped on her back for the smaller ship, with the human cradled clear of water. Her calf swam at her side. The bull blatted her a warning, then an order to drop the man and flee. She did not hear. For new explosions were deafening her, from one of the ships ahead. Confused, she slowed.

He rocketed for the surface to try to cut her off. He was too late.

He breached, behind her, into wispy fog. A hundred yards to his right the enormous vessel he had led to the north loomed like a coastal range. Ahead, the smaller ship knifed through the water. A black-coated group of men at her bow were training one of man's weapons at the cow, or himself, he could not tell: His mind flew back to a day off Spain, with harpoon guns slamming and the ocean running red. He bellowed at his half-sister. Now she heard and dropped her burden.

She arched her back and dove, and the little bull tried too. But too late.

There was a jarring crack from the weapon, a shriek from the little calf, and the taste of blood in the water in their wake. He moved to the side of the quivering baby, who was floating where he had been hit. The mother, moaning, surfaced on the other side to help. Together, they supported him between two pectoral fins.

There was another shot. Something smacked the water a half-fluke length away and went wailing into the mist.

Then the fog drifted closer, shrouding both vessels.

The two, with the motionless calf between, swam slowly to the north.

❦ 20 ❦

The mate stood on the wing of the bridge with the captain. They peered down at the bloody water as the ship slowly gathered way. Soon the blood slipped aft, and there was only the fading rumble of the Coast Guard lifeboat plucking at debris from what they were calling, since they had picked up the Russian, a Soviet sub.

If he didn't get his hands on a drink, he'd dive over the side himself. The fog turned suddenly solid, heavy in his lungs.

The captain was still sulking over the delay. "You happy now, you seen 'em shoot?" he asked bitterly.

"The whale," the mate said evenly, "was a killer. He had *one* in his mouth, and he damn near got another."

"Well, he is *still* a killer, no? Because I think your 'Ooligan Navy, they got baby instead."

The son of a bitch was right, they had. "Coast Guard," he shrugged. "What do you expect?"

"I *expect* we gonna be twelve hours late, this fog. I expect maybe man from Scheduling. Maybe *main* office, too."

"Screw 'em. We reported a menace to navigation. Look, they saved one poor bastard! That's something!"

About the Russian he couldn't have cared less, but to admit he had been wrong to this undersize Sea Scout was more than he could bear.

"Saved? For why? Chart say he come up from six hundred feet! My brother-law sponge diver. Come up from two hundred. Live in wheel chair. That commie bastard by now, he gonna look like a square-knot."

"They got a decompression chamber," he said, nodding into the fog. God, he wanted a drink.

"Good, they maybe save him, send him back, he come again, blow up New York. You *like* Russian Navy, hey? I got communist mate. Good! I tell main office, next passage, new mate." He suddenly grabbed the mate's arm. "You damn well next time leave fish for fishermen, hokay? Sheeyut...."

The mate knocked his hand away. The foghorn bellowed ten yards above them like a tortured bull. The mate jumped a foot. The captain looked at him, shook his head, and said, "Go get a drink, rummy. I take the conn."

The bottle-shaped radio officer loomed out of the

mist. Fog glistened on his ebony skin. "Chief? Notice to Mariners, just in from Commandant, First Coast Guard District." He handed him a dispatch. "Read it." His Oxford accent was suddenly edged with steel. "I'd say your whale got a bloody bum rap. Or rather, his wee one did. Would you agree?"

The Jamaican glared into his eyes for a moment, spun on his heel, and left. Dusk had fallen: The light was poor. The mate held the flimsy paper to the glow from the pilot house window.

His hand began to shake.

The man-killing whale had crushed its own skull attacking a steel trawler off North Carolina.

Almost twenty-four hours before.

"Goddamn Coast Guard!" he yelled, after the black. "*I* didn't shoot the son of a bitch!"

He heard the radioman clattering down the ladder.

"I *didn't*!" he yelled again.

He clung to the rail, racked with shudders. He must be losing his mind. What did he care what the black bastard thought? Or what happened to a frigging fish?

The foghorn roared with laughter, scrambling his brain.

He stumbled to his cabin for a drink.

✤ 21 ✤

Lieutenant Peter Rostov had been drifting in and out of consciousness for hours while somewhere the compressor that was saving his life whirred faintly and the pain in his body eased. Conscious again, he began to study his surroundings cautiously, feigning sleep beneath half-lowered eyelids.

He lay stripped on a table in a gleaming white tank, which he knew to be a decompression chamber not much unlike the one he had known after his training ascent at submarine school. He had a dim memory of being carried here, screaming, by those who had plucked him from the water. The man who had been left to tend him had covered him with blankets, eased a blood-pressure cuff on his bicep. Now he sat reading a paperback book, only a foot away.

Rostov knew that the vessel was small, for he had seen it as it fired. To find it equipped with a chamber seemed miraculous: It must be some sort of coastal patrol boat, ready for oil-rig diving accidents or commercial salvage disasters. It was certainly not a naval vessel, as he had thought when he heard the two shots that had panicked his saviors and very likely killed their little calf.

The Americans had obviously not been shooting at

him, though the *zampolit* would have said so. Or else why were they trying now to save his life?

But why had they fired at their own trained animals? He felt his heart racing. Perhaps the whales had not been trained at all, but wild.

Ridiculous. Fantasy. He must be going mad....

Still, trained or wild, the Americans must have thought the whales were attacking him, and fired to save his life. And might be hunting them still: He could hear the whine of a deck gun through deck-plates somewhere above, and feel the vessel heeling as it turned and turned again.

He tried to sit up and fell back weakly.

The compressor roared again. Each time it did, the gauges on the cylindrical walls trembled, the heat in the tiny chamber soared, and the air grew heavier. But the ache would ease in his elbows and knees, and he welcomed the sound. The bubbles in his blood were slowly collapsing, he knew, under enormous pressures surrounding him and the attendant. He waved a hand, testing its mobility. The air was so thick it felt like water over his fingers, but the motion was there: no paralysis. He was sure that he could talk: no aphasia. He would see Anna and Marina and his mother again; he knew it in the marrow of his bones. Though never Natasha, whom the *zampolit* had killed, or Olga, or the rest...

His mind was wandering. There was something he must do.

The whales!

With an effort, he sat up.

The young man, startled, tried to press him down. Rostov shook his head: "*Kashalot,*" he stumbled. "Good! *Kashalot* okay!" He cursed his lack of English. "*Bon! Gut! Verstehen sie?*"

The young man shook his head, spread his hands in puzzlement, and smiled. Rostov reached for the paperback book and made a scribbling motion. The young man took a pencil from a clipboard on the side of the tank.

In the flyleaf Rostov drew a sperm whale outline with a stick-figure man clasped to its chest. He made a cradling motion, as if he were being carried in the arms of a mother.

The young man seemed perplexed.

Rostov knew no English. Russian lullabies would not do. But he never forgot a tune or a lyric in any language. A vision of Anna with tiny Marina in her arms plucked at his musical memory. English, he thought the song was, not American, but it would have to serve.

"*Rockabye baby, in the treetop,*" he crooned, as best he could. "*When the wind blows....*"

He had forgotten the rest. The young man patted his wrist, smiled tolerantly, tried to press him down again. He obviously thought he suffered, still, the raptures of the deep.

"*Nyet!*" Rostov wracked his brain. "Me, baby! *Kashalot*, mama!" He cradled his arms, rocking. "*When the wind blows?*"

He pointed to the depths, to himself, to the whale in the picture.

"*The cradle will fall,*" murmured the young man.

"*Da!* Yes!"

The young man's mouth fell open. He grabbed the paperback, scrawled a submarine under the whale, an arrow to the surface, and shoved it in Rostov's face.

"That whale? *Saved* you?"

"Yes! Yes! Yes!"

The compressor groaned. A foghorn blasted. The

gun on the fo'c'sle whined, stopped, whined again, as if sniffing the fog.

The young man grabbed a red telephone by the hatchway of the tank. In a moment he was yelling to whomever picked it up.

Rostov had heard that in America a whisper soon became a shout. He had begun to whisper. The young man was shouting now.

Thank you, *bogodoo*. And to your mate, thanks too. I wish your little baby and your family very well. And Anna and Marina, and my mother, wish this too.

Rostov lay back. The whole world must be told. He might finish in a psycho ward, but he'd do his very best.

⚜ 22 ⚜

The aging sperm remembered the cove exactly. Slowly the arms of the crescent opened as they approached. A great blunt hill rose behind the inlet like the upthrust head of a female sperm. The twin headlands became pectorals, welcoming them to her clasp. There was no breath of morning breeze and inside the cove the waters were unruffled, like those of a coral lagoon.

He had left the place three years ago in sorrow, moving slowly past the headlands in the surge of the dying storm. The man who had comforted the first little bull had waved to him from the height of the bluff they were passing now.

Were there more than one species of man? the pilot whale had asked.

Now the sperm did not care.

He raised his body and peered at the beach. Three years had mounded the sand where the calf had been; somewhere under it were his bones. Near them would lay his, too late, and perhaps the little calf's too soon.

The sandhills, which before had been grey and sodden, were golden now in the sunlight. The surface of the water was dappled with brassy mirrors, each with its own rising dune, as if the hills were slipping down to join the sea.

The little calf, supported between him and his half-sister, had been drifting away toward the Ocean of Thought all through the long, long night. Each time he slept and ceased to breathe the cow would sense it and slap him gently with her fins until he awoke.

The thing the ship had hurled at him was lodged beneath blubber and muscle, near a rib. It had the shape of a conus shell, found on tropic sand.

The aging sperm could not understand the device. It was easy to understand the function of a harpoon: Man wanted the victim tied to his vessel for butchering. But what the ship had spat at the calf had no such function; it was a simple message to Cetacea that man, for no purpose, would destroy a living thing. The pilot whale, who had had the wit to flee, had warned him that this was so.

The sperm was heavy with shame. Currents in the Ocean of Thought had brought the pilot and him together to make the warning clear. He had ignored the warning, trusting his larger brain to sound the Ocean of Thought. But the Ocean of Thought was turned foul by man, and the prophecy was false. Now this second calf might die for his mistakes.

All through the foggy night, and now in the crystal dawn, he groped with all his senses for the pull of the friendly moon. Only the moon with its tides, and the shoreline the ancients had left, could save the little bull.

He caressed his half-sister, forbade her to come farther, and nudged the calf into the slap of the shoreline surf. When he felt the rasp of sand on his belly, he sheltered him and waited for the flood.

As the tide flowed in he eased him further and further onto the beach, always keeping him in his shade, for the little one's skin was tender. He was dooming himself to strand with his bulk, and never swim again, but if the calf could breathe until next high tide it would return to his mother refreshed; she would feed it and teach it to return to the beach and lie awash again. Offshore and on, resting and feeding, the calf might heal and live. He was healthy and young. The shock might pass and the flesh turn whole again.

To beach when sick or dying had always been Cetacea's way.

The aging sperm was half out of the water, with the tide about to turn, when he heard the shrill high piping of a human on the beach. The calf whimpered and the bull blared a warning. He thrashed himself around in the shallows until he could see along the strand.

A child was racing down the sand. It waded into the water, but when it had splashed to the calf, it stopped.

The little whale ceased whimpering. For a long

moment the two were still. The child patted the wound
and scampered away.

A gull screamed.

A wave whispered along the beach, sighed closer,
lapped at the bull's gnarled flank, and rippled to the
reaches of the cove. He heard a mighty thumping
above, rolled to his side, and cast an eye aloft.

One of man's great insects was hovering. As he
watched, it landed on the beach. Men ran from it. He
waved his flukes to keep them off as they waded to
the calf. But he could get no purchase, and they simply stepped aside. Soon something in their manner
made him stop.

They touched the wound, milled in the surf and
began to work together. He heard the cow bellowing
in anger past the breakers, but the men paid no attention. They cooled the calf with water, as they had its
brother, and even dared to cool the bull besides. More
men arrived, then hundreds, from the fields behind
the dunes, in snorting noisy ships of land he had never
seen before.

He was helpless now, and frightened, but the little
bull seemed calm. They heard a strange and liquid
sound, and somehow writhed to see.

A man was standing in the water. In his mouth was
a tube like a stalk of kelp. He trilled a song of beluga
whales that echoed of the north.

As he listened the bull had a vision of blue depths
pierced by golden shafts and heard the song of ancient
dolphins pulling children in the sea.

That night, as the moon rose high, the tide groped
for the calf, and even the bull felt its lift. He had
meant to stay on the beach to die, but the calf was
rested and could swim free, and he ordered him out
to the cow.

The little one moaned but wallowed loose, and the bull heard him blow in the cove. He heard his half-sister welcome the calf and cry for her aging mate. His jaw might become better; the pain might leave. If he were free, she thought, he soon could hunt.

He shifted and strained, and writhed and pulled, but the sand kept him deep in its folds. Men scurried around and dug the sand, like crabs on the ocean floor. As the tide rolled in they cleared a way and cheered and urged him on. On a seventh wave he strained and heaved, and the ocean took him home. He joined the calf and the mother and stayed with the little one at dawn, when his half-sister left to hunt.

For weeks they remained in the friendly cove. Each evening when the hot sun set, they sent the calf ashore. Men working by lights like great lantern-fish would tend his wound. At dawn, to avoid the heat of the day, the calf would return to the sea.

His wound was healing quickly from something man had brought.

Men put up tents on the dunes above; some slept with no shelter at all. Gentle boats with skins like blubber floated out from the golden sand. More boats came with every rising sun. From these boats men and their young reached out to caress the little calf and even the bull's scarred brow.

Men seemed to notice his shattered jaw, and spilled him nets of cod. His jaw ached less; he did not need to die. Soon he could feed himself, and did, taking squid outside the entrance and returning.

For eighteen days and eighteen nights they stayed within the cove.

Some men left, but others came. Their great birds and insects roared by aloft, but never flew too close.

Children began to swim with the calf, who towed chains of them in play.

One glorious day, when the calf's wound healed, he breached three fluke-widths high. It was a sign to the bull.

There were richer waters across the sea, on Europe's eastern shore. He would first find a herd for the cow and the calf, then return to the frozen north.

He breached three times with the little calf, and man seemed to understand. That morning they left as the cliffs turned live with men and their cheering young.

The dolphin had brought her herd to play, and the dolphins stayed behind. It was later said that if one fell sick, man fed him every day.

The aging sperm sounded often of what he had learned of men. He roared it off Gibraltar, and later in the north. He spoke of it to pilot whales, and humpbacks made it song; orcas squealed his learning to their young.

The thing he had been taught was this: The prophecy was true.

In oceans where whales swam that day men's voices were noise indeed.

But in Oceans east of tomorrow's sun men's voices and whales' were one.

Acknowledgments

To those scientists and observers of Cetacea who gave us their time, we and our readers owe the basis of this book.

First, to John Lilly, M.D., and his lovely wife, Toni, who insisted that we learn cetacean body language by swimming with his dolphins, and that we try to penetrate the cetacean mind by floating in his Samhadi isolation tank. When John's Human-Dolphin Foundation learns from dolphins how to speak their language he may prove us all correct.

To William Cummings, Ph.D., for his help on sperm whale sound, and to William Evans, Ph.D., for his on the body of the sperm. To Ray Gillmore, Ph.D., father of gray-whale studies, and to Ken Norris, Ph.D., for the hours in Santa Cruz, and for compiling that bible of cetacean science, *Whales, Dolphins, & Porpoises*. To Don Patten, Ph.D., for taking us to Mexico to meet whales in the wild, and to Sam Ridgeway, D.V.M., for his help on cetacean respiration and Andy Pilmanis, Ph.D., of the USC decompression chamber, Catalina Island, for his help on understanding the limits of the human body beneath the sea. And to Michael Cahalan, Ph.D., for his help on the sperm whale's food, giant squid.

To those who work with orcas, whose cooperation was so kind: Tim Andrews, Shauna Baird, Angus Matthew, and Ceef Schraga of Sealand, in British Columbia. To

Milt Shedd, founder of Sea World, whose love of all sea life has done so much to save it for us all.

To those who endured the nights of strain and rain treating the little sperm whale Physty on Fire Island: the Ocean Research Foundation's Sam Sadove, who imposed order on chaos; Mike Sandlofer, whose diving team administered the medicine; Bill Rossiter and his rubber boat; Guy and Nancy D'Angelo, of the New York Chapter of the American Cetacean Society; and above all Dr. Jay Hyman, D.V.M., who cured him of pneumonia in the end. And to Physty, for surviving, wherever he may be.

To those Warriors of the Rainbow who risked their lives to save Pacific sperm, and to Robert Hunter of Vancouver, who was there. To Paul Watson and the crew of Sea Shepherd. To the little group of Moclips men and women studying orcas on the tip of Friday Island, in the islands of San Juan; to Wendy Cooper and to Millie Payne, of the A.C.S.

If Cetacea survives, it will have all of them to thank.

Slowly—perhaps too slowly—they are stopping the murder of whales.

—Hank Searls

About the Author

Hank Searls has lived most of his life on or under the ocean. He's been an underwater photographer, a naval officer, and a scuba diver. He's lived aboard a forty-foot ketch for three years and has swum with dolphins and whales. Born in San Francisco, Hank Searls now lives ashore with his wife in Newport Beach, California. He is the author of OVERBOARD; JAWS II; and BLOOD SONG.